The Secrets of the
Black Canons

Also by Iris Collier

Day of Wrath
Reluctant Spy
Death at Candlemas

The Secrets of the Black Canons

Iris Collier

PIATKUS

✿ *Visit the Piatkus website!*

Piatkus publishes a wide range of bestselling fiction and non-fiction, including books on health, mind, body & spirit, sex, self-help, cookery, biography and the paranormal.

If you want to:

- read descriptions of our popular titles
- buy our books over the internet
- take advantage of our special offers
- enter our monthly competition
- learn more about your favourite Piatkus authors

VISIT OUR WEBSITE AT: www.piatkus.co.uk

For more information on other books published by Piatkus, visit our website at www.piatkus.co.uk

First published in Great Britain in 2006 by
Judy Piatkus (Publishers) Ltd of
5 Windmill Street, London W1T 2JA
email: info@piatkus.co.uk

The moral right of the author has been asserted

A catalogue record for this book is available from the British Library

ISBN 0 7499 0786 X

Set in Times by
Action Publishing Technology Ltd, Gloucester

Printed and bound in Great Britain by
William Clowes Ltd, Beccles, Suffolk

To Arthur

Chapter One

Still half asleep, young Juppy stumbled across the field, squeezed through the hole in the hawthorn hedge, and went down onto the shore where, looming through the thick sea mist, the other fishermen's boats looked like a herd of basking seals. But, glancing up at the sky, Juppy could just make out the pale outline of the sun and knew that in an hour or two it would be another glorious autumn day. The sea was as smooth as a mill pond; the waves, tiny ripples of water lapping against the shingle. Juppy rubbed his eyes and yawned. A day like this made his job a pleasure. The lobster pots would be full. He could drift out on the tide to where the markers were, idle away a few hours, empty the pots and row back to the shore with the first of the flood. Then home to where his father would be waiting for him with a piece of bread and cheese and a beaker of ale; old Tom already harnessed to the cart. A short journey to the castle where Lord Gilbert's stewards would pay good money for the lobsters.

He was all alone on the beach. None of the others had yet arrived. He was always first; his father saw to that. Glancing along the shore to where the rocks began, he saw a dark mass of something which moved gently around at the water's edge. Seaweed, he thought, loosened from the rocks and brought ashore by the incoming tide. Seaweed was useful; especially the thick, juicy variety. Dry it out and it became

1

good winter fuel. He decided to walk over to it and pull it above the high water mark to be collected later.

But it wasn't seaweed. As he stared down at the waterlogged bundle, he saw it was a woman dressed in a dark-coloured robe, her black hair clinging round her tiny, pale face and falling in a tangled mass around her shoulders. She was a small lass, he noticed. Small, neat waist, slender wrists and dainty hands. Had she a tail, she could have been a mermaid; but the thin legs which he could see clearly through the soaked dress were undoubtedly human.

There was something familiar about her face. Tiny, well-shaped, brown eyes staring up him; the terror still apparent in them. Hastily, he bent down and closed them. And then he saw the bruise marks round her slender throat. He felt a surge of anger. So the poor lass had not drowned herself. Someone had strangled her and dumped her in the water, hoping the sea water and the fish would dispose of the body. But whoever it was had forgotten about the tide. He reached out and pulled her further up the beach, her body surprisingly light despite having been in the sea for several hours. Not long enough, he thought, to cause that sweet face to become bloated or the crabs to get at her eyes. In fact there was no signs of that deterioration he was used to seeing when bodies were retrieved from the sea. She was as beautiful in death as she had been in life. Because now he remembered who she was. Sarah. Old Mother Bowman's granddaughter who lived up at the edge of Willet's wood in Monksmere, the next village to his own.

She'd always been a bit of a mystery, he remembered. Beautiful as the new moon in a cloudless night sky. But quiet. Clever, people said; a bit haughty. But he'd admired her as one would admire a beautiful princess shut away in a castle, unapproachable and unobtainable. However, Sarah hadn't been standoffish to everyone because, one day, two years ago, she'd been seen with a babe in her arms. A bonny child. She called him Henry. And folks laughed, of course, as they always did in these cases. They soon got

2

used to the situation and she never flaunted herself round the village. Her grandmother saw to that. But who, in God's name, would want to kill her? Gently he eased her over to see if there were any bruises on her back. He pushed aside the mass of hair and saw the marks on her skull; deep indentations as if she'd been hit with a heavy object. He took a deep breath and glanced nervously around as if he expected to see the murderer there waiting for him. Then he pulled himself together. These marks must have been made as the sea caught hold of her and dashed her against the cruel, barnacle-encrusted rocks. How could it be otherwise? Her killer had strangled her; the bruises round her neck proved that. Why kill her twice? Unless her attacker was in a frenzy of rage. But who could be so angry with her? Unless it was some monster with a deranged mind. Probably he had succumbed to lust and was anxious to destroy the evidence of his handiwork. This was a case for the sheriff if ever there was one, he thought. But first he had to get the lass up to the barn and lay her on some clean straw. Give her the respect which was due to her.

He heard the others arriving and shouted to them. He'd leave his own pots for the moment. They came running over to him and together they lifted up the girl called Sarah and carried her up to the barn already half-full with the harvest. Young Juppy turned to one of the other fishermen, an older man with an air of authority about him.

'What'll we do now, Billy?'

'You go and tell Old Mother Bowman and I'll get Master Fuller to get off and find the sheriff. We can't just leave her here and say nothing.'

'Don't see why not,' mumbled one of the others. 'The lass probably got what was coming to her. Having a babe with no husband and not telling anyone who the father is, is asking for trouble. Could have been the Devil's child. She's got the look of a witch about her. Why should we lose an hour's valuable fishing time for the Devil's whore?'

'Because we're Christian folk, that's why, John Bates.

3

And I'll have no talk of the Devil. Young Henry's father was a man right enough. Now get on up to Master Fuller and tell him to saddle that horse of his and go find the sheriff. The fish'll still be there when you get back and you can work away with a clear conscience knowing that the lass's killer will be caught and strung up on Marchester Heath as an example to others. We can't have people murdered and dumped in the sea and nothing done about it. And just because the maid's unwed and has got a child doesn't mean she's not entitled to the same treatment as other more respectable folk. Now get off with you!'

Sickened by what he had just seen on the execution ground on Marchester Heath, and with the stench of burning flesh still filling his head, Nicholas Peverell turned his horse, Harry, towards the Downs instead of going straight back to his manor house in Dean Peverell. The sheriff had insisted he went with him to see the burning of the witch, Jess Hobbes, as he said it was Nicholas's duty as Justice of the Peace to see the law in action. But Nicholas had no stomach for cruelty and the sight of the crowd shouting obscenities at the poor old soul had only depressed him. Maybe old Jess had supped with the Devil. Maybe she had tamed two hares who shared her hovel with her and her cat, and maybe she had the marks of the Devil on her wizened old body, but what harm had she done? Admittedly two women had lost their babies, both in the same week, but that had happened before and nobody had attributed the deaths to witchcraft. A cow's milk had dried up. A calf had died. It happened all the time. Most people got on with their lives and accepted these tragedies as part of existence. More to the point, he thought, as Harry, sensing his master's mood, bounded up the chalky path, she had ranted and raged against the King and his divorce from Queen Katharine. However, it was obvious the poor soul's brain was deranged and it would have been better if everyone had ignored her mumblings. But the neighbours had taken

4

against her – a witch-hunt was still going on and the new archdeacon was determined to clean up the parishes. So Jess had died today outside the city walls. He thanked God that her end had been swift. Despite the crowd's insistence that no mercy should be shown to her, the sheriff had ordered one of his men to strangle her before the pile of kindling was lit.

They reached the highest point of the Downs and Nicholas reined Harry in. They were in the middle of some ancient earth walls, built long before his ancestors had come over from France with Duke William. There were several of these earthworks along the ridge of the Downs, built, so it was said, by the ancient people to defend themselves from invaders coming over from the Continent. He dismounted and let Harry crop the short, sweet Downland grass. All around them, the sheep were doing the same thing. He noticed that their short summer coats were now thickening up ready for the winter and that the lambs which gambolled round their mothers were large and sturdy and ready for the Michaelmas slaughter. These were his sheep, his lambs and he should have felt proud at this evidence of his wealth. But Jess's death had lowered his spirits. Looking round at the gently undulating curves of the hills and then down to the coastal plain where the spire of Marchester cathedral was clearly visible, he thought that there was no spot on earth more beautiful than this; yet the scene he had just witnessed had been ugly and brutal. And in no way could he find it justified.

The early morning mist had cleared and he could see the island with its cliffs and inlets quite clearly. The five creeks which made up Marchester harbour, like the fingers of a hand, shone brightly in the sunshine. This was his land; he owned a considerable part of it. His ancestors had acquired it from King William who had rewarded his followers generously. This was his inheritance which he would pass on, God willing, to his own son, when Jane, his wife of eight months, produced an heir. Not that there was any sign of one at the moment; but she was young and all in good time. There was his manor house below him, next to the priory of which he had been patron until the king dismissed the monks. Now it was his parish church and its square tower would be a landmark for centuries to come.

His mood began to lighten. He tugged Harry's head up from the grass, mounted him and patted his glossy neck.

'Come on, old fellow. Let's put Marchester Heath behind us. Let's go home.'

Handing his horse over to the stable boy who was waiting for him, Nicholas walked quickly across the cobbled courtyard and into the great hall of his manor house, which, as always, looked bright and clean and smelled delicious from the fresh herbs strewn on the floor. The fire, which was never allowed to go out whatever the time of year, crackled in the huge fireplace. In the distance came the sound of music and women's laughter. This, he thought, was how things should be: a well-ordered house, a loving and talented wife, a great estate. Why should he concern himself with other people's sordid lives?

He went into the small room which led off the hall. It was Jane's room and the music room. The three of them were grouped together around the virginals where Jane was seated with Balthazar sitting on a stool by her side. The singer was Philippa, the Bishop of Marchester's young daughter whom Jane had become friendly with in the spring when Philippa's father had been dean. They had become strongly attached to one another, bound together by the dreadful ordeal they had experienced at that time. She often came to stay with them and Nicholas was pleased to see her. She was company for Jane as well as a gifted singer and a willing student of Greek and Latin, in which Jane was proficient. Balthazar had come with Jane when she left the court after the death of Queen Jane. For reasons which Nicholas never enquired about, he had made an enemy of the king and it was expedient for him to leave court. Jane had offered him sanctuary with her and Nicholas, who,

6

after a period of suspicion, had got used to him and saw in him no threat. Balthazar loved Jane; that was obvious. But for him love could not be expressed with a woman, and, for the duration of his stay at Dean Peverell, he accepted his celibate state. Perhaps, one day, when there was a new king on the throne, he would return to court, Nicholas thought. Or more likely go back to his native Venice.

For a moment, Nicholas stood quietly in the doorway enjoying the scene which had all the beauty of one of Master Holbein's paintings. Three extraordinarily attractive people in the prime of their lives: Jane, slim and elegant, her glorious red-gold hair framing her face and tumbling round her shoulders, her creamy skin perfectly set off by her pale green morning gown; Balthazar's dark Italianate looks complemented by his crimson velvet doublet and soft leather hose; and Philippa. How beautiful she looked. Her golden hair, unplaited, fell to her waist and her rosy face, still childish, was animated with the pleasure of the music they were making. It was one of Balthazar's own compositions. The king, thought Nicholas, had lost a talented musician. But the king's loss was his gain.

Jane looked up and saw him and the tableau disintegrated. She jumped up and ran over to him.

'Why, Nicholas, you're back early. Let me order you some wine, and you must come over and listen to our new song which Balthazar's just finished writing.'

She beckoned to one of the servants who had followed Nicholas into the room, and ordered refreshment for Nicholas. The wine, when it came, was cool and refreshing and made by his own servants under Jane's direction, from his own grapes which grew on the southern slope of one of his gardens. The cakes were soft and delicious and made with honey from his own bees. Glass in hand – Jane had introduced his household to glasses when she came from court – he walked over to the other two and sat down on one of the oak armchairs which Jane had softened by the addition of cushions. The floor of this room was covered

7

with rugs, not with straw and rushes as in the hall, and he felt enveloped in softness and comfort. He was, he thought, a most fortunate man.

The sound of horses' hooves on the cobbled yard shattered his peace. A servant entered and went over to Nicholas.

'The sheriff's here, my lord,' he said.

'Richard? What the devil does he want? I only saw him a couple of hours ago.'

'Your help, my lord,' said Richard Landstock, Sheriff of Marchester, who strode into the room, filling it with his boisterous energy. 'We've got a murder on our hands. Over at Atherington. I'd be grateful if you'd come with me and take a look at the body. After all, you'll be the one to sentence the culprit when we find him.'

'Atherington?' said Jane sweetly. 'That's a good ride from here. Surely you'll stay and eat some dinner with us first? It's not good to start a murder investigation on an empty stomach.'

'I'd never turn down the offer of good food, Lady Jane; especially when it comes out of your kitchen. Just a bite, mind. We must get on our way soon if we are to be back by dark.'

Chapter Two

'What's so special about this girl, Richard, that you need my help?' said Nicholas as they mounted their horses and clattered out of the main gate and down the drive towards the coastal road, two of the sheriff's men following them.

'Just a hunch that this is not a straightforward case. Jack Fuller, who came to fetch me, hinted at there being more than meets the eye to this lass's death. Now, I don't take remarks like that lightly. Great men could be involved; and when it comes to great men who would be the best person to consult? Why, Lord Nicholas Peverell, I think. Besides, if this does turn out to be a murder investigation, and until I've seen the body I don't jump to conclusions, you'll be trying her murderer at the next Quarter Sessions; so you'd best come along and help me find him.'

The road east ran across the coastal plain, parallel to the coast. They rode past tranquil fields surrounding prosperous villages, each one with its little church with pointed spire. The cattle grazing on the rich pastureland looked fat and sleek at the end of the summer. They passed carts stuffed with hay and corn slowly making their way to the barns where there would be ample food during the winter months for both humans and beasts. The harvest was good this year, thought Nicholas, as he cantered along beside the sheriff. A few more weeks of this dry weather and all would be well for another year.

He was not as familiar with this part of Sussex as he was with the western half where business took him to Marchester, the county town, or to Portsmouth when he needed to speak to Ralph Paget, the Earl of Southampton. This was the lord lieutenant's territory whose castle was just coming into view. Lord Gilbert Fitzherbert, the richest landowner in the county, whose family had come over, like his own, with Duke William of Normandy, was a powerful man who, so far, had escaped the covetousness of the king, who seldom visited him. He seemed to prefer Nicholas's modest manor house which King Henry charmingly called his 'hunting lodge'.

Nicholas knew little about Lord Gilbert. Rumours abounded, of course, as they always did when great men were involved. He was known to be unsociable, preferring his own company to that of others, and seldom went outside his castle walls. They had reached these walls now as the coastal road passed by them. They were massive fortifications made of local flint stone and strongly buttressed. The main gate was a huge iron-studded door which was shut that day. Only once had Nicholas penetrated these defences and he had ridden through that door and across the drawbridge, under the portcullis and into the main courtyard. He had felt, that day, as if the centuries had rolled away and he was back in some earlier age when powerful barons had ruled the land and occupied castles like this one from which they could overawe the terrified peasantry.

The visit had been mundane enough: the confirmation of some fields which the prior of his own priory in Dean Peverell had owned and, when the monks left, the king had given to Nicholas as a reward for his services. The land had been farmed by the canons of Monksmere Priory, which, when they too had been turned out, had reverted to their overlord Lord Gilbert, who had supervised the distribution of the priory's assets. That had been last year, and Nicholas had done nothing about it. It was time, he thought, that he put his affairs in order and recovered that piece of land.

At the castle gate, they turned right onto a track that went down to the coast. This took them over lush water meadows, past Monksmere Priory which stood on a piece of high ground well above the flood water. It had been an estate of considerable size but now only the church, whose tower was a landmark for miles around, was still intact. The other buildings which had made up the priory estate were already falling into disrepair, the stone having been taken by local people to strengthen, or, in some cases, rebuild their homes and farms. It was said that Lord Gilbert himself had ordered the removal of the chapter house in order to make an extension to his castle – a summer house, built in the modern style with windows and a chimney. Make it too comfortable, thought Nicholas grimly, and the king would want to stay there and maybe, just as Wolsey had been forced to give up Hampton Court, Lord Gilbert might have to hand over his castle to the king to serve as a summer retreat from the heat and plagues of London. Better to own a modest place like his own, he reasoned, where the king could play at being a country squire but never dream of owning it.

All such thoughts vanished when Nicholas stood beside the sheriff in a barn in the coastal village of Atherington, looking down at the pale face and slender body of Sarah Bowman laid out on a bundle of straw. She looked so young, so fragile, that he felt a wave of compassion for her and sadness that such youth and beauty should come to such a tragic end.

'Who is she?' he said to the young man who had found her that morning.

'She's called Sarah Bowman, sir,' said young Juppy, overawed by the presence of such important people. 'She lives up in Monksmere with her grandmother. She's a widow lady – the grandmother I mean. The lass is unmarried but has a child. I don't know what happened to the father.'

11

'Well, one thing's for sure,' said the sheriff, pointing to the livid marks round the girl's throat, 'she didn't take her own life. She couldn't have made those marks with her own hands. Turn her over,' he instructed Juppy.

Juppy and one of the sheriff's men gently turned her over and they looked down at the indentations on the back of her head.

'Could be he bashed her on the head and then strangled her to make sure,' said the sheriff.

'Or most likely these were made by the rocks as she drifted around in the sea. No one would want to kill her twice,' said Nicholas.

'Unless he was a madman. We'll move her up to her own village so that the coroner's men can take a look at her. They'll be here tomorrow; not that there'll be any difficulty in establishing the cause of death. There's a church at Monksmere and we'll put her there for the night. Does the grandmother know?' he asked Juppy.

'Yes sir. No details, mind you; just that I found her drowned.'

'Good lad. Best not jump to conclusions. I'll have you working for me if you continue to be so sensible. Now, get someone with a horse and cart to take her up to Monksmere church and we'll go ahead and tell her grandmother a few more details. Here, take this and see you pay the carter well.'

Juppy took the money and rushed off to tell his companions who were waiting outside expectantly. He had become a hero. No longer a boy, but a man to be reckoned with.

For someone whose husband had died and whose granddaughter was a girl with a child and no husband, the Bowmans' house was surprisingly large and well kept. It was made of flint and brick with a tiled roof which set it apart from the other cottages which were made of a more modest cob with thatched roofs. There was a wooden gate, which the sheriff opened, and a brick path

12

leading to a front door which stood open. Chickens rooted around amongst the cabbages and carrots planted in neat rows in the front garden and logs of wood were piled against the side of the house ready for the winter. And Mistress Bowman, whom they saw as they entered the house, was not the wizened old hag Nicholas had expected to see. She was sitting in a rocking chair, a child on her lap, and she looked up, startled, when they knocked and went in. Her strong, pleasant face was streaked with tears, but unlined. Her blue eyes were undimmed and the only indication of her age was the few wisps of white hair which strayed out from under her spotless white cap. Her arms which clasped the child to her were stout and strong as were her hands, which were large and capable and darkened by exposure to the sun. The child was dark-haired like his mother and he stared at them sadly with huge brown eyes, not knowing what had happened but sensing his great-grandmother's distress.

'I'm sorry to disturb you, mistress,' said the sheriff. 'This is a sorry day for you. We're bringing your granddaughter to lie in the church where the coroner's men will see her tomorrow.'

'I'll not have her lying in that godforsaken place,' said Mistress Bowman, setting the child down on the floor and rising to her feet. 'This is her home and here she'll stay as long as it takes to lay her in the churchyard. And bury her we shall, along with all the other Christian folk, whatever the priests say, because she would never take her own life. Why should she, sirs? She had everything to live for and this child was the apple of her eye. No, someone's done this to her and she deserves a proper burial alongside her grandfather.'

Mistress Bowman stood before them like an avenging angel. Her face was flushed with anger and her thick-set body quivered with passion. Although old, she was still fit and healthy and still retaining the smooth skin and clear

13

complexion which had made her a beauty when she was young. Her voice, too, was well modulated and had but a trace of the local dialect.

'If you want her brought here, then so be it,' said the sheriff meekly. 'It will make no difference to the coroner's men where they see her. The cause of death, I am sorry to say, is only too apparent.'

'I'll not believe it,' she said, bending down to pick up the child who was beginning to cry, obviously upset by her vehemence. 'She would never want to inflict this disgrace on us. She'd not want Henry to grow up knowing his mother deliberately drowned herself. What would he think? That his own mother rejected him and committed a mortal sin? No, sirs; there's been a mistake, and I want it set right.'

'She didn't take her own life, Mistress Bowman,' said Nicholas quietly. 'Someone strangled her. There are very clear marks on her neck. You'll soon see them for yourself. I am sorry to be the bearer of such shocking news. Now, please sit down, wipe you eyes, and let us ask you some questions.'

She picked up a piece of cloth and wiped her eyes. Then the child, Henry, curled up against her bosom and put a thumb into his mouth. She rocked him soothingly whilst staring in horror at them.

'Why should anyone want to harm her, sirs? My Sarah was a quiet girl, did no harm to anyone. Was she ...? Had anyone done anything else to her before he strangled her?'

'We can't tell, mistress,' said the sheriff; 'the sea would have washed all signs away. The coroner's men might find something when they take a proper look at her; but I don't think her murderer harmed her in the way you are think- ing. There are marks on the back of her head, but they could have been made by the rocks.'

The sheriff then left them to give orders for the body of Sarah Bowman to be brought to her house. He didn't like to tell her grandmother that the reason for bringing Sarah

to the church rather than to her home was that the hovels
of the poor were not a suitable place for the coroner's men
to make their examination. However, this obviously didn't
apply to the Bowman house which had more than enough
room for the coroner's investigation.

Nicholas drew a chair up next to Mistress Bowman and
sat down for a few minutes in silent sympathy. The child
had snuggled up against her breast and had gone to sleep.

'Your granddaughter was a lovely girl,' he said. 'We
shall do all we can to catch the person who did this terrible thing. Now, if it won't distress you too much, may I
ask some questions?'

'Ask away, sir,' she said, 'although I can't guarantee to
be able to answer them. Forgive me, sir,' she went on as
her eyes filled with tears and trickled down her face and
onto the sleeping child's head. 'I still can't take hold of this
news. I wondered where she'd got to last night as she didn't
come home; but that's not unusual. She knows Henry is
quite safe with me and she had her work to do. I thought it
was good for her to get out a bit; mind you, it now seems
I was wrong and should have insisted she came home to
sleep. But some of her friends live a fair way away and it's
customary in these parts to offer a night's lodging to visitors.'

'What time did she go out, mistress?' said Nicholas,
handing her the cloth to wipe her face

'Late afternoon. She said she felt like a walk before
darkness fell. She'd been working all day and I thought the
fresh air would be good for her. It was such a lovely
evening.'

'What sort of work did she do?'

'She was a needlewoman, sir, like her mother and me. I
always did plain work but she loved making beautiful
things. My daughter, Agnes, Sarah's mother, embroidered
for the good fathers up at Monksmere, before they were
turned out. She embroidered altar frontals, the fathers'
vestments, that sort of thing. She died soon after Sarah's

15

birth, but Sarah followed the tradition and learned how to do marvellous embroidery. I taught her the main stitches and she made up her own designs; beautiful they were – birds and flowers and seashells for example. She worked in that room over there,' she said, indicating a door which led off the room they were sitting in. 'It's got a good-sized window and lets in lots of light, even in the winter months.'

'Where did Sarah sell her work?'

'She sold it to anyone who wanted to buy it. Recently she went up to Tredgosse, to Lord Gilbert; not that she ever saw him, of course; she took her work to the housekeeper. Lord Gilbert's a widower, as you know, for some years now. He paid her well – in advance – so that she could buy her silks. The housekeeper said he valued her work highly. She was hoping to offer her services to Sir John Woodcock who bought Monksmere manor house last year, but that was not to be. Such talent; all come to nothing. It would have been better if she'd made her own winding sheet.'

She cried silently to herself until the sound of horses' hooves disturbed them. The sheriff came in.

'She'll be here soon, mistress. Best make up a bed for her to lie on.'

Nicholas glanced at the sheriff who took the hint and sat down at the long table which filled the middle of the room.

'Perhaps she went to see Sir John last night?' said Nicholas after a pause.

'No sir, she'd not do that; not at that hour of the day. Besides, she'd tell me if she was going up there. No, she most likely went to see Matilda. She's to be wed soon and wanted Sarah to embroider her wedding gown. She would stay the night if she went there. I've never worried about her, sir; you must believe me. Sarah was a good girl and knew what was right and wrong and how to look after herself. But last night she came face to face with evil and her bed was the sea.'

'And we'll find the person who put her there, mistress,' said the sheriff. 'We'll catch him and see he hangs for his

16

crime. Now get a place ready to lay out your granddaughter. She'll be here very soon.'

They rode side by side along the road to Dean Peverell as the daylight was fading. The sheriff had left his two men behind to guard the body and ask the woman called Matilda whether Sarah had been to see her yesterday evening.

'Well, what do you think, Lord Nicholas? Have we a straightforward murder of a pretty lass on our hands, or do you sense complications?'

'What do I think? Well, first, Richard, I think you should drop the title and call me Nicholas. We've worked together now for a long time and we shall probably continue in our partnership until one of us gives up and retires. So Nicholas it is. Now, as to the lass's death, I must admit that I am sure there is more to it than meets the eye; but it's too soon for me to jump to any conclusions. Girls get murdered not infrequently. If they are victims of lust their attacker might kill them afterwards to stop them reporting him. They can be victims of robbery and the same thing goes there. Sarah might have been carrying some valuable pieces of embroidery – she was a needlewoman, you know. Her attacker might have thought she was carrying money.'

'A robber might have inflicted those blows to the back of her head, but why then did he strangle her?'

'No, but a rapist would strangle his victim and maybe inflict the blows afterwards to make it look as if the girl had thown herself in the sea and her body was dashed against the rocks.'

'But he must have known people would see the marks round her neck? You can't hide those,' said the sheriff.

'No, but he might have hoped that by the time the body was found the sea would have removed the strangle marks. As it happened she was found sooner than he expected.'

'Then the man was a fool.'

'Murderers are not known for their wisdom, Richard.'

*

17

As they rode westward, a full, orange harvest moon illuminated the way ahead. A white mist hung low over the water meadows which gave Monksmere its name. Through the mist loomed the faces of cattle making them feel that they were being watched by a ghostly regiment. The farm carts had all gone home. The road was deserted.

'Mistress Bowman was well set up in that house, er, Nicholas,' said the sheriff after some hesitation over the use of Nicholas's name. 'I wonder where the money came from? There's no men around to provide the means to build such a fine place.'

'The same thought occurred to me, Richard,' Nicholas answered. 'She's a widow so I suppose her husband could have prospered and left her well provided for.'

'I suppose so. Sarah's mother, by all accounts, died soon after she was born. What happened to her husband? Did he not provide her with a house before he died?'

'Too many questions, Richard. It'll take us some time to find the answers. I fear we shall have to return to Monksmere tomorrow.'

'I shall certainly have to accompany the coroner's men. They will establish the cause of death so that Sarah can be given a decent burial. Then I shall send my men off round the neighbouring villages to find out more about the Bowman family. Somewhere, someone must have heard something last night; the lass must have screamed out at some point. Someone will know something that can help us in our investigations. There are always witnesses to these crimes. The difficulty is to get them to come forward.'

'I'll come with you,' said Nicholas decisively. 'I own some land in Monksmere, you might remember me telling you. Now, if Sir John Woodcock bought the manor of Monksmere off Lord Gilbert, then he probably bought my piece of land as well; and Lord Gilbert's keeping quiet about it. I shall need his confirmation that that part of the manor is mine. There won't be any dispute about it as the king signed the deed of transfer himself. Besides, it's time

18

I saw Lord Gilbert again and introduced myself to Sir John Woodcock. We may have him on the bench when there's a vacancy. I've been a bit negligent in welcoming new-comers to the district, so it's time I started to do my duty.'

'I've not made the acquaintance of the Woodcock family,' said the sheriff, urging his cob forward to keep up with Nicholas, whose horse, sensing he was on the home straight, had broken into a canter.

'Lord Gilbert's a strange man,' he said as he caught up. 'Likes his privacy and I don't trust people like that. Gentry's gentry and they should be seen about the county attending dinners and making speeches. People who hide themselves away, in my experience, are probably hiding something.'

'He might have sunk into melancholy after his wife died, Richard.'

'Humph! She's been dead a few years now and rumour has it that he's not short of female company.'

'Then it's time I paid him a visit. Let's hope he's at home tomorrow.'

'At home? He never goes out of that great place of his. Ask the people of Tredgosse; they don't even know what he looks like.'

The tower of his own priory church of Dean Peverell came into sight just as the twilight deepened into night. And there, to the north, the peaceful sight of his manor house; not a moated castle, but a gentleman's residence with an elegant gatehouse and turreted walls of a modest height, surrounded by a well-kept park and gardens which were the admiration of the county.

Chapter Three

As Nicholas rode across the drawbridge and into the court-yard, he felt as if he had left the sunshine behind and was entering a dark world of sorcerers and dragons – a world of legend and fairy tale. No one came to take his horse. No one came to welcome him. He looked round, half expecting to see a contingent of soldiers, wearing the Fitzherbert livery, emerge from the keep which was situated at the far end of the courtyard. Shrugging off these fanciful ideas, he tied Harry to a post and walked across to the main door. He tugged at the rope which hung at one side of the door and heard the strident tone of the bell; a sound which echoed round the courtyard like demonic laughter. What, he thought, was Lord Gilbert playing at? Castles like this were a thing of the past. All over the country gentlemen were building themselves civilised houses, places of beauty and refinement. Strongholds like Tredgosse were relics of a barbaric past.

He waited with growing impatience until, finally, the door creaked open and a small, frightened face peered out.

'Is Lord Gilbert at home?' said Nicholas.

'He might be,' said the face, 'depends who wants to see him.'

'Tell him I'm his neighbour, Lord Nicholas Peverell. He's met me before so no doubt he'll not object to seeing me again. Are you going to let me in?'

Slowly the door creaked open and Nicholas stepped inside the castle. The owner of the face turned out to be a diminutive man dressed in a plain doublet and hose which did nothing to conceal his spindly legs. Sparse hair covered his head and his beard was neatly trimmed. His grey eyes were wary as they surveyed Nicholas from head to foot, as if he was looking at a dog of unpredictable habits.

'Wait here, sir. Lord Gilbert is not yet dressed. He seldom emerges from his bedchamber until noon.'

'Tell him I apologise for disturbing his rest, but I have come to see him about a matter of some urgency.'

The servant disappeared leaving Nicholas wondering what sort of man could afford to get up from his bed at so late an hour.

Whilst he was waiting for Lord Gilbert to emerge from his chamber, Nicholas glanced round at his surroundings. He had been shown into the main hall of the castle, a massive room with a ceiling which disappeared up into the rafters. A great stone fireplace stood at one end, the fire unlit. As far as he could tell there was no chimney and looking up he saw that there was a hole in the roof which would let out any smoke – a custom that had rapidly gone out of fashion amongst the gentry. The surrounds of the fireplace were elaborately carved with heraldic emblems; unicorns and other mythical beasts capered along the top of the fireplace and down the stone columns at the sides. The stone floor was strewn with rushes; not as sweet-smelling as those which covered his own floor. Jane changed them frequently so that they always smelled fragrant and she always added fresh herbs daily.

A huge oak table occupied the centre of the hall, surrounded by twelve chairs. The chair at the end nearest the fireplace was a fine armchair elaborately carved with the same beasts which cavorted round the fireplace. The room felt cold and dank as if the sun had never penetrated these walls. There was an air of desolation about it, Nicholas thought, as if no one had sat at this table or lit the

21

fire for centuries. He could imagine it as it might have been in the past when guests were served with wild boar and venison and servants brought in flagons of ale and the logs roared up in the fireplace. Minstrels would have played up in that gallery, he thought, glancing up at the wooden gallery at the far end of the room, and a space would have been cleared for dancing. Instead there was silence except for the rustling sounds in the straw caused by small creatures who no doubt had made their nests there.

At last there was a sound of loud barking. The door at the far end of the hall opened; a huge wolfhound came leaping in and made straight for Nicholas, who ordered it to stop. With a growl of protest, the dog obeyed and collapsed on the floor beside him looking up at him suspiciously. He was a fine hound, thought Nicholas, very useful in the hunt or in catching escaping prisoners.

'I see you've made a friend, Lord Nicholas,' said a voice from the doorway. 'You are no doubt familiar with the breed.'

'It's a very brave breed. They serve you more faithfully than any human.'

Nicholas watched Lord Gilbert closely as he walked the length of the hall to where Nicholas was standing by the fireplace. He was much as he remembered him from the previous year; a little stouter, the streaks of grey in his dark hair, which he wore long, a little more plentiful. With a full beard he looked, except for his colouring, not unlike King Henry. He wore a dark robe over what was obviously a nightshirt and leather slippers on his bare feet. His short, podgy fingers were covered with rings of amazing patterns and stones and thick gold bracelets circled the wrists of both hands. His face was flushed as if he had indeed just got out of bed but somehow he managed to greet Nicholas with a smile of welcome and a shake of the hand.

'What brings you to Tredgosse, my lord? I am not accustomed to visitors at such an early hour, but as you are here, come and join me in a glass of mead, or whatever else you fancy. The day is fine, I understand. You must be thirsty.'

Lord Gilbert led the way out of the hall and into a smaller room where tapestries of hunting scenes covered the stone walls and the stone floor was partly covered with woollen rugs. There was a fire burning in this room and at the far end a window let in some daylight. Two armchairs with embroidered cushions stood on either side of the fireplace. Lord Gilbert seated himself in one and indicated to Nicholas to take a seat in the other. A servant entered and Nicholas accepted a tankard of ale.

'Well, what do you want from me, my lord?' said Lord Gilbert, who liked to get straight to the point.

'Nothing that's not mine,' said Nicholas, draining his tankard and accepting a refill. 'Also I need to ask you a few questions in connection with a case we are investigating.'

'How very interesting. Let's deal with what is yours first, shall we? How can I help you?'

'I need your confirmation that the piece of land in Monksmere which the king gave me is still mine. I have the deed here with the king's signature if you would like to see it.'

Lord Gilbert waved it away dismissively. 'There's no problem with your right to the land, my lord. The coming of Sir John Woodcock has made no difference to how things stood at your last visit. Come with me.'

He stood up and walked towards a door at the far end of the room, near the window. Nicholas followed him along a passageway which ended in a low door which Lord Gilbert opened, revealing a narrow stone spiral staircase.

'Come,' he said, turning to look at Nicholas. 'Let's take a look at your fields – water meadows, if I remember; good grazing, good for wildfowl, poor arable land.'

The staircase was very steep and the treads of the steps had been worn down through centuries of use. The only light came in through narrow slits in the wall and it was a relief to see the daylight in front of them at the last bend of the stair. They came out onto the top of the tower through

23

a narrow archway. A slight breeze had got up and brought with it the smell of the sea. They walked over to the turreted wall, where, through an embrasure, they could look down at the surrounding countryside. It was a peaceful sight; the sea glittering on the horizon, the small spire of Monksmere church and the great priory church of the Monksmere canons, still intact with its high square tower and gabled east end. There was a long, low, stone-built house to the right of the priory buildings and Lord Gilbert pointed to it.

'Woodcock's place. Nice little house. Used to belong to the prior's bailiff. Woodcock wanted to buy it and I saw no reason why I shouldn't lease it to him. Nice enough fellow. Came from Suffolk. Family were haberdashers. Can't think how Sir John got himself a knighthood and raised enough money to pay for the lease on that place. He's got a coat-of-arms, too, damn me, and his own heraldic crest. It's a boar's head surmounted by crossed swords. Damn cheek, I say. The man's never hunted boar in his life and as for the swords, he's never been near a battlefield. But so it is and no business of mine how he got his money. Must have known the right people at the right time and had enough money to pay the College of Arms. Now, your fields are to the south of his house and the road cuts them in half. Not as bad as it sounds, because the meadows to the east of the road run down to the river and there is a water mill there, which, I believe is yours by rights. That will be the most valuable bit. You'll have to find a miller to work the mill and a steward to manage the fields. Or you could, of course, sell it to Woodcock.'

'Thank you, my lord. You've given me a lot to think about. It's time I sorted my affairs out.'

Lord Gilbert made for the stairs and descended to the passage with considerable agility considering his size. Nicholas followed him back to the room where the wolfhound was now sprawled out in front of the fire.

'Now, help yourself to some more ale, and tell me how

24

I can help with your investigations,' said Lord Gilbert, settling himself back in his chair.

'The sheriff and I are investigating the death of a girl called Sarah Bowman,' said Nicholas. 'Can you tell us anything about her?'

'Who the devil is Sarah Bowman?' said Lord Gilbert, fondling the ear of the wolfhound.

'I thought you knew her. She did some work for you, I understand. She was an expert needlewoman.'

'A needlewoman? Damn it, my lord, I leave such matters to my housekeeper. Well, if she did some work for me, I expect I paid her well. Why come all this way to ask me about her?'

'Because her body was found early on Wednesday morning and there were signs on her body indicating that she'd been murdered. The coroner's men are taking a look at her body now.'

Nicholas watched Lord Gilbert carefully but there was no change of expression on his face and the brown eyes returned his scrutiny without a flicker of unease.

'Well I'm sorry for her. Has she any family? Where was her body found and who found it?'

'She lived with her grandmother. Her body was found on the shore at Atherington by a fisherman, name of Juppy.'

'My, my, what excitement. A murder! All the great and the good descending on this small place. Have you got any witnesses yet? Brought in any suspects?'

'I am seeing the sheriff later. It's early days so far.'

'But why tell me about the wench? I can't recall ever having seen her.'

'Because you might remember something which could help us. She has a child. There's no talk of a husband. Your housekeeper might have mentioned something about Sarah which would be of use to us.'

'I hardly discuss visiting needlewomen with my servants, Lord Nicholas. I can't help you, I'm afraid. Yes, what is it?' he said to the woman who entered the room at that

25

moment. She was quite extraordinarily beautiful: tall with a full figure, black hair brushed back from a high forehead and hanging down her back in a glossy stream. She wore a wine-red robe of simple design but heavily encrusted with elaborate embroidery around the neck and sleeves, and jewelled slippers that matched her dress.

'My lord,' she said hesitatingly as she looked at Nicholas.

'Not now, Adeliza; can't you see that I have a visitor?'

'But Justin is asking for you.'

'Justin, Justin, always Justin. Tell him he must wait a while. I am busy,'

'But, if I might ask, my lord, and not meaning to be presumptious,' said Nicholas, 'who did the beautiful embroidery on this lady's dress? Maybe it is Sarah Bowman's work?'

'Sarah?' said the woman, looking at Nicholas in surprise. 'Yes, this is her work. She embroidered these slippers too. Has something happened to Sarah, my lord?'

'Yes, yes,' said Lord Gilbert impatiently as if he wanted rid of the subject, 'she's dead, I'm sorry to say. So you will have to find a new needlewoman. Now, no more questions. Be off to your domestic duties.'

'But how can she be dead? I only saw her last week when she came up here with Henry to deliver some table napkins. Tell me what happened, my lord,' she said, looking at Gilbert beseechingly.

'Leave it, Adeliza. It's nothing to do with you. I don't like you interfering.'

'But she was invaluable. A gifted needlewoman as were her mother and grandmother,' she said, turning to Nicholas. 'Her mother embroidered lovely things for the priory church when the canons were here. I believe she also did some work for you, too, my lord, before I came here.'

'No, no, you've got it wrong. I never employed Agnes Bowman but I think she did do some work for the canons.'

'But you told me ...'

26

'I am sure that I never discussed the Bowman family with you or with anyone else, madam. Now get back to your duties and try to keep that child of yours under control.'

She flashed him an angry look with her dark eyes, and left the room. Nicholas prepared to leave.

'I must get back to the sheriff, my lord, and see how his enquiries are getting along. Thank you for your hospitality and for showing me the extent of my property.'

'It's nothing. I'm sorry I can't help you more with your investigation. Take no notice of Adeliza. I have been far too lenient with her. She has to learn her place.'

Nicholas walked out to the courtyard where Harry was waiting patiently. He mounted, and rode slowly across the drawbridge and out onto the main road, turning west towards the inn where he had arranged to meet the sheriff and the coroner's man. It was only a short ride but he was glad of the brief interval for thought. Why had Lord Gilbert pretended to know nothing about Sarah Bowman's family when the woman called Adeliza obviously assumed he did? How did he know the name of Sarah's mother? And who, in fact, was Adeliza? Not his wife, that was for sure, because Lord Gilbert had not introduced her to him which he would have done had she been. A most beautiful woman, he thought, as the Dog and Bell inn came in sight. Not aristocratic. Her voice, although well modulated, was that of the people – not local but from the area around St Paul's cathedral in the City of London. And who was Justin?

The sheriff was waiting for him when he went into the main room of the Dog and Bell. He was sitting in a corner seat along with his two men, Peter, whom Nicholas had met before, and another, younger man whom he didn't know but was introduced to him by the name of Dickon.

The landlord came up with another tankard and a flagon of ale. Nicholas took the tankard, accepted the ale, and sat down opposite the sheriff.

'Any news?' he said, taking them all in with his glance.

27

'Coroner agreed that death was due to unlawful killing. The lower part of her body had not been interfered with so she wasn't raped. The blow to the head could have been accidental or inflicted by her attacker. The marks round her neck were conclusive. So it's official, a murder hunt, Lord Nicholas,' he said, reverting to Nicholas's title in the presence of his men. 'He's gone off to Marchester and will announce the verdict. The funeral can take place tomorrow. It's at noon. I've told the grandmother.'

Nicholas nodded. All was as expected.

'So what have you discovered, Peter?' said Nicholas glancing at the dark, heavily bearded man who had worked with them on a previous case.

'I interviewed the woman called Matilda; Matilda Rushman is her full name. Her parents are well-to-do local farmers. Says she knew Sarah Bowman but she didn't come to see her on Tuesday evening. It's the best part of three weeks since she's seen her. However, I continued to ask around along with Dickon and one of the fishermen came up with something that could be important. He said he had seen a girl walking along the shore on Tuesday evening. He watched her for a few minutes as he thought it unwise for a lass to be walking on her own at that time of the day. But when she got to the rocks at Atherington a man came up to her. The fisherman hadn't seen him before. They continued to walk together and became engrossed in conversation. The fisherman's description of the lass fitted Sarah Bowman pretty well, but he wasn't much help with the man. He said he watched them for a little while, but as they seemed to know one another and the girl wasn't making any protest, he went home. He now regrets that he didn't stay longer.'

'So that man could have been her murderer?'

'Could have been, yes, if the lass was Sarah Bowman. His description of the man could have fitted almost any man of a certain age – medium height, stocky build, no horse that he could see but he could have left it up in a field. Not

28

much to go on. If he was the murderer and a stranger to these parts, then he'll be well away from here by now.'

'So we have a possible scene of a murder, a description of two people, one of whom could have been Sarah, but absolutely no motive. Who in God's name, Richard, would murder a young girl in cold blood? Unless her attacker was a madman, and in that case, we would have found him by now because everyone would know him,' said Nicholas.

'Not if he wasn't from these parts,' put in Peter.

'A madman on the loose would surely be seen by someone. This is a small village. Atherington has but a handful of fisherfolk and they would know each other intimately.'

'Unless the murderer was one of their own and someone is protecting him,' said the sheriff.

'That's possible,' said Peter, brightening up. 'And if that is the case, then we'll soon find him. You can't hide a man with an unsound mind for long in a small community. Someone will tell us. No one wants a murderer on the loose. Yes, I'd better get back to Atherington when we finish here.'

They drank their ale in silence, each one lost in thought. Suddenly the sheriff looked across at Nicholas.

'And you, my lord? How did you find the lord of Tredgosse Castle?'

'An interesting set-up, Richard. Like something out of an old minstrel's tale. A powerful-looking man, courteous enough, took me up to the top of the tower and showed me my fields, and lives with a dark-haired beauty and someone called Justin. Knows nothing about Sarah Bowman, but the woman confirmed that she had worked for the household, as did her mother. Lord Gilbert appeared not to know anything about this.'

'That'll be the woman called Adeliza,' said Dickon.

'He likes a gossip, does Dickon,' said Peter gruffly. 'You mustn't mind him.'

'Don't stop him, Peter. Gossip is just what we need at

this moment,' said Nicholas. 'You see, I can't go along with the madman theory. You can't hide a madman and if he was on the loose, someone would have seen him and reported him to us by now. Sarah Bowman was murdered by a cunning man who tried to make it look as if she had drowned herself. We have to find out why he wanted her out of the way. The answer to that will only emerge from gossip. So, Dickon, what do you know about this Adeliza?'

'She's someone who's lived with him for some years now; ever since his wife died, in fact. They call her Lord Gilbert's concubine down in Monksmere. Comes from London. People round here don't like her as they say she thinks she's a bit superior. She doesn't welcome visitors and doesn't know the meaning of the word charity. Not like your wife, sir, if I might be so bold. Now this Adeliza's got a child by Lord Gilbert. A boy called Justin. He's four now – a strong fellow, already handy with a sword and bow and arrow. Not like Lord Gilbert's real son and heir by his wife, who died having him, God rest her soul.'

'So he has an heir. What is the matter with him? Carry on, Dickon, you are being very helpful. The sheriff will be mighty pleased with you.'

'The ladies like him, that's why he knows so much,' grunted the sheriff. 'It'll get him into trouble one of these days if he doesn't watch out.'

'I am always discreet,' protested Dickon, 'I only listen.'

'Then let it stay that way,' said the sheriff. 'But carry on, man. You can talk to us. Lord Nicholas has asked you a question.'

'I am coming to that but I was interrupted. Lord Gilbert's son, so I was told, is a poor twisted boy of ten years old. His name is Marcus. Mind you, folk like to exaggerate but I heard he has a twisted back and short, bent legs that can scarcely support his body. He's just a slip of a lad, but he's got a good brain in that head of his and is fond of Justin who can do all the things he can't do, but hasn't much of a brain for letters and such.'

30

'That probably accounts for Lord Gilbert's melancholy,' said Nicholas, 'but it still doesn't give us a motive for Sarah Bowman's murder. However somewhere we'll unearth it. I suggest you carry on talking to people, Richard, and give Dickon here another tankard of ale. He's done well. I'm off to meet Sir John Woodcock now and see if he knows anything about Sarah Bowman. Sooner or later things will fall into place. These are small communities and everyone knows everyone else's business.'

'And I'll get back to Marchester,' said the sheriff, standing up. 'Keep listening, lads,' he went on. 'Routine work. I'll send a cart down just in case you want to bring in any suspects. Let's hope Sir John can tell us something useful.'

'He's well liked,' said Dickon, sitting back in the corner of the oak settle with his second flagon of ale. 'Got a nice wife, too. Very charitable. Not like the ogre up there in his castle.'

'Then I look forward to meeting him,' said Nicholas, making for the door. Outside, he unhitched his patient horse from the post and rode back to Monksmere.

Nothing could be less like Tredgosse Castle than Sir John's manor house which Nicholas reached early that afternoon. He approached it from the main road down a narrow, grassy track which skirted the deserted priory's boundary wall. The house had been there since earliest times; the lord of the manor invariably a nominee of the lords of Tredgosse and a tenant of the priory. The eviction of the canons, however, had changed these customs; King Henry had appropriated the priory and the surrounding lands and sold off the manor house to the highest bidder. Lord Gilbert had simply administered these changes.

Monksmere manor stood in its own modest park with a driveway leading up to the front door situated in the centre of the building. The house was strongly built in local stone, with a tiled roof and windows which Sir John had already had enlarged. At the moment, a chimney stack of ornate design was under construction. Sir John, it seemed, was a man of modern tastes, thought Nicholas as he rode up to the door. He suspected that there were stables at the back of the building where Sir John would keep his horses and a carriage to take his wife on her visits around the neighbourhood. It all looked peaceful and prosperous, the grass neatly trimmed, the flower beds well stocked with unusual plants. Nicholas dismounted at the front door and looked around him. To the south stood the ruins of the priory, and on the horizon the sea glittered in the sunlight. A stable hand appeared and led Harry away. The door opened immediately to his knock and a neatly dressed servant invited him inside. Nicholas found himself in a large, comfortable room which obviously had once been the main hall of the old manor house but was now furnished with good quality oak furniture, tapestries of scenes from classical mythology on the walls and, instead of the usual rushes, carpets on the floor. Everything indicated a gentleman's residence; a gentleman, thought Nicholas, of considerable fortune.

If Lord Gilbert had looked like a baron of the old days, Sir John Woodcock looked every inch the retired Ipswich haberdasher which he had been in his old life. He was a man in his middle years, of medium height, stocky with a large, good-natured face. He was beardless and his hair, which he wore on the long side, was of an indiscriminate shade of brown streaked with grey. His eyes, pale blue and slightly watery, looked shrewdly at Nicholas as if calculating his worth. He was dressed in plain, good quality countryman's clothes and his riding boots looked as if they were made of the finest leather. He came up to Nicholas with a welcoming smile, rubbing his hands together nervously as if uncertain how to greet someone of Nicholas's rank.

'My lord,' he said, 'what an honour. My, my, Lord Nicholas Peverell here, in my small house. What can I do for you, my lord?'

It seemed churlish to introduce the subject of his fields

32

so early in their acquaintance; instead he assumed the role of the sheriff's constable and asked Sir John if he knew Sarah Bowman.

'I've heard of her, of course. She is an accomplished needlewoman, I've been told. Ah, here comes my wife. You'd best talk to her, I think. Joan, dear, come and meet Lord Nicholas Peverell who has honoured us with a visit.'

Joan Woodcock advanced towards Nicholas, smiling shyly. She was about the same age as her husband, a comfortable woman with a homely face, her hair covered by a neat, unfashionable cap. Her brown linen dress and spotless white apron indicated that she was performing some domestic task.

'Welcome to Monksmere, madam,' said Nicholas, acknowledging her curtsy. 'I am sorry that I have not welcomed you before; we live but a few miles from here, but unfortunately I don't often have a reason to visit Monksmere.'

'Well, we can change that,' said Sir John heartily. 'You are most welcome to my house any time you choose to call.'

'Certainly you must come again and bring your wife. I hear she is a most beautiful and accomplished lady who has sung before the king at court,' said Joan Woodcock.

'Thank you, madam, we shall be delighted to take up your offer. But I hope you find the company hereabouts agreeable?'

'Oh yes, my lord. Everyone is very kind. I still can't get used to my husband's good fortune. A knighthood and the purchase of a place here in Sussex – it all seems a long way away from our modest house in Ipswich.'

'You must miss your family and friends, madam?' said Nicholas, sensing a certain wistfulness in her expression when she thought of her previous life.

'Oh, there's too much to keep her occupied here, Lord Nicholas. I don't like her harking back to the past. Soon, before the autumn rains set in, some of the members of both our families will pay us a visit. We've no shortage of accom-modation here, as you can see. Now stop talking about Ipswich and fetch Lord Nicholas some of our wine. We have good quality wine here, my lord, all the way from Bordeaux. Soon, I hope our own vines will be as good as those of France. But now we have to be content with the wine which our good friends, the Ipswich vintners, gave us as a leaving present. The best glasses, remember,' he said to his wife who turned round and scowled at him from the doorway.

'Of course, husband. As you said, we are not in Ipswich now.'

Whilst they waited for the wine, Nicholas brought up the subject of his land which the king had given him. After Sir John had glanced at the deed of transfer signed by the king, he conceded Nicholas's claim with gracious acquiescence.

'It will be good to have the mill working again, my lord,' said Sir John as his wife came back into the room followed by a servant carrying a tray with glasses on it and a flagon of wine. She had removed her apron and put on another cap decorated with lace and ribbons.

'Then may I leave it to you to find me a miller and start work as soon as possible, Sir John. I will send my steward to draw up an agreement dividing the profits between us. As for the fields, you are welcome to make use of them and help yourself to whatever wildfowl you might want. In return, a small rent would suit me fine. I am sure we can arrange things to suit both of us.'

'You are most kind, my lord. I have an interest in farming; it hurts me to see a good working mill not earning its keep. The canons, I understand, enjoyed a healthy profit from the sale of the flour. They were shrewd businessmen.'

'You say "canons", Sir John. The monks who lived in my priory were black monks, following the Rule of St Benedict. Yours were obviously a different breed.'

'Oh yes, I believe so,' said Sir John, delighted to show off his knowledge to such an important guest. 'The inhabi-tants of Monksmere Priory were canons following the Rule

34

of St Augustine. They were black canons, you know, because they wore black cloaks. They were priests who were allowed out of the priory to help out in the parishes around here when there was a shortage of parish clergy. A very worthy bunch of holy men, I understand. Not that I am supporting an outdated religious order, my lord. I support King Henry completely. Changes were urgently needed.'

'And not before time,' put in his wife, refilling Nicholas's glass. 'By all accounts, they were a bunch of rogues; frequenters of the alehouse up in Tredgosse and everything else that goes on in such places.'

'Be quiet, woman, you don't know what you're talking about. Now Lord Peverell has also come here to ask us about Sarah Bowman. Might I enquire why you are interested in her, my lord?'

'She was murdered last Tuesday night and her body dumped in the sea near Atherington rocks. She is to be buried tomorrow. At the moment, she lies in her grandmother's house. It's all a bit of a mystery. We have heard that someone saw a girl answering to Sarah's description down on the shore by the rocks last Tuesday evening talking to a stranger. And that's all we have to go on at the moment. Her grandmother, Kate Bowman, told us that Sarah's mother used to work for the canons and Sarah herself did fine embroidery and was planning to come and see you about doing some work for you. Did she ever do that, madam?' he asked Joan Woodcock, who seemed to be upset at the news.

'Oh the poor lass. Who would want to murder her? And the child, my lord? Who's looking after him?'

'Hush, woman, control yourself,' said her husband roughly. 'Lord Nicholas doesn't want to see you weeping and wailing. You are not with your Ipswich gossips now, you know.'

'I am sorry to distress you, madam,' said Nicholas, watching, with sudden interest, Joan Woodcock's attempts to control her agitation. 'I didn't realise Sarah meant so much to you.'

'Oh no, my lord. My wife hardly knew her. She's a soft-hearted woman, that's what. Always getting involved in everyone's troubles. A great shame we had no children; she finds it very hard.'

'I'm sorry, Lord Nicholas,' Joan Woodcock said, wiping her face with the edge of her sleeve. 'It's the child Henry I feel sorry for. No father and now no mother and brought up by an old woman.'

'Kate Bowman seems very capable, madam. She will look after the child very well.'

'Perhaps we could have him here with us,' said Joan looking pleadingly at her husband, whose irritation was increasing by the minute.

'Have him here? Are you out of your mind, woman? We can't bring up every lass's unwanted bastard.'

'But Sarah was special.'

'Of course she wasn't; an unwed girl with a talent for embroidery, that's all she was. Now get back to your dairy, or whatever you're doing, and leave Lord Nicholas and me to talk about important matters. You must forgive her, my lord,' he said when his wife had left the room. 'A childless wife is very hard to live with.'

'Her compassion is very commendable, sir,' said Nicholas. 'Not many people would offer to shelter the child of an unwed, murdered girl.'

'Oh, she'd gather up all the bastards in the neighbour-hood if she had her way. I must see to it that I find her some comfortable dog on which she can lavish her affections. Poor soul, I pity her. I trust that your wife bears you fine offspring, my lord?'

Nicholas smiled as he made ready to leave. 'We were only wed last January, Sir John. My wife has years ahead of her to bear us children. All in God's good time.'

'I wish you joy of her, Lord Nicholas. You will come again? And maybe bring her with you?'

'Certainly. She is a great enthusiast for the sport of falconry. Also, I have still to find the answers to a lot of questions concerning Sarah Bowman's death. You will probably get a visit from the sheriff soon. Or, most probably from one of his men. The sheriff never leaves a murder case unsolved. Good day to you, sir.'

He left the manor house and rode slowly back to Dean Peverell. There was much to think about. He would have to attend Sarah Bowman's funeral and talk again with the grandmother. He also would have to see Woodcock again and Lord Gilbert. Just because they were gentry he couldn't eliminate them from the investigation. He was puzzled by Joan Woodcock's reaction to Sarah's death. She might, of course, be someone easily upset by the news of a girl's murder; and she might be concerned over the fate of a motherless child; but her distress did seem a bit excessive for someone she didn't know.

He arrived home just as the daylight was deepening into a rich twilight. Enquiring where Jane might be, he was told that she had gone down to the village to attend to her father who had developed a high fever and taken to his bed. Alarmed that Jane might succumb to the same infection, he decided to ride down to the village and bring her home. Others could look after an old man who had always suffered from infections of the lungs.

Chapter Four

Nicholas reached Guy Warrener's house just as Jane was coming out of the front door. She carried the basket she always used when she visited the sick and for a moment she stood there deep in thought. Then she saw Nicholas and her face broke into a wonderful smile of welcome.

'Come,' he called down to her; 'Jump up on Harry and we'll ride home together. Here, give the basket to me.'

She handed up the basket and, ignoring the mounting block by the gate, leapt up behind Nicholas. Harry danced around, showing off, and when Jane was firmly in place set off home at a brisk pace.

'How is he, Jane?' Nicholas called back to her.

'As well as can be expected. He's got his usual cough and fever; a bit worse than usual, though. I've given him something for the cough, but had to add feverfew and a tiny bit of an opiate for the pain. He'll live, I'm sure. Can't you tell Harry to slow down a bit? I'm being tossed about like a ship in a storm.'

Nicholas laughed and checked Harry, who tossed his head in protest. Nicholas was proud of his wife's skills with herbs. Old Agnes Myles had taught her a great deal before she died last year, leaving her cottage with all its phials of medicines and her garden stuffed with herbs to Jane, who had turned it into an apothecary's shop for the benefit of the villagers. Jane spent a lot of time there, mixing up her potions and attending to all and sundry. Too much time, he thought as they turned into the drive leading up to their manor house. It wasn't good for a young woman to pore over old herbal books and worry herself over other people's aches and pains. However it made her happy and he felt everything would change once babies came.

They dismounted in the courtyard and Nicholas sniffed appreciatively at the contents of the basket.

'One day I'll be ill and you can mix me up one of your potions. Make sure there's plenty of wine in it.'

She laughed and took the basket from him. 'It'll be water for you, if you should be laid low, Nicholas. You sound like my father; he's always suggesting a flagon of wine would do him more good than my juniper berries. He's taken to his bed with this sickness which isn't like him, but Anna said she'd stay with him and Hugh will come if he gets any worse.'

'Then put him out of your mind and see what Mary's planning for supper. And tell Balthazar to get ready to entertain us after we've eaten.'

The roast goose stuffed with apricots and raisins was delicious and Balthazar was in fine form. Then, after a deeply satisfying lovemaking, Nicholas and Jane slept soundly in one another's arms.

The next morning, Nicholas rode down to Monksmere to attend Sarah Bowman's funeral. Through long experience in investigations of this sort, he knew funerals were valuable sources of information. Frequently there were surprises: old friends of the family could turn up unexpectedly; members of the family whom no one had seen for years nearly always came to funerals. And there were the strangers who stood awkwardly at the back of the church and slipped away as soon as the service was over. These were the people he would have to look out for.

It was a hot, still day. Summer was dissolving into autumn in a golden haze and dewy nights. The little church at Monksmere was packed with parishioners. Although the Bowman family was not particularly popular, everyone was sorry that a pretty young girl's life had been cut off so brutally and people were anxious to support Kate Bowman in her grief.

Nicholas joined the sheriff and his two men at the back of the church and they exchanged subdued greetings. Nicholas glanced at the congregation. The sheriff saw his look and shook his head.

'Nothing untoward,' he said. 'Only friends. There's no family to speak of except for the old lady and the young lad, of course.'

Kate Bowman was sitting on one of the benches placed in front of the bier on which rested the slight figure of Sarah Bowman, wrapped in a white linen shroud. The child Henry was next to her. A group of the village men stood awkwardly at the side of the church waiting to carry Sarah's body to her resting place in the churchyard. The service was soon over. The people shuffled out in the bright sunshine and walked over to where a grave had been dug in the churchyard, the priest leading the way. Then they grouped round the grave whilst the last words were said. Nicholas and the sheriff stood at a respectful distance.

Suddenly, the sheriff nudged Nicholas. 'Now who might this be?' he said, nodding towards a figure of a woman who had entered the churchyard and stood by the gate watching the proceedings. She was dressed in a grey gown and her head and shoulders were covered by a loose veil. Through the white material, Nicholas could just make out the features of Joan Woodcock.

'Now what brings Woodcock's wife here?' he muttered to the sheriff. 'And there's no sign of her husband. Does he know she's here, I wonder?'

The priest had finished the final prayers and the gravediggers set about their work of filling in the hole. The mourners turned to leave. Kate Bowman had offered refreshments before people went back to their homes and

40

everyone began to drift off down the church lane towards her house. Suddenly, the veiled figure rushed forward and seized the child, Henry, who clung to his grandmother's skirt and started to cry.

'Please, please,' Joan Woodcock said, 'please let me take care of him – just for a little while. He's so precious.'

She had thrown back her veil and now everyone could see her. Kate Bowman looked at her with hatred and gathered the child up in her arms. Nicholas and the sheriff, sensing trouble, stepped forward.

'You will never have him, never. He is my granddaughter's child and he is my responsibility until he grows up. Get back to your husband and leave us alone. Look, here he is; he's come to find you, and by his appearance he's very angry. This child is none of your business; get away from us.'

Then, to Nicholas's amazement, Joan Woodcock fell on her knees in front of Kate Bowman, clutching at her dress and preventing her from joining the other parishioners who were now well on their way to the Bowman house. Sir John Woodcock, his face blazing with anger, darted across the grass and seized hold of his wife, hauling her roughly to her feet.

'For God's sake, woman, what are you doing here? Get up and leave Mistress Bowman alone. The child is not your concern. My apologies, mistress,' he said to Kate Bowman who still clutched the child to her possessively. 'My wife doesn't know what she's doing. Please forgive her. Let me pay for the cakes and ale, it's the least I can do, and I'll take my wife home.'

He thrust some coins into Kate Bowman's hands and pushed his wife away from her. Half carrying, half dragging, he forced her across the grass towards the carriage that stood in the lane outside the church.

Nicholas looked at Kate Bowman, who still looked shocked, but as the carriage went away she relaxed and put the child down.

41

'I'm sorry, Mistress Bowman,' he said. 'This is most upsetting for you. We didn't expect anything of this kind to happen today. How well do you know Lady Woodcock?'

'Know her? Why, not at all, sir. We are used to seeing her in church, of course, and she always looked at Henry, sort of longingly, I thought, but she never behaved like she has today. Poor soul; I fear her mind is deranged. You'll come back to the house, sirs,' she said. 'There's only ale and some cakes and a bit of bread and cheese, but it will refresh you.'

'Thank you, mistress, we'll be pleased to join you. Peter and Dickon here will see that you get back to your house safely and Lord Nicholas and I will ride on ahead.'

Nicholas untied Harry from the gatepost and slowly mounted, deliberately letting the sheriff and Peter and Dickon get a head start. The scene he had just witnessed had disturbed him. Something was not right. Joan Woodcock's behaviour was too extreme; even if one took into consideration the natural longing of a childless wife for a child. And her husband's reaction had seemed heartless, cruel even. There was much more to be revealed, he thought, as he gathered up the reins in order to urge Harry forward. Then, suddenly, he heard something. A sound so slight that normally he wouldn't have taken any notice. It was just the sound of a twig breaking and the slight rustle of a leaf. He turned round in his saddle and looked back at the graveyard. No one was there. There was the yew tree by the gate but no one lurked in its shade. A fox, he thought; a cat on the prowl. Even so ... He waited. Nothing materialised. No more sounds. So he ordered Harry forward and rode after the sheriff to the Bowmans' house.

Despite the tragic manner of her granddaughter's death, Kate Bowman had not stinted on the food and ale required on these sad occasions. When Nicholas joined the throng of people crammed into the Bowmans' main room, faces were already flushed with the first round of ale and hands were stretching out for refills. The central table was heaped high with slices of bread, rounds of cheese and a huge side of beef. But, because the death had been a tragedy and people were uncertain of how to behave in such circumstances, the room was strangely quiet. Everyone's eyes were fixed on the table, but no one was bold enough to help himself. Nicholas accepted a tankard of ale and went over to offer his condolences to Kate Bowman who was sitting at the far end of the room by the window. She was surrounded by her female neighbours who took turns to keep the child Henry occupied. She started to get up when she saw Nicholas but he told her to rest whilst she could. The women drew back respectfully when he spoke to her.

'I just want to say how sorry I am about this tragedy. This is a sad occasion for you and the child,' he said, groping for suitable words and falling back on familiar sentences.

'Indeed it is, sir. She was young and fair and had such a talent ... But there it is, God called her to be with Him.'

'But her end was untimely, mistress. God had not prepared her for this.'

'Have you got any idea yet, sir, about who might have done this to her? The sheriff says no arrest has been made.'

'I'm afraid not; but we continue to search the area and will question everyone in the vicinity. Forgive me asking this, Mistress Bowman, but had Sarah any enemies who might have wanted to harm her? A jealous suitor, for instance? I understand that the father of her child is no longer around so there must have been others wanting to marry her. A child is no impediment in such circumstances, and a child as bonny as Henry would be a positive inducement to offer matrimony.'

Kate Bowman shook her head. 'Alas, no, sir. I don't know of anyone who was wooing her. She kept herself to herself. She was much respected, see. Despite having a child, no one condemned her. She kept quiet about Henry's

43

father. The first I knew of it was when she could hide the baby's presence no longer under her apron. Whoever was responsible for her condition never came to this house. He never saw his son. A fly-by-night, I expect. A moment of weakness on Sarah's part when summer was here and the flowers blooming and a young man passing through the village caught her fancy.'

'She never mentioned him, mistress? Not even after the child was born and you sat together of a winter's evening and she felt the urge to confide in you?'

'No sir, never. It was the same with her mother, my daughter Agnes. Beautiful she was – the Bowman women have all been beautiful. Even I turned heads when I was young. Agnes, too, concealed her baby as long as she could. I, sir, am the only respectably married woman of the Bowman household and my husband's grave is up there in the churchyard to prove the point,' she said, with a sudden flash of anger which gave colour to her face which had been white and strained with fatigue during the funeral service. 'A daughter and a granddaughter, both with mysterious lovers. It is as if the fairies took them into their care and gave them babies. And much inconvenience it has caused me. But Jack, my husband, sir, left me well provided for and I was able to cope. He worked up there with the canons who lived well and wanted good farmers to work their lands and rear their herds. Goodness knows what he'd do now that they've gone. Anyway it was a good thing that one member of our family did the right thing and married the man she loved before she considered bearing children. So be it; Henry is a delightful child and I shall see to it that he's brought up properly.'

Nicholas bowed and left her with her women. The signal had been given for everyone to start eating and the heaps of food piled on the table were steadily diminishing.

'Funerals always makes me hungry, sir,' said one of the guests, an old man whose piled-up plate caught Nicholas's eye. 'Soon, it'll be my turn for the last rites and I want to make the most of this life whilst I can.'

44

Nicholas smiled and walked over to where the sheriff and Peter and Dickon were tucking into plates of cold beef. They were standing apart from the other guests, very much aware that everyone was watching them. They made a space for Nicholas.

'No help from Mistress Bowman, my lord?' said the sheriff.

'I'm afraid not. By all accounts both her daughter and her granddaughter kept quiet about their lovers.'

'Well, one thing's certain, ruling out the miraculous, someone helped Sarah Bowman make that baby. You would think the wench would want to name her lover; even if she only wanted to get some money out of him.'

'Mistress Bowman said she was left enough money by her husband to support them all.'

'That's mighty generous of him. What did he do for a living?'

'Worked for the canons up at the priory.'

'They must have paid him very well. A meal like this doesn't come cheap. Something's not right, my lord. Everyone here is as tight-lipped as a basketful of oysters. Look at them all; eating, yes; watching us, yes; that's only natural. But just notice how they lower their eyes when you look at them. Now, you may rest assured that I am going to get to the bottom of this. What went on here in this village of Monksmere that makes everyone look so shifty? Damn me, I intend to speak to them. Peter, call for silence.'

Peter, however, didn't need to utter a word. As soon as the sheriff put down his plate and stepped forward, silence fell. Outside a cart rumbled by. Through the open front door came the heady scent of lavender and the sound of the seagulls shouting to one another with their raucous cries whilst they waited hopefully for scraps from the feast.

'Now listen to me, everyone,' said the sheriff, his tongue loosened by the two tankards of ale he'd drunk. 'We are here to offer our sympathies to Mistress Bowman on the tragic death of her granddaughter. And we thank you, mistress, for your generous hospitality on such a day as this.'

The company growled their thanks and Kate Bowman nodded her head in acknowledgement.

'Now, I am here with my men and Lord Nicholas, who, in his capacity of Justice of the Peace, is helping us and we are going to find the wicked person who took the life of Sarah Bowman. We are a law-abiding people in Sussex and we cannot allow a murderer to remain on the loose. We shall do our utmost to find him and Lord Nicholas will see to it that he is suitably punished in accordance with the law. However we want you to help us. We want to know everything about Sarah Bowman. Who were her friends? Had she any admirers? Did she reject a suitor who set about getting his revenge? Any information will be helpful; any tittle-tattle – we want to hear it. We shall be making our headquarters up at the Dog and Bell and one of us will always be there to talk to any of you who come forward. There will be good money for any information that might lead us to the killer. Peter, show them.'

Peter took a small leather bag out of his pocket and held it up for everyone to see. 'Ten marks, sirs. And more where this has come from for any information which might help us. And if you're frightened to come forward, there's no need to be. We'll protect you.'

A murmur of excitement followed this speech, but still Nicholas was conscious of a certain sullenness in the faces of the people watching them. Some were even edging their way towards the door; a thing unheard of when there was still food on the table and ale in the cask. The sheriff turned to Nicholas in exasperation.

'Damn me, my lord, what a surly collection of rogues. You'd think the sight of money would jog someone's memory.'

'Neither ten marks nor ten hundred marks would make us tell what went on here,' said a voice from the back of the room. Silence fell as a tiny figure pushed his way to the front. He was small in stature, thin as a rake with a tiny elfin face and scanty grey hair. He had obviously drunk his fill of Kate Bowman's ale because his cheeks were flushed and his eyes wild. Before he could say any more, Kate rose to her feet and rushed forward. She seized him by the shoulders and spun him round to face her.

'Cease your drunken nonsense, Morriss,' she said. 'Take no notice of him, sirs,' she advised the sheriff's party. 'He's a right troublemaker. Get back to your moles; there's more molehills in the graveyard than graves at the moment. Be off with you!' And she pushed him with such vehemence that he flew through the door and bolted off down the path.

'Stop him,' shouted the sheriff. Then, as no one did, 'After him, Peter,' as the little figure ran out of the gate and disappeared.

'Who was that man, mistress?' he asked Kate. 'What does he know?'

'Nothing, sir. Nothing at all. He's just a blabbermouth. A dimwit ever since he was born. His name's Morriss. We call him Morriss the mole-taker and he lives in an old shack on the edge of the parish. It's a disgusting place covered in moleskins.'

'Seems to me we should go and speak to this Morriss the mole-taker, Lord Nicholas. We'll go and find him now. Things are looking up. The offer of more money should loosen some tongues,' said the sheriff.

'And I'll make for home, Richard. Jane's father took a turn for the worse last night and I must get back to her. Let me know what you find here and we'll meet up in Marchester sometime tomorrow. Good day to you, mistress,' he said to Kate, who was still looking angry. 'Thank you again for your hospitality.'

It was late afternoon when Nicholas arrived home. Something was wrong, he thought, as he rode into the courtyard. No one came to take Harry. The silence was

47

ominous. Then his steward appeared, flustered and ill-at-ease.

'What is it?' Nicholas said. 'Speak up, man. What's happened?'

'It's my lady's father, my lord. He died this morning. Lady Jane is with him now.'

'Then we must bring his body up here and lay him in the chapel. See to it that there's a table ready to put his body on. And get the priest and prepare a coffin for him. He must be laid to rest in the plot where my family lies. Make haste now.'

As he watched his steward, Cecil Hunter, only appointed last year, a reliable and faithful servant, he thought of Jane and how sad she would be at the death of her father. There had been little love lost between him and Guy Warrener, his father-in-law, who always spoke his mind with alarming frankness. However, he loved his only child and wanted to protect her from all possible hurt. Life was changing, he thought; he didn't yet know in which direction it was pointing.

Chapter Five

With Guy Warrener's body laid out in his family chapel and Jane and her great-aunt supervising the funeral arrangements, Nicholas set off to see the sheriff in Marchester. He was reluctant to leave Jane as she had spent a restless night grieving for her father, but with the coming of daylight she had gathered her strength and turned her mind to organising the funeral arrangements. Mixed with her grief there was a concern about the cause of her father's death, and Nicholas knew that she would not be satisfied until she had checked every ingredient and every measurement in the medicine which she had prescribed for her father over those last days. Nicholas had tried to reassure her that she had done all she could. The old man was getting on; he'd been ill with a fever and a cough; he was prone to chest infections. This time he had not recovered. But she was not convinced.

The day was warm, the roads were still in good condition. With the coming of the autumn rains it would all change. He joined the steady stream of carts and horses making their way to Marchester for market day. When he reached the town he made straight for the centre of the town, past the newly built cross where crowds had gathered to watch the tumblers and gossip with friends. The taverns were doing well and as the weather was fine people had spilled out into the road adding to the congestion. He pushed his way past pedlars selling their fripperies to the country folk eager for novelties. Piemen were doing a roaring trade and the stallholders selling cheeses and local produce in the shade of the market cross were quietly relieving people of their money.

Turning into the road that ran north from the cross he rode up to the sheriff's house. Leaving Harry with a stable hand he pushed open the door to the sheriff's office – a large room in the comfortable wooden-framed house built long ago in times when the upper storey, where the sheriff lived with his family, jutted out across the street. Peter, the sheriff's man, was there and he rose to his feet when he saw Nicholas.

'I'll get the sheriff for you, my lord. He's not gone far. Two thieves were caught red-handed last night. No doubt you'll be meeting them soon at the next Sessions.'

Nicholas sat down. Ale was brought to him and he drank it readily. Two flies buzzed disconsolately round the closed window. Time passed and still he waited. Suddenly he jumped to his feet, not prepared to wait any longer. What was the world coming to when the gentry were kept waiting for an unreasonable time, he thought?

Then the door opened and the sheriff came in followed by Peter. Something was wrong. Nicholas, who knew his friend well, could see that immediately. The sheriff was not the same man. Gone was the exuberant self-confidence, the cheerful handshake, the bursting energy.

'Good God, Richard, what's amiss? You look like a man awaiting execution.'

To his surprise, the sheriff didn't laugh. In fact he looked even more worried, terrified even.

'Sit down, man,' said Nicholas, much surprised, 'and let Peter fetch you some ale. You look all in. Have the thieves been giving you stick?'

'No, no, my lord; they are safely locked away pending trial. Take no notice of me. I am a little fatigued, that's all.'

50

'Fatigued? You? Don't talk rubbish, man. You were as lively as a young cockerel yesterday evening. Best let my wife make you up a restorative cordial. Are you sick in the stomach?'

'Indeed I am. I've taken nothing to eat this morning. It must have been the rabbit my wife cooked last night which is doing this to me.'

Saying this, he flopped down into a chair and drank down, in one draught, the tankard of ale which Peter handed him.

'Now pull yourself together, man,' said Nicholas impatiently, 'we have an investigation on our hands. Have you any further thoughts on the murder of the girl, Sarah Bowman, or have you forgotten all about her in your sufferings?'

'The investigation? Yes, I have given it some thought and I have come to the conclusion that there is little more we can do for the time being. It appears to be a straight-forward case of death by drowning. That's all.'

Nicholas stared at the sheriff in astonishment. What on earth had happened to his old friend who never gave up on a case until it was solved and the culprit caught? He'd always had the tenacity of a ferret. Nicholas glanced at Peter, whose dark, bearded face gave nothing away. But was there something in those dark eyes? Nicholas wondered. A wariness? A warning? Nicholas began to feel uneasy.

'Richard, what is this? Why have you suddenly lost heart? You know Sarah Bowman was murdered. You saw her body. You know something had been going on down in Monksmere. You heard what that mole-catcher fellow said at the funeral feast yesterday. We've got work to do, man. It's no use moping around here nursing a sick belly.'

Wearily, the sheriff got to his feet. 'Lord Nicholas, I can do no more. I have other, more important thing to see to. I am deeply sorry to hear of the death of your father-in-law. Do send my condolences to your wife. Will the funeral take place on Monday? If so, my wife and I will be honoured to attend. And now I really must go. If I might be so bold, I would like to give you a piece of advice, my lord, and I do so with all sincerity and forgive my impertinence: drop this case. It is not worth your efforts. Keep away from Monksmere. Keep away from the Bowman household. Look after your own affairs, my lord, and be happy in your good fortune; but remember things can change suddenly. We live in uncertain times. Now it is more than my life's worth to say more. And I mean that. Forgive me, I am a most unhappy man.'

So saying, he rushed from the room. Nicholas looked at Peter. 'What, in God's name, is going on, Peter?'

'I can't say a word, my lord. If I do, then I am a dead man. But let me repeat what the sheriff has said: look after your own and be happy in your present good fortune. Let Sarah Bowman lie in peace in Monksmere churchyard.'

'I understand your concern, Peter, but, damn me, you can't tell me what I should do. A murder has been committed. A village has been frightened into silence. My sheriff has been reduced to a terrified wreck of a man and now you, too, advise me to go home and forget all about the case. Now, let me tell you, I for one will never give up until this mystery is solved. I intend to ride straight down to Monksmere and find that mole-catcher fellow. He knows something, and, by God, he's going to tell me. Now are you coming with me, or not? And Dickon? Or is he down in Monksmere?'

'No, my lord. No one is allowed to go to that place. We dare not. But, let me say this: if you must pursue this case, then take care. Watch your back, my lord. Take nothing at face value. Expect the worst; it might not happen, but at least you will be prepared. Now, I will help all I can, but it will be without the sheriff's knowledge. Leave any message for me at the Dog and Bell. Matt, the tavern owner, is a friend of mine. He'll not want to get involved in any investigation but he'll pass on messages. After you've seen Morriss the mole-taker go and see Master

Fuller, the person who came to tell the sheriff about Sarah Bowman's death. He told the sheriff that there was more to this case than meets the eye and that's why the sheriff brought you into the investigation, remember? Now, I can't say any more. Good luck, my lord; you have much to lose and enemies are not always recognisable.'

Peter, his face troubled, turned to leave. Nicholas tried to restrain him. 'I'm indebted to you, Peter. I'll not forget this. Now, you'll need a horse to get down to the Dog and Bell. You can hardly use one of the sheriff's after what you've just told me. I'll get one of my men to bring you one of my horses. He'll leave it at the Rose and Crown on the eastern outskirts of the city. You know it?'

Peter nodded. Then Nicholas shook Peter's hand and watched as he left the room. He stood for a moment, lost in thought, then went out and retrieved Harry and rode home using the north road that went across the Downs. So, he thought, it was happening again. The death of a seemingly innocent person, then the ramifications. And once again he was in the centre of it. But he would not be put off. The Peverells could not be frightened. The sheriff could lose his job, but no one could touch the Peverell estates. But could they? Suddenly the image of his former neighbour, Sir Roger Mortimer, stretched out in agony on the rack in the Tower of London, came before his eyes. He shuddered. However, Mortimer had been a traitor. The Peverells had always been loyal. Their motto, 'Toujours Loyal', said it all. He had nothing to be afraid of. Just a case to solve. He was sorry that the sheriff had turned faint-hearted, but he might change his mind when his belly settled down.

He arrived back in Dean Peverell and saw everything was in order. The great-aunt was ensconced in the kitchen with his cook and steward planning the funeral feast. Jane, they told him, had gone to her cottage to check on her herbal remedies. Philippa had been despatched back to her parents in Marchester in one of his carriages. Picking up a trencher of bread and a slice of cold beef he rode off to Monksmere munching the food as he went along.

After Nicholas had gone to Marchester to see the sheriff, Jane had gone into the chapel to sit for a while beside her father's body. She felt an immense sadness that part of her life had come to an end. Since her marriage to Nicholas she had seen less of her father and his influence had weakened. Looking down at that familiar face, calm now that he was at peace, she realised how much she owed him and how much she had taken for granted. Ever since she was a young child, barely out of her baby smocks, he had supervised her upbringing and planned her education. She had never known her mother who had died bringing her into the world. Always her father had been there and a kindly nurse had looked after her personal needs. He had chosen her tutor, an elderly and erudite cathedral canon, to teach her Latin and Greek. A music teacher had come from Marchester to teach her music and French and Italian. The same man had introduced her to courtly dances. Her father had taken great pleasure in her progress and encouraged her. When Nicholas came into her life, her father had been wary of him, but that was only natural. He had wanted only the best for her and had mistrusted all suitors for her hand. But lately, over the summer, she had spent more time with her father and seen that he was well looked after by her great-aunt who had moved over from Midhurst to live with him. She had nursed him through several of his frequent feverish chills. This last illness, she thought, had been more severe. Even so, she had not expected it to be fatal.

She thought back over the last few days when he had taken to his bed and complained of chest pains. Had she missed something? Perhaps it wasn't the fever that had caused his death. Maybe his heart had just given up on him. But even so ... Had she slipped up with the dosage? She recalled what she had given him – the usual remedy for a person suffering from a high fever and a cough: juniper

54

berries steeped in honey to ease the cough, feverfew to reduce the fever, St John's wort to help fight the infection, and a dose of Agnes Myles's opiate to ease the pain, which had been more severe than usual. Had she given him too much?

Jane always kept a record of her prescriptions and the book was in the cottage which Agnes Myles had left her in her will. It was also Saturday and people would be waiting for her at the cottage to ask her advice on all manner of ailments. She rose to her feet, took one more look at her father's face, and left the room. She checked that Great-Aunt Anna and Mary, her cook, were busy in the kitchen and told them she was going to the cottage. They hardly heard her as they were busy making the puddings and pies which people would expect to eat at Monday's funeral feast.

The cottage was only a mile away from the manor house tucked away up its own track leading off the main Marchester road. Jane walked briskly along, not wanting to be away from her house too long. At the crossroads at the bottom of the drive which led up to the manor house, she saw Mistress Burton coming up the village street. She was not one of Jane's favourite people; however there was no avoiding her that morning. She would, Jane thought, want to offer her condolences and be ready to listen to all the gruesome details about her father's death; a pleasure which Jane intended to deny her.

Jane crossed the road and approached Mistress Burton, who, much to her surprise, didn't stop, but looked away and hurried past her, gathering up the skirts of her dress so that they didn't brush against Jane's morning gown.

'Good morning, Mistress Burton,' Jane said, stepping aside to let the woman pass. There was no response. With her face averted, her skirts bunched up in her hands, Mistress Burton rushed past, turning right at the cross-roads.

Jane stood still in amazement, trying hard not to burst

out laughing. What was Mistress Burton thinking of? Had she heard that there was the plague up at the manor house and she was scared of contagion? Or was she not feeling well and did not want to give Jane an infection? It was all very puzzling. She knew the Burton household very well. She'd treated them all for various ailments and only two weeks ago the grandfather had sent a fat goose up to the house as a thank-you present for the ointment she had made up for him to ease the aches in his joints. What had happened to make the mistress of the house behave so rudely?

However, Jane was not easily offended. Maybe, she thought, Mistress Burton did not want to intrude on her grief. Many people, she knew, were uneasy in the presence of the recently bereaved. But usually they communicated a silent sympathy; not this abrupt dismissal.

She reached the cottage, known as Thyme Cottage to the villagers, and walked up the garden path to the front door, breathing in the scent of the herbs which filled the garden. She opened the door with the special key Nicholas had had cut for her in Marchester, and entered the room which had once been Agnes Myles's living room. Now it was her storeroom. She stood there inhaling the pungent smell of the herbs, gathered in early summer and now hanging in bundles from the rafters. She loved the smell: lavender and thyme, rosemary and sage, parsley and gillyflowers, garlic and fennel, rose petals and marjoram.

On the shelf at the back of the room was a row of pottery jars, each one labelled and dated. These were the precious opiates which Agnes had left her; opiates that eased the pain of the dying and were beyond price. The opiates were made from special poppies which she knew she could not cultivate in the English climate, but which Agnes had bought from a merchant in Portsmouth who traded with the Levant. Jane had never enquired how Agnes had come to meet the merchant. In fact there was a lot about Agnes which Jane did not know. Enough that she was a wise woman with a tremendous knowledge of human ailments. Jane had only been pleased to learn all that Agnes could teach her.

Jane took one of the jars off the shelf and checked its contents. All was as it should be. She opened the cupboard next to the opiate shelf and took out her book of remedies. Her father's mixture was the last on the list. The dose she had recorded was absolutely in accordance with Agnes's instructions and her own experience. No, her father's death had to be heart failure induced by the high fever; not a result of any potion she had given him. Satisfied, she shut and locked the cupboard, then looked around for her first patient. All was quiet. Usually there would be half a dozen people waiting at her gate, noisily discussing their ailments. But not today. It was as if everyone in the village had decided not to be ill. Even the regulars had not turned up. Then the thought came to her that people would think that she wouldn't want to be bothered with their troubles until after her father's funeral. That was the answer, she decided as she put her book back in the cupboard and shut the door. They'd all come back on Tuesday. She locked the cottage door, picked a big bunch of fresh parsley which she knew Mary, the cook, could make use of, and set off home, her mind at rest.

However, when she opened the garden gate she saw young Tom Miller, one of her helpers, who liked to watch her mix up her potions. He was a great help with the pestle and mortar. She gave him a cheerful wave but, to her astonishment, he stuck out his tongue in a rude way and ran off calling out something that she couldn't hear. This time she felt her heart miss a beat. What was going on? Why should two people, one of whom had always been her devoted helper, suddenly turn against her? It was with a feeling of relief that she turned into the drive leading up to her house and she only felt safe when she walked into the courtyard and saw the familiar sight of her steward, Cecil Hunter,

57

carrying a basket of freshly caught rabbits to the store-rooms.

Nicholas arrived at the Dog and Bell early that afternoon. The main room was strangely quiet when he opened the door; the inn keeper was nowhere in sight. The logs in the fireplace were lying in heaps of ash; no one had bothered to rekindle the flames. Nicholas called out impatiently: 'Is anyone around?'

Suddenly the door at the side of the counter opened and Matt, the innkeeper, came forward reluctantly as if the sight of Nicholas put the fear of God into him.

'Yes, my lord. What can I get for you?'

'Some ale to start with. Don't look so scared, man, I'm not a ghost.'

Matt didn't smile, didn't attempt a quick repartee. He scuttled behind the counter and poured Nicholas some ale from an earthenware jug.

'Where's everyone today?' asked Nicholas after he had quenched his thirst.

'It's too early for business, my lord. Folk'll come in later.'

'There seemed no lack of drinkers the last time I came. Well, never mind, it's you I want to speak to. Willet's wood; can you tell me where that is? I want to speak to that mole-catcher fellow. And after that, Master Fuller. Can you give me directions to his house?'

'You'll have to ride down to Atherington to find him, my lord. Biggish farmhouse on the right, just as you enter the village. As for Moley, his house is just a collection of skins and sticks on the edge of the water meadows where it borders the wood. Go out of the village, our village that is, Monksmere, and turn down the first track you come to after the church.'

It was quite extraordinary, Nicholas thought, how much the man had changed since he'd last seen him with the sheriff and his men. He was now deathly pale and his eyes were frightened, like a hunted rabbit. Nicholas drank down his ale, put some money on the counter, and went out. As he mounted Harry and turned into the Monksmere road, he knew that something was indeed amiss with this case of the murdered girl. First the sheriff, and now the innkeeper; no one, it seemed, wanted to talk to him today.

The mole-catcher's hut was as he had been told a ramshackle place. The framework was made up of some saplings bent and twisted together to give the place a sort of shape. Over this frame, a mixture of mud, dung and straw had been daubed and, on top, a great number of skins of all sorts of woodland animals had been draped. Inside it was snug enough. A heap of skins in one corner served as a bed. A patch of ash on the mud floor showed where the fire had been. A wooden shovel had been propped up against the rear wall next to an iron cauldron. These were all the mole-catcher's possessions. The man himself was not there. Thinking that he was probably about his business of catching moles up in the churchyard, Nicholas rode back to the church and tethered Harry to the gate. Then he went into the churchyard, which was deserted. Sarah Bowman's grave stood out with its fresh mound of earth. Someone had put a bunch of wild flowers on it, ox-eye daisies, dog roses and wild thyme, and he was glad whoever it was had paid her some attention.

He walked round the graveyard, quite small and compact for a small parish, and noted that the moles were still hard at work, judging by the neat piles of freshly dug earth scattered, like a rash of pimples, over the newly scythed grass. There was no sign of Morriss. And no sign of any other human being. The only sound was the doleful call of the wood pigeons.

Nicholas felt a slight shiver of unease. Monksmere was like a village of the dead; or a village that had been visited by the pestilence during the night and people had locked themselves away in their houses to avoid giving the contagion to outsiders.

Shaking off these fancies, Nicholas rode off towards the sea in the direction of the village of Atherington. Much to his relief, Jack Fuller, who had ridden to Marchester to fetch the sheriff when Sarah Bowman's body had been found on Wednesday morning, was there, in his yard, loading up his barn with bales of straw. He was a stout, red-faced farmer, dressed in a peasant's smock and tough leather breeches. He was in his middle years, still strong, if the ease with which he tossed the bales of straw to his workmen was any indication. He stopped working when he saw Nicholas and stood there looking at him stolidly, waiting for Nicholas to speak first.

'Master Fuller?' said Nicholas, dismounting.

'That's me.'

'Can I have a few words with you?'

'You can; though I don't know that I can help you much.'

'You know who I am?'

'Indeed I do. You're Lord Nicholas and come from Dean Peverell and you've been helping the sheriff.'

'And you fetched him from Marchester. We want to catch the person who murdered Sarah Bowman. Can you help us?'

'I can't say that I can. I'm sorry about the lass. She died a cruel death, but I have no idea who would want to kill her.'

'But you'd like to help us catch him?'

'It's none of my business. I do my work and keep my nose clean.'

'But you might have heard things?'

'If you say so. I don't listen to gossip.'

Nicholas was aware that the other men had stopped work and were staring at him with looks of feigned indifference on their faces. Master Fuller was also aware of their interest and whirled round ordering them back to work.

'There's much to do here, Lord Nicholas,' he said, 'if we're to get this stuff stored away before the autumn rains come. You must allow me to get on.'

'I see you are a man of substance,' said Nicholas, glancing round at the well-stocked barn and the strongly built stone farmhouse where Jack Fuller lived with his wife and family. 'You must know what goes on around here. Be so good as to answer me two questions and them I'll leave you to your business. Do you know who fathered Sarah Bowman's child, and can you tell me where Morriss the mole-catcher is?'

The man's reaction to Nicholas's questions took him by surprise. He jumped as if someone had just punched him in the chest and his sunburnt face visibly paled. And there was now this new expression on his face which was becoming familiar to Nicholas when he asked people questions. Fear. The man was plainly terrified. He took up his pitchfork and turned to resume work.

'Master Fuller, you are a man of standing in this community and a juror at Quarter Sessions. You know how important it is that murderers do not roam free. Now give me an answer to both questions and then I'll leave you in peace.'

Jack Fuller turned and faced Nicholas. He could not look him in the eyes.

'There are some things best left alone, my lord, and Sarah Bowman's death is one of them. No, I don't know who fathered her child, though there's many of us would have liked the pleasure; and no, I don't know of Morriss's whereabouts. Best get back to Monksmere; folk there are more likely to help you.'

'There's no one around in that village.'

'Most probably they're in the fields getting in the harvest. The women will be out gleaning.'

He resumed his work. Nicholas mounted Harry. No one wished him God speed. So it was happening again, Nicholas thought as he rode off, just as it had in the past in another part of the county. But this, he thought, was worse. Someone had put the fear of God into these people. They would never talk to him, or to the sheriff and his men. One thing, though, was certain – he would get to the bottom of this, even if he had to do it single-handed. These people had a right to live in peace. No one had a right to terrorise them. Those days were over.

He rode back to Monksmere, and, on impulse, turned off to visit the mole-catcher's hut again. Maybe he had returned from his work, he thought. The sound of a child sobbing made him rein in Harry and stand there listening. The sound came from inside the hut. He dismounted and approached the shack cautiously. He looked inside and saw a young boy crouched on the pile of skins which served as a bed. He was painfully thin, no more than ten or eleven years old, Nicholas thought, and he was sobbing his heart out.

'What's the matter, child?' said Nicholas quietly.

The boy jumped up and looked at Nicholas in terror. He tried to run away but Nicholas was blocking the doorway and caught hold of the boy's thin shoulders and held him tightly.

'What's your name, child?' he said.

'Edwin, sir. Though everyone calls me Eddy.'

'How old are you?'

'I don't know, sir. No one's told me.'

The boy was dressed in rags and looked as if he hadn't eaten for days. He was shaking with fear and seemed to have no strength to struggle against Nicholas.

'Here child, take this; it will buy you a meal up at the inn,' said Nicholas, offering the boy a few coins which he snatched up lest Nicholas should change his mind. 'Now, tell me, what are you doing here?'

'I came to see Moley.'

'Is he a friend of yours?'

'Yes, he was my friend. He shared his dinner with me sometimes and I helped him skin his moles.'

'And where's Moley now?'

'Over there, sir. And he won't talk to me. He won't wake up.'

Nicholas felt his heart miss a beat. So, he'd come too late. Moley had known too much.

'Take me to see him, Eddy. Maybe I can make him wake up.'

Suddenly, Eddy seemed to come to life. Stuffing the coins which Nicholas had given him into a pocket of the rags which covered the lower half of his body, he ran out of the shack and went up to the corner of the field. Nicholas followed him. Then Eddy disappeared through a hole in the hedge which separated the field from Willet's wood. Nicholas forced his way through the hedge. There was Eddy, standing in front of a mound of twigs and muck-laden straw; and there was Morriss the mole-catcher, whose wizened face Nicholas saw staring up at him out of the pile of muck. He stooped down and pushed back the debris. There was the little man whom Nicholas had last seen at Sarah Bowman's funeral feast. Now his chest was caved in under the heavy blows which someone had inflicted on him, and his skull was fractured. His clothes, face and hair were all covered with blood. His eyes stared upwards in terror. Nicholas took hold of the child's hand.

'Come, we'll go and get help. I'll take you somewhere safe and I'll see that the man or men who did this will be punished.'

Nicholas led the crying child back to Harry and lifted him up onto the saddle. Then he jumped up behind him and set off back to the Dog and Bell. This time he ordered Matt the landlord to retrieve Morriss's body and handed him money to look after Eddy. As Matt left to get help, Nicholas looked at the boy.

'You are my friend, now. I've given Matt some money to keep you in food and drink and you are to sleep here. In return, I want you to work for me. I shall come and see you again soon and I shall want you to tell me everything you see and hear in this place. Do you understand?'

The boy nodded. 'Yes, sir. Will this help to catch the bad men who murdered Moley?'

63

'Oh yes, indeed it will. And if Matt doesn't look after you properly I shall have words with him. I must go now, but I'll come again soon. Remember, keep your eyes and ears open, say nothing to anyone about what I've just said, and keep out of trouble. This way we'll soon have Moley's murderers under lock and key.'

The boy seemed reinvigorated. His face took on a new look of determination as he watched Nicholas ride off, He would, thought Nicholas, be a good ally; an intelligent one, too.

Chapter Six

Dean Peverell
31st August

Dear Richard,

I feel compelled to write to you as you do not seem to appreciate the seriousness of the situation in Monksmere.

When I came to see you yesterday you appeared to have lost interest in the investigation into the death of Sarah Bowman. For the life of me I cannot understand what has brought about this change in you. Let me now inform you that someone else has been murdered in that village. The man known as Morriss the mole-taker was found by me yesterday afternoon lying dead in a dung heap at the edge of Willet's wood. Now is this not a serious matter? Don't you think it is possible that there could be a connection between these two murders? Could it be that someone is trying to get rid of a witness, or, at least, someone who knows too much for his own good? Haven't we experienced such a thing many times in the past? What did Sarah Bowman know? What did the mole-taker know? And who will be next?

I am seriously worried about the safety of Mistress Kate Bowman and the child, Henry. She, I am sure, knows more than she is prepared to tell us at the

65

moment and consequently could be in danger.

If you are not prepared to investigate further, then I shall have to take measures into my own hands, and, for the sake of law and order in the county, continue the investigations on my own and, in my capacity of Justice of the Peace, make the appropriate arrests when the time comes. I shall also feel obliged to report your dereliction of duty to his majesty the king who might find it necessary to remove you from office. I should hate to do this as we have had a long and successful partnership in keeping the peace.

Nicholas paused, then signed the letter. It had not been an easy one to write. He was fond of the sheriff and they had been a good team. But with the number of deaths increasing, action had to be taken. Richard Landstock would have to pull himself together.

'That's a strong letter, Nicholas,' said a familiar voice behind him. 'Not good for your digestion just before dinner.'

Jane was standing behind him unashamedly reading his letter over his shoulder. She handed him a glass of cordial.

'Peppermint; to soothe you before you eat,' she said, smiling as he took the glass. 'Now tell me what has poor Richard done to deserve such a reprimand.'

Nicholas pushed back his chair and looked up at her, noting with appreciation that she had unbound her hair after coming back from church and it hung down her back like a stream of molten copper. She had exchanged her formal Sunday dress for one of simple linen, the colour of forget-me-nots.

'Jane, I don't know what's come over the man,' he said. 'He appears to have lost his wits. First, he tells me that what is obviously a murder, and the coroner has confirmed that in his verdict, is an accident, and then he warns me off the case. I can't imagine what's gone wrong. He said he was out of sorts with a bellyache, which is rubbish. He's got the constitution of an ox. And, just to make matters worse, he seems to have infected his constable, Peter, who also appears to have lost his nerve and warned me off the case. However, he did agree that I could leave messages for him at the Dog and Bell and he would help me if I needed him.

'And now we have a second murder on our hands – a poor, miserable fellow, who earns his living by catching moles. It's murder all right. His body was in a bad state. So I had to tell the sheriff. No good me going to him – he'd probably refuse to see me – but he'll be obliged to read the letter. Now, I would be pleased if you would ask Cecil to get one of the men to take this to Richard. Tell him to tell the sheriff I shall want a reply and he can wait for it as long as he has to.'

Nicholas then folded the letter, sealed it, and handed it to Jane.

'This is all very perplexing, Nicholas,' she said. 'What went on in Monksmere which necessitated the murder of two people? Maybe more will follow. Who is this Kate Bowman and the child Henry?'

Nicholas told her. When he finished, Jane looked at him keenly. 'Maybe she has been frightened into silence and consequently won't be in any danger; as long as she keeps her mouth shut, of course. The mole-taker was a blabber-mouth and had to be silenced. Did you really find him, or did someone else take you to him?'

'A boy; a poor wretch who lived with the mole-taker. His name's Eddy. He doesn't appear to have a family and he lives by his wits.'

'Is he in danger?'

'I don't think so. I left him with the innkeeper of the Dog and Bell and told him to lie low. He's used to that. All his short life he's had to keep his head down to avoid the kicks and blows of people around him. I left some money for his keep with the innkeeper and the boy said he would earn that money by reporting anything untoward to me.'

'Poor child. If he's in danger, Nicholas, you must bring him here. Mary will fatten him up.'

67

'I'm sure she will; and I'll have another mouth to feed. He's all right for the time being and he could be very useful to me if the sheriff refuses to step forward.'

Jane bent down and kissed him on the top of his head. 'Come and eat dinner, my love, and at least for an hour or two forget about all these things. Although. . .'

Nicholas looked at her and saw something was bothering her. 'What is it, Jane? Tell me now before you forget about it.'

'It's not important.'

'Anything's important if it's troubling you.'

'Well then, yesterday I went to Thyme Cottage as I usually do on a Saturday morning. I met two people who avoided me. One of them, the boy, Tom Miller, who always helps me mix up my medicines, was positively rude to me. He stuck out his tongue and ran off. The other, Mistress Burton, walked straight past me with not even a "good morning". I can't think what I've done wrong to deserve this rudeness.'

'You've done nothing wrong, my love. They were probably tongue-tied in case they said the wrong thing to you. Some people don't know what to say to the bereaved. Young Miller wants a good beating, I think. You spoil him too much. Wait until I get hold of him.'

'Maybe you're right, Nicholas. I am probably too sensitive. My father's death has upset me more than I realised. Now, let's see what Mary's produced for dinner. We'll need to preserve our strength for the funeral tomorrow. My father was well respected and we are expecting a full church and a lot of hungry people.'

When dinner was over and Jane was getting ready to supervise the arrangements for tomorrow's funeral feast, Mary, the cook, approached them hesitantly. She was a handsome woman with a plump, serene face. However, that afternoon she looked worried.

'Sir,' she began, then stopped.

'What is it, Mary? You seem upset. What's happened?'

'Nothing's happened, sir. At least, not yet, but I feel obliged to ...'

She stopped, groping for the right word. Jane got up from the table and went over to her and put an arm round her shoulders.

'Obliged to what, Mary? Come, we know each other too well to mince words. Have we not got enough ale? Has Cecil upset you? If so, Nicholas will speak to him.'

'No, no, my lady; nothing like that; nothing to do with the kitchens. It's you I'm worried about. I feel I have to ... yes, that's it, that's the word I want, warn you.'

'Mary, what are you saying? Warn me? What about?'

'My lady, madam,' said Mary becoming more and more agitated, 'it goes without saying that I would give my life for you. We all would. You are the kindest, most honourable of all the ladies I have met. You are goodness itself. But now I've heard that there is a rumour going round, oh, my lady, it's too terrible even to speak about it,' and she turned to burrow her face into Jane's breast and burst into tears.

Nicholas felt the familiar ripple of fear. First the sheriff had turned against him and now people were turning against Jane.

'Tell us, Mary, what you have heard. Don't be afraid. You know you are safe with us. Nothing you tell us will go beyond these walls.'

His voice seemed to have a calming effect on Mary who drew away from Jane and looked fearfully at Nicholas.

'Sir, they do say down in the village that my lady has poisoned her father. They say she's too fond of giving people potions. Some have even called her ... a witch. It's her red hair, see.'

'My hair, Mary?' said Jane, astonished. 'I'm not responsible for it. It's what God gave me. I can't change it. Some even like it.'

'You've beautiful hair, my lady,' said Mary, 'but it's rare to have such a rich colour and witches, as you know, are said to have something about them that's uncommon.'

'Yes, usually warts and pimples and an ugly face. This is nonsense, Mary, and you know it. I don't believe in witches; they're just a collection of lonely, deluded old women. As to my medicines, they are all well attested for and my father was given a safe dose. I checked yesterday.'

Mary began to look relieved, but, even so, Nicholas knew he could not ignore what she had just told them. Suddenly, an image of Agnes Myles came into his mind. She had been dubbed a witch and people had killed her cat and set fire to her shed where she kept her herbs. People, he knew, were very fickle. They loved sensation. They were always ready to believe the worst. They could also be dangerous.

'Perhaps it would not be a good idea, Jane, to go to your cottage just at this moment; not until all these rumours have died down.'

'But the herbs need turning over and there are people in the village who are dependent on my medicines.'

'Then they must do what they did before you came – either go without, or visit the apothecary in Marchester.'

'Nicholas, you know my patients have no money to pay an apothecary and can't leave the fields at this moment to walk to Marchester.'

Nicholas sighed. Why hadn't he married a docile woman who would always do what was bidden? Looking at Jane now, her face flushed with indignation, her bright hair standing up round her head like a halo, her blue eyes flashing dangerous lights at him, he knew the answer; he desired her every time he looked at her and loved her quick mind. He would never tire of her.

'Then you must do as you please. But Mary has given you a warning and I repeat it. Remember what happened to Agnes Myles.'

'That was because she was tricked.'

'Yes, and it could happen to you. If it gets around that

you are involved in the black arts, then you could be arrested. And they would have me to contend with. And that, my love, could lead to my arrest and a journey to the Tower of London.'

Jane gasped and looked at him in disbelief. 'That could never happen. You are one of his majesty's justices and a Knight of the Garter and a member of his Council. No one would dare lay hands on you.'

'Oh yes they would; if it was necessary for the furtherance of their evil plans.'

'But why should anyone want to harm us?'

'Ah, that's the question! I don't know, I really don't. But until I do, then we must be careful in what we do so that no one can accuse us of witchcraft or anything else. We must be above reproach. Mary,' he said, looking at his cook who was dabbing her eyes with the corner of her apron, 'you have done very well in reporting these things to us. Please feel that you can come to see us at any time and tell us what is going on. Have you gathered why these rumour-mongers think that Jane poisoned her father? Everyone knew they thought a lot of one another.'

'My lord, how can I say this? It's too shocking to be repeated. Please don't ask me to speak of such things.'

'You must tell us, Mary. Nothing can shock us, you know. I am only too aware of human wickedness. We can't blame you for repeating what the villagers say.'

'Then they say that my lady poisoned her father to get his house as she has no money of her own; and also, that she wants his . . . body parts, my lord. Oh, please forgive me.'

'Body parts?' repeated Nicholas.

'For my lady to grind up into her concoctions. It's what witches are supposed to do. How can anyone be so wicked as to think that my lady's healing medicines bear any resemblance to a wicked witch's dirty potions?'

'Because someone has been spreading lies about me,' said Jane, her face pale with anger. 'They want me accused of

71

witchcraft. You see, if it's not the lungs and livers of old men witches are accused of using for their potions then it's the brains of young children. These are wicked accusations, Mary, and I shall see to it that they are refuted. We shall bring my father to the church in an open coffin so that everyone can see that his body has not been interfered with, and you can tell everyone you meet that my Great-Aunt Anna is to inherit my father's house. Now, we have a feast to prepare and a great amount of shifting of chairs and tables and I must see Cecil about my lord's letter. We shall show everyone how much we revered my father and we would be obliged if everyone would leave us alone to grieve over his death, through natural causes, you can also tell them.'

Looking much relieved and anxious to get back to the work she understood, Mary curtsied and left the room. Only then did Jane give way to a storm of grief. Nicholas took her in his arms and held her tightly.

'How could they? How dare they say such things?' she said. 'I thought these people were my friends. They were only too pleased to let me help them when they were ill. And now, because someone wants to destroy us, they turn on me and say these disgusting things about me.'

'My darling, it will only be one or two people who spread these rumours; and I am sure they were put up to it. Someone wants me off this investigation. He has frightened away the sheriff and his men, they have murdered innocent witnesses and now they want to frighten me, which they do by spreading these vile rumours about you. They will never prevent me from doing my duty, Jane. I cannot tolerate intimidation. But you, my darling, are all the world to me and I'll not have you subjected to these slanderous lies. Tomorrow, we bury your father. Until then, you must stay here with Mary and Anna. Don't, I beg you, leave the house. Let others go to your father's house and prepare the feast. And when we go down to the church tomorrow, behind your father's hearse, you will hold your head high and be proud of your beautiful hair and behave as if nothing has happened. Meanwhile I must speak to the bailiff and see that he tells all the tenants that if I hear one more slanderous rumour about either of us, by God, I'll turn them all out of their miserable cottages and send them packing to the next parish where they will have to beg for their bread. Joseph will get the names of the ringleaders and I shall have great pleasure in passing sentence on them at the next Sessions.

'Now, dry your tears, Jane, and try to put out of your mind everything Mary has just said. I shall see to it that these wicked rumours are suppressed.'

Gradually, Jane calmed down, and when she looked at Nicholas there was a new determination in her face.

'I shall never give up my work of finding cures for people's ailments; and I hope that, in time, these people will come to know the difference between medicine that heals and the stupid and dangerous potions thought up in the deranged minds of those people they call witches. There is much ignorance and superstition in our village, Nicholas.'

'Not only in the village; don't take on the whole world, my darling.'

Guy Warrener had never been a churchgoer. In fact he had scant respect for priest or religion of any kind. He had told Jane that he did not believe in heaven or hell or the resurrection of the body. If he had had his way he would have wanted his body to be disposed of by burying it in the bottom of the field at the back of his property; 'Not under the oak tree,' he'd said, 'because the pigs will root me up looking for acorns; but under the yew, a noble tree and its wood makes good long bows.'

Jane had spent many a long winter's evening discussing theology with him, and the parish priest had made futile attempts to make him change his views. But he was adamant. 'This is my body and my brain is here, part of my body. The brain is responsible for inventing the soul and heaven and hell and God and the Devil and, when I am dead, everything dies with me. Yet I must be buried because this vile body will decay and the smell with offend the neighbours.' Certainly he didn't want a funeral; but he liked to think of people enjoying themselves after he was disposed of.

Nicholas finally intervened in the discussion and said his father-in-law must be buried with the Peverells and from now on the new family plot was to be in the cloister garth of the old priory. The vicar, Alfred Hobbes, a man of small stature but not easily dissuaded, said that Guy Warrener should have the simplest funeral service possible, in order to give a seemly end to the old man's life.

'People will expect me to say a few words, my lady,' he'd said when he came to see them to discuss the service. 'They'll want the old prayers – no incense mind; he didn't like ritual, but I'll have to wear suitable vestments otherwise the bishop will chastise me. He'll be coming, I suppose? The bishop, I mean, my lord?'

'Certainly, if he can. He's a friend of the family. He'll come unofficially, of course.'

'And the sheriff?'

'Possibly.'

'Then I'll put a seat ready for him.'

Looking agitated because he didn't like uncertainties, Alfred Hobbes dashed off.

Monday morning dawned with a blue sky and not a cloud in sight. By midday the heat was oppressive and it was a relief to go into the priory church which used to be the monks' choir before they were turned out. Now the parish used it for their own services, preferring it to the part of the building which the monks had given them four hundred years ago. Nicholas and Jane had walked behind the hearse, the coffin lid open as Jane had instructed. Following them came the whole household ushered along by Cecil, the steward. The coffin was brought into the church and put down before the high altar. Jane and Nicholas took their seats in front of the coffin. There were chairs for the bishop and his wife, the sheriff and his wife; the rest stood around respectfully at a distance.

As soon as they were seated, Humphrey Catchpole, formerly Dean of Marchester, recently made bishop, and his wife, Katharine, were escorted to the seats next to them by a nervous vicar. There was no sign of the sheriff. In fact, there was no sign of anyone else. Not a single villager had turned out to pay his respects to one of their number. Nicholas saw Jane turn and look round the church, which was only a quarter filled by their own household. He noted the puzzled look on her face, followed by a flash of anger, then a sadness.

'Nicholas,' she said, 'where is everyone? Why are they shunning us?'

'Don't worry now, my love. We shall give your father a good send-off.'

At twelve noon, Alfred Hobbes began the service and Guy Warrener was buried with due ceremony in the peaceful cloister garth with a congregation of jackdaws watching them from the deserted guest house on the other side of the cloister.

The funeral feast was an anticlimax. The servants had produced a huge feast of cold roast pigeons, capons, and roast beef. Mary had made custards and pies and the best cheeses had been laid out because Guy Warrener had loved his food. Gallons of ale stood waiting. But no one came. The bishop looked at Nicholas in surprise.

'Where's everyone? Was the old man not liked?'

'He was liked well enough for everyone to want to attend his funeral. Something is going on in my village, Humphrey. I am afraid that certain people are trying to intimidate us. Even the sheriff has not come. Someone has frightened him out of his wits.'

'Don't tell me that you are involved in another case, Nicholas? Pray God it doesn't go the way of your last one. Do you know what's behind all this?' the bishop said, waving a hand round the half-empty room. 'I heard you were investigating the death of a girl over in Atherington. Surely there can't be any connection between that death and this avoidance of your father-in-law's funeral?'

'Humphrey, I just don't know. If there is a cord connecting these events, then I have not yet found it, let alone traced it to its source. I feel as if I am trapped in a maze and can't find my way out. But it is only a matter of time before I find the person or persons causing all this trouble.

'However things could turn ugly, and I fear for Jane's safety. Yes, Jane. Don't look so shocked. The person who is behind all this is trying to undermine my family. His message is clear, isn't it? Peverell, keep off; or else . . .'

'Then Jane must come and stay with us,' said a firm voice behind them. Nicholas looked round and saw Katharine, the bishop's plump and sensible wife, listening to their conversation. 'You and Jane have been so good to our daughter Philippa; now it's our turn to look after Jane.'

Nicholas felt his spirits lift. Here was a solution to one of his problems. Jane would be safe in the bishop's palace. But would she go? Looking at his wife's set face as she handed round food to her own servants, he doubted it.

'Katharine, you are kindness itself and I accept your offer most gratefully should the need arise. However, at the moment, I fear Jane is as stubborn as me in seeing this case through. She will feel this slight against her father most keenly and will want to put an end to the rumours that are circulating round the village. I, for one, must find out who murdered Sarah Bowman and another innocent person in Monksmere. And I want to know who is intimidating the sheriff and the tenants on my own manor.'

'Then take care, Nicholas. You might uncover a nest of hornets. But whatever happens you know you can always rely on us; whatever the circumstances.'

'Thank you, your grace,' said Nicholas using the official title for the first time. 'It is good to know that, should I have to go away, Jane can find shelter in a safe haven with friends around her.'

Just then he heard the sound of a horse's hooves thudding along the road outside the house. The sound stopped and the room became suddenly quiet as everyone looked towards the front door which stood open to allow people to come and go as they wished. A man entered, ducking his head to avoid the low lintel over the door frame. He looked as if he had ridden hard and long. His jerkin was caked with dust, his face gleamed with sweat and his hair was matted to his head.

'Lord Nicholas?' he said. Nicholas stepped forward.

'What is it, Drayford?' said Nicholas, recognising one of the king's messengers.

'The king wishes to speak with you, my lord. At once, if you please.'

'Where am I to go?' said Nicholas, used to these peremptory summonses.

'The king's at Hampton Court and will expect you tomorrow for dinner.'

'Then I shall leave today and stay overnight at Merrow. My horse will have to be rested. And you, sir, are welcome to stay with us tonight and follow on tomorrow. If you have to return with me, then you are welcome to make use of one of my horses. '

'Thank you, my lord. You are most kind. The king won't want to see me again just yet and I am sure you know your way to Hampton Court so I, most gratefully, accept your offer of hospitality.'

The messenger bowed and Jane told one of the servants to bring him ale and a plateful of cold meats. Nicholas instructed a groom to see to his horse.

The feast was over and Nicholas ordered the servants home, Jane left with them to supervise the arrangements for their guest, Nicholas and Bishop Humphrey joined Drayford as he sat at the table.

'What news of the court, Drayford? How is the king?'

'In good humour, my lord. He has come out of mourning for Queen Jane and I have heard talk about him looking for another queen. I believe Baron Cromwell has someone in mind.'

'No doubt. And so will many others,' said Nicholas, thinking that the king's matrimonial affairs kept a lot of courtiers on their toes. What with the Howards waiting in the wings with a selection of highly attractive nieces, and Cromwell at loggerheads with the Howards, the court would once again become a hotbed of plot and counter-plot. He hoped the king didn't want to consult him, Nicholas Peverell, about the choice of a suitable Queen of England. That would be putting his head on the block for sure.

Jane was used to Nicholas's comings and goings and when Nicholas returned to the manor she had already ordered his horse Harry to be made ready and had packed a change of clothing. He kissed Jane and made ready to leave for the court.

'Goodbye, my love; I shan't be away long. The king has these sudden whims to see me and no doubt all sorts of inconveniences will follow this visit. But you must take great care not to leave the house. Keep away from your cottage and tell Anna to stay here with you. Lock up your father's house for the time being – no harm will come to it, I'm sure – and when I return I'll put a steward in it for the time being. Remember Jane, I love you and will do so until the end of my life. I could not bear it if any harm came to you.'

'Don't worry about me, Nicholas. The Peverell house makes a tolerable prison and Mary and Anna are the kindest of jailers. We shall occupy ourselves with household duties and Balthazar shall entertain us in the evenings. God speed you, my darling husband.'

Reluctantly, Nicholas mounted Harry and rode off down the driveway, turning left along the Roman road which would bring him to London and the king.

Chapter Seven

Hampton Court. Former home of Cardinal Wolsey. Now the favourite residence of King Henry; particularly in the hot summer months when the pestilence stalked the stinking alleys and streets of London. As Nicholas approached the familiar red-brick building, riding across the bridge to the great gateway, he wondered how many more times he would be summoned here to pander to an unpredictable monarch's whims.

A groom took his horse. A steward showed him to his usual room above the gateway and told him that refreshments were on their way as well as water to wash away the dust of the journey. The king, the steward said, bowing as he left the room, would be expecting him at half past three in the anteroom to the Chapel Royal where his majesty would be saying prayers for his late wife. Dinner would be at a quarter past four. After he had left the room, Nicholas collapsed in the chair provided for guests of his rank. He had an hour to make himself presentable and order his wits.

King Henry had finished his prayers and was waiting for Nicholas by one of the small windows which looked down onto the courtyard. He turned when he heard the door open and Nicholas noticed that he had put on a lot of weight since he had last seen him in the spring. But the small eyes still looked at him appraisingly out of his heavily jowled face. His beard was still a youthful red and what little he could see of his hair beneath the flat velvet cap which Henry always wore whatever the weather, had not yet turned grey. At forty-six he was still a fine figure of a man despite his increasing girth. However, when he walked across to greet him, Nicholas noticed that one leg was bandaged and he leaned heavily on a stick.

'So, Peverell, it's good to see you again. Not too wearied by the journey, I trust?'

'Thank you, your grace; I am well. Thank God the roads are still in good condition.'

'And that fine horse of yours? He took no harm?'

Nicholas glanced quickly at the king. Was there a covetous look in those shifting eyes? Was Harry to be sacrificed to the King just as Wolsey had been forced to hand over his own house which he had built and paid for himself? Not if he could help it! Then the king laughed and Nicholas realised that the monarch could read his mind like a book and, what was more, enjoyed tormenting him.

'Thank you, he can still manage a long journey, even though he's getting a bit long in the tooth and soon I shall have to put him aside for another from my stables.'

'Very wise, Peverell. I look forward to inspecting these stables of yours. I hear the grazing is very fine in your part of Sussex. I must come soon before the autumn rains set in. We'll settle on a date before you leave us.'

Nicholas inwardly groaned. He thought of the inconveniences they would all have to suffer; and the expense of it all. However, he forced himself to smile enthusiastically and bowed.

'Your grace is always welcome at my humble manor and I shall see to it that all your needs are catered for.'

'Of course you will. You know me – simple fare – can't eat a lot these days. Informal, mind. No ceremony. I like the simple rural pleasures as a contrast to court life. I like your manor, Peverell. It gives me a chance to put aside the cares of state which exact such a toll on my health. I trust your delightful wife is well? No sign of any future Peverell on the way?'

'My wife is in excellent health and as to future genera- tions, I leave that in God's hands, your grace.'

'Good, good, quite right, Peverell. Mind you, God needs a helping hand occasionally, isn't that so? I should never have let that wench leave court. She was an adornment. Still, she stayed with my dear wife right until the end, and I suppose I could not ask for more; not when you were waiting for her so impatiently, eh?'

He laughed and poked Nicholas playfully in the ribs with his stick. The same old Henry, Nicholas thought. Ben- evolent one minute; malevolent the next. One could never drop one's guard.

'And you, your grace? I trust you still enjoy good health?'

'Yes, yes. This leg causes me much pain, though. These damn doctors can't seem to mend it. I shall have to ask that wife of yours for some of her healing ointment. I've heard she is a skilled apothecary?'

'She takes an interest in the healing arts, yes.'

'Well, as long as she keeps away from the black arts she'll come to no harm, eh?'

Again the laugh. Again the playful jab with the stick.

'Now relax, Peverell. Stop looking at me as if I am a venomous snake. Tell me what goes on in that county of yours. A damn troublesome county it is, you know. What with nests of Yorkists seething with discontent and others plotting with my Continental counterparts, it doesn't give me a minute's peace. And you? What do you with yourself all day? You do a bit of hunting, I suppose, and you preside over Quarter Sessions and send highway robbers to the gallows; but it seems to me that you are too much occupied with these unimportant matters. Now, take this girl, for instance. I heard she drowned herself and you waste your energy rushing round the county saying it was murder and you have to find the culprit. You even expect the Sheriff of

81

Marchester to waste time and money in joining you in this unnecessary investigation. Now what have you to say about that, Peverell?'

Nicholas's heart missed a beat. It was only a week ago that Sarah Bowman's body was found and yet, already, the king knew about it.

'News travels fast, sire. I would have thought such an unimportant event would have had little interest for you.'

'Everything interests me, Peverell. Especially when it involves a breach of the peace in Sussex.'

'May I ask where you got this information from, your grace?'

'No, you may not. I have my spies, you know. Thomas sees to that. Oh, by the way,' he said as he placed an arm affectionately across Nicholas's shoulders and steered him over to the window which looked down onto the courtyard. 'He wants to see you, Peverell. The fellow's plotting something, no doubt. Probably concerns my next wife. They want me to marry again, Peverell, and I suppose they are right. My dear Edward is not strong and I need more heirs. We don't want to raise the hopes of those Yorkists too much, do we? Now, he's expecting you tomorrow. He's at my palace of Whitehall which the fellow thinks he owns. He spends most of his time there. Says it's handy for keeping my parliament under control. Now, listen carefully.'

They stood together, looking down into the courtyard where courtiers strolled across the grass waiting to be summoned to dinner in the Great Hall. It was a scene of utmost tranquillity: a great king, in a great palace, surrounded by his courtiers. And yet, Henry was not at ease.

'When you've finished with your investigation concerning this girl, Peverell – and don't take too long about it – I want you to do a bit of visiting for me.'

'Visiting?' said Nicholas, his heart sinking to his boots. The last time he had gone visiting at the king's request, he thought, it had involved him in a Continental invasion.

'That's right; the lord of Tredgosse's castle. Lord Gilbert Fitzherbert. Now, I know very little about him; and that worries me. Not like you, Peverell; I know you inside out. He's kept his nose clean. Took the Oath of Supremacy, so no trouble on that score. He's also my lord lieutenant and fulfils his obligations. But what sort of man is he? When I come to see you, probably at the end of this month, I shall call on him and take stock. But I need to be prepared. What do you know about him, Peverell?'

'Like you, your grace, very little. I had to see him recently about the transference of land which you gave me when you last honoured us with a visit, and he seemed agreeable. He lives a quiet life in that great castle of his. It's not a comfortable place. A bit behind the times. More like an old-fashioned fortress – not a magnificent palace like your grace's here at Hampton Court.'

'Hm, the cardinal had good taste, I'll give him that. Has Fitzherbert remarried?'

'Not that I've heard. He lives with a woman named Adeliza. A beauty. And there is a child by her. And another child from his wife.'

'A beauty, eh? Is she of noble birth?'

'No, your grace. They say she comes from London and is one of the people.'

'So, that's why he doesn't want to marry her; though I expect she wishes it. Well, what does he do all day? Entertain my Yorkist cousins? Does this Adeliza aspire to become Queen of England?'

Henry laughed and squeezed Nicholas's shoulders playfully.

'There's no talk of that, your grace. Fitzherbert is a recluse. He's got a great castle, extensive grounds stretching down to the river on the eastern side. He sees no need to ride round the countryside. I shall invite him over to Dean Peverell to take dinner with us, if your grace wishes.'

'Good idea, Peverell. Get to know him. Make friends

with him. And make out a full report for me by the time I come to see you. I can't have my subjects skulking in their castles. They could be up to anything.

'Now you, Peverell, are my loyal and faithful subject. You have not got a drop of Yorkist blood in your veins and you have never let me down. God damn it, man, you saved my life and thwarted an invasion. What more proof of your loyalty could I ask for? And I love you, as a friend, and I enjoy your company. Don't let me down, Peverell. Don't get tempted by other people's offers of wealth and power. I shall see to it that you are always well rewarded for your services. Stick to me, Peverell, and I shall see you want for nothing.'

'Your grace, you know I shall always be of service to you. My ancestors fought against England's enemies. Not one of them has been charged with treason. I shall do my best to keep the county clean of rogues and murderers. I want the place safe to live in. I ask only to be left in peace to tend my estate and love my wife.'

'And so you shall, Peverell. But as long as there are people out there who want me off the throne, I shall have to keep vigilant. They're all at it,' he said, waving a hand in the direction of the courtiers below them in the court-yard. 'Look at them. What are they talking about? The latest fashions from France? The new music from Italy? But how many of them would stay loyal if a fleet came up the Thames and landed troops in my capital? How many would fight to the death for me? They are not all like you, Peverell. You, I know, would stay with me to the last. But the others? No, they watch me closely, waiting for the first sign of weakness. Time servers, every one of them. At the moment it's down with the Bishop of Rome! King Henry is the supreme head of our church. Tomorrow, it could all change. Down with King Henry! Let the Pope rule us again.

'But you will never change, Peverell. I trust you implic-itly. Now get to know Fitzherbert and winkle him out of

84

that castle of his. Tell him I shall be seeing him soon. That'll wake him up.'

'I'll do my best, your grace. But I can foresee difficulties.'

'I daresay. But you will know what to do. You see, Peverell, I don't worry unnecessarily, as Thomas keeps telling me I do. It's not long since we had to stamp out that troublesome rebellion in the north. And I am not convinced it's over yet. That rebel, Robert Aske, was executed last year and two hundred of his followers went with him to the gallows. Suffolk did a good job up there and taught the northern lords a lesson. But some of Aske's followers are still unaccounted for: Dudley, Reginald Haughty, Robert of York, and all those priests who left their parishes to march with Aske on London. What happened to them? They didn't return to their livings when the rebellion was crushed. We didn't execute them all, you know. Now, are they still in hiding? Or are they out of the country stirring up trouble with my enemies? I can't trust anyone, Peverell. And I want your loyal eyes to spot trouble coming.'

'I shall certainly do my best, your grace, but I doubt whether Fitzherbert had anything to do with the northern rebellion. He's too comfortable in that castle of his. His family's been there since the Conquest and his name has never been linked with any traitor.'

'And let's hope he stays that way. But I shall need that report, Peverell. So don't waste any time on drowned maidens. Now, let's to dinner. You must be in need of sustenance after your long journey.'

That night, Nicholas slept uneasily in his uncomfortable bed. The moon shone through the window lighting up the bare walls of his room and its sparse furnishings. It reminded him all too vividly of the room he had occupied in the Tower only eighteen months ago. Maybe, he thought, it was a good thing to be reminded of the fickleness of the king's affections. Henry had been lavish with them at dinner, insisting that he, Nicholas, sat at his right hand and before the whole company had slipped the ruby ring off his

85

finger and given it to him. 'For that wife of yours. It will match her red hair,' he'd said.

As Nicholas tossed around in his narrow bed, he wondered whether he was ever to be left in peace. Was he always to be the servant of a king who was becoming increasingly suspicious of everyone around him as he grew older and the succession to the throne was still uncertain? Admittedly, he now had a son and heir, but Prince Edward was a sickly child and it was rumoured he probably would not live to adulthood. The king needed more heirs. Well, Baron Cromwell, no doubt, would have his own plans. All would be revealed tomorrow.

And then, just as he fell asleep, he thought of Jane. Pray God she had taken no harm whilst he was away.

Looking at Thomas Cromwell, seated, as usual, behind his desk in the room which he had made his own in the palace of Whitehall, it was difficult to appreciate the full power of the man who had smoothed the way for his master's drastic legislation which had severed the country from Rome and buttressed up the royal authority. This man, thought Nicholas, understood the king better than anyone else. This was the man who knew how to manipulate parliament, control the King's Council, and whose spies were despatched to every corner of the country. That pale, slightly puffy face, now relaxed into an ingratiating smile, housed a shrewd and calculating brain. He also had an infinite capacity for hard work. Without him, King Henry would be lost. And Cromwell saw to it that he was indispensable to his royal master. And yet, and yet, thought Nicholas, here was simply a servant; a servant of a capricious ruler who would dismiss him from office without a moment's hesitation if he failed to give him what he wanted. Nicholas thought of Wolsey – richer, greater than Cromwell in every way, even considered as a candidate for the papacy at one stage of his career – yet he died alone in Leicester Abbey on his way to certain execution. Cromwell, in serving such a master, would always have to look to his own safety. One false step and he was doomed; no one would raise a finger to help him. At the moment, though, he was all-powerful.

It was oppressively hot in the small room. Cromwell felt the cold and was dressed, as usual, in a heavy robe trimmed round the neck with fur. The windows were closed, shutting out the stench of the river which flowed nearby. Cromwell looked up.

'Good morning, my lord. I trust you had a comfortable night's sleep. The air is fresher at Hampton Court and further away from this noxious pestilence which afflicts our city at this time of year. Alas, I am bound to stay here, to be near his majesty's parliament and the Tower where two traitors are waiting to be interrogated.'

'Thank you, yes. I am much refreshed and the boatmen brought me here in record time.'

'Good, good, then you will need to return when the tide turns. Not long now. Some ale, my lord, or a glass of wine from my humble cellars?'

'Some ale would be be most refreshing,' said Nicholas inwardly writhing at the man's false modesty. Everyone knew Cromwell was a hearty eater and his cellars contained some of the finest wines in the country.

'I am glad to hear that the disturbances that afflicted your county last spring are over, Lord Peverell,' said Cromwell as ale and honey cakes were served. 'There are no more aggravations, I trust, to cause you any anxiety?'

Nicholas looked at Cromwell keenly. He did not trust a word he said. Cromwell's spies were notoriously efficient at reporting every incident to him, however unimportant it might seem at the time.

'Thank you, Baron, we have had only the usual number of highway robberies and two, recent, deaths.'

'Natural causes, I trust?' said Cromwell impassively.

'I shall have to make further enquiries when I return. Both appear suspicious and the coroner returned a verdict of unlawful killing on one of them.'

'The young girl, I assume? I heard otherwise. I shouldn't waste time on suicides, my lord, or accidental death. Coroners' verdicts are often wrong. The Sheriff of Marchester appears untroubled by the wench's death. So my advice to you is leave well alone. The sheriff has much experience in these matters and when he says that there is no evidence of foul play then we should believe him. You stick to what you do superbly well – a Justice of the Peace passing sentence on the guilty brought to you at the Sessions by the sheriff.'

Nicholas could hardly believe what he had just heard. Was the king's minister warning him off an investigation which was still unresolved? First the sheriff, now Cromwell? What was going on?

'Now don't look so worried, my lord. These are unimportant matters. There are weightier concerns to occupy your mind. I shall be needing you soon to help me with a delicate mission. The king, as I am sure you are aware, has a mind to marry again, and has asked me to find him a suitable maid.'

Cromwell coughed and looked slyly at Nicholas. 'He thinks me expert in these matters, and I shall do my best. The king, as we all know, wants more heirs so I shall have to find him someone young enough to endure the perils of childbirth safely, fair enough to arouse the king's passion, and without carnal knowledge of any other man. And, believe me, it is difficult to find these qualities in any of the court ladies, so I shall have to look elswhere. And that's where you come in, my lord.'

'Baron, I am hardly expert in these delicate matters. I have my own wife whom I love dearly and hope to return to as soon as possible. There must be many other men more suitable than me who would be honoured to find his majesty a new wife.'

'Indeed, I am surrounded by such men offering their hussies for the king's pleasure. But none would be suitable to be the Queen of England, who must be a virgin, my lord, and modest, and free from any connection to the old faith. The king requires a maid from the reformed churches, and my quest, at the moment, has taken me to one of the German courts. The king favours an alliance with one of the German princes which would provide a good counterbalance to the Catholic kings of France and Spain.

'Now, I am not talking of you going over to the continent this year. First, Master Holbein must go to the court of the Duke of Cleves and paint his daughter's picture. Then the king must approve it. After that, we have to conduct the negotiations and Cleves will be hard to win over; but he'll agree if we offer him a good settlement. Then we have to keep an eye on the Howard clan, who always have a clutch of pretty wenches at hand – not virgins by any means and certainly not above reproach – but pretty all the same.

'No, a German alliance would be a sound diplomatic move. I am thinking of asking you, Peverell, to go to Cleves some time next year and talk that tight-fisted Duke of Cleves over to our side. He's got a virtuous daughter, I understand, well protected by her mother. Her name's Anne. Not an auspicious name, I agree, but his majesty will have to put up with it, or change it after he marries her. It'll do you good to broaden your horizons a little, my lord. It will also bring you honours; the king will be grateful to you if you arrange a good match for him and you can conduct the lady across the Channel and bring her to the king. You can teach her English, as well, as his majesty doesn't take to the German tongue.

'Now, return to your beautiful wife and think about what I have said and look forward to the many honours which will come your way next year. And leave these trivial matters of accidental death to the sheriff. Concern yourself with weightier matters as befits your rank. The king, I understand, wants to visit your manor at the end of the month. Let me see; I have it here ...' And Cromwell reached for a leather-bound book and turned over the pages. 'Yes, here we are. The twenty-third of September. He wants to take a short holiday in Sussex, staying first with you, and then on to Fitzherbert. You are to give him warning, understand?'

Nicholas nodded, thinking that Fitzerbert was in for a shock. He was also amazed at Cromwell's efficiency. Everything had been discussed with the king. Everything had been arranged before he had been summoned to court. Not once had he been consulted. Only given orders.

He stood up to leave. Suddenly, there was a knock at the door and a servant came in and whispered something to Cromwell who nodded agreement and stood up.

'Stay for just a moment longer, my lord. The tide will wait for a few minutes. Let me introduce you to the new Bishop of Lincoln – you'll be hearing a lot about him in the future. He and Thomas Cranmer will sort out all the king's ecclesiastical concerns. Good morning, Edward, come in. Lord Peverell is just leaving.'

It was the first time that Nicholas had seen the Bishop of Lincoln, whose huge diocese stretched from the Humber to the Thames. It was a position of enormous responsibility. The bishop entered the room. He was tall, in his middle years, dressed soberly as befitted his calling, with a lean, intelligent face, shrewd blue eyes and short-cropped hair which barely concealed what was once a monk's tonsure. So, thought Nicholas, another monk had fallen on his feet, remembering how the prior of his local priory had become Bishop of Marchester – an appointment which had ended so tragically.

The bishop and Cromwell were obviously on good terms, and after wishing Nicholas a safe journey the two men settled down to a convivial meeting.

Cromwell was in his element, thought Nicholas as he walked down to the landing stage where the boat which had brought him to Whitehall would now take him back to Hampton Court. He was a spider in a web, spinning endless plots and counterplots, busily gathering information from

90

all over the country, waiting to pounce on the king's enemies. Now, Nicholas thought, he was being drawn into the web. Cromwell had given him much food for thought: the promise of a royal visit, a venture into diplomacy for next year, the promise of honours; and a firm warning to drop the case of Sarah Bowman.

But as he rode back to Sussex, pressing Harry hard and resting only briefly at the inn in Merrow in order to change Harry for one of his other horses from the supply which he kept there, he resolved that not even Cromwell could frighten him off the investigation.

As he approached his own village in the early hours of Thursday morning, he saw something that, tired as he was, filled him with dread. His first thought was that the dawn had come early; but that was impossible. Ahead of him the sky had a reddish hue, and as he drew near to his house, he choked on the acrid smell of burning wood. Dear God, he prayed. Not that. Had they burned down his house? With Jane asleep inside?

But it wasn't his house, the outline of which he could see, still intact, at the end of the drive. The glow was coming from the far end of the village. Urging his horse forward, he rode down the street where all the houses were shuttered and no lights burned. At the end of the street stood the local inn, and behind that was a field which the villagers used for their celebrations. Someone had built an enormous pyre of wood and straw and animal carcases. Someone had built an effigy which had not quite burned away. Almost, but not quite. The hank of wool which served as the hair on the effigy's head had not been totally destroyed. And the colour of the hair was bright red.

Chapter Eight

Nicholas stared at the messy remains of the bonfire and the pathetic red wig smouldering in the hot ash and felt white-hot anger surge through his body; an anger so intense that it made his heart pound as if it would burst out of his chest. He leapt on his tired horse, who bounded off in fright up the village street and into the courtyard of his house. Tossing the reins to the frightened groom, who ran out of the stables when he heard him arrive, Nicholas strode into the great hall where Great-Aunt Anna, like a stern shepherd, was standing over the huddle of frightened servants clustered together like a flock of terrified sheep. Anna, tall and angular, dressed in her night robe, her grey hair unbound, was berating her flock with harsh words. When she saw Nicholas she fell silent.

'Where is my wife?' shouted Nicholas, as if he thought she might have spirited her away.

'She's in her boudoir, Nicholas,' said Anna calmly. 'She's taken no harm.'

Thrusting aside the servants who vociferously began to proclaim their innocence, Nicholas went into the little room which Jane had made her own and saw her sitting calmly by the fire, like Anna dressed in her night robe, comforting a distraught Mary. He went across to her and she rose to his embrace. He held her tightly as if he would never let her go and sobbed out his relief that she was safe. After the first surge of emotion had run its course, Jane gently drew back from him.

'Nicholas, I am unhurt. None of us has been harmed. We saw the fire and Joseph went down to the village with some men to see what was going on. By the time he got there, the pranksters had gone home so he returned here and told us to go back to bed. But by that time everyone was awake and it's going to take a long time to calm everyone down.'

'Pranksters, you say?' said Nicholas. 'This is not the work of pranksters. This is serious intimidation.'

'Joseph doesn't think so. He says it's the work of young men having drunk too much ale and wanting to fool around. They probably heard these rumours going around about my supposed involvement in the black arts and thought they'd have some fun at my expense. You must calm down. You've ridden a long way and this agitation is bad for you. Now Mary,' she said, turning to the cook who was still sobbing loudly and mopping up the tears with the sleeve of her nightdress. 'Take a hold on yourself and get Lord Nicholas some of that spiced ale I made. See that it's warmed properly; not hot, mind, just tepid.'

'How can you take this so calmly, Jane?' said Nicholas as Mary stumbled away. 'Don't you see that this is a deliberate attack on us? And I'll not stand for it. Whoever wants to harm you will have me to contend with. Now, get dressed and I shall conduct you to the bishop's house as soon as I have seen to those reprobates who dare to call themselves my tenants.'

'Nicholas, stop! You don't know ...' Jane began. But it was no use trying to reason with Nicholas whose anger had surged up again. Striding back into the hall, he shouted for his bailiff.

'Joseph,' said Nicholas to the elderly man who stepped forward. 'What is all this? Who's responsible?'

'Hotheads, my lord. No tenant of yours would dream of doing this to you.'

'Who else is there, apart from my tenants? Everyone in

the village is part of my manor. Someone must have planned this and we'll go and find him now, before the wretch has time to go back to sleep. Come, get your men together, and arm them with staves. We'll drag everyone out of their miserable hovels and haul them up to the top field. I shall speak to them all and find out who was responsible. And, if necessary, I shall keep them there all night and turn them all out of their hovels and push them along to the next parish if no one comes forward. I cannot countenance this insult to my family, Joseph. I have been too soft with them. All I expected of them is that they should be loyal to me.'

Joseph Oakes had been his father's bailiff and Nicholas had grown up with him and knew he was utterly trustworthy. Joseph had introduced him to his first horse and supervised his lessons in horsemanship. Joseph had been his father's constant companion and many a flagon of good French wine they had enjoyed together. Now Joseph was looking apprehensively at him and taking it upon himself to contradict him.

'My lord, stop, I beg of you. Don't be too hasty. I know the people on your manor; I have lived here all my life. I am one of them. None of your tenants would ever do such a thing.'

'Hasty? Did I hear you say hasty? What do you expect me to do? Sit down calmly and do nothing when my wife's effigy has been put on public display and burnt to ashes? No, I cannot condone this. Get down to the village and turn them all out of their beds and order them up to the field; the field I gave them, incidentally, for their own pleasurable pursuits. If they haven't taken any part in this contemptible act, then they have nothing to fear. But I want them all there. Someone might know who's responsible and, if he does, he must speak up. Then they can go home. Come, let's away. All of you,' he shouted at the servants. 'Go with Joseph. Take sticks, and the dogs and get everyone up to the top field.'

Jane had come out of her room and stood listening to Nicholas. When he'd finished and the servants had dispersed, she tried to reason with him; but nothing would make him change his mind. Drunkenness, cheating, lying, he could tolerate and was known to treat mercifully but this insult to his family and his beloved wife he could not forgive. After kissing her passionately, he left her with Anna who put a restraining arm round her shoulders. Then, accompanied by Joseph Oakes who also realised that Nicholas's anger would have to run its course, they marched down to the village where the terrified tenantry were summoned out of their beds and forced to walk to the top field.

Nicholas surveyed the raggle-taggle group of people standing huddled together and gazing up at him in abject terror. He'd taken his stand on a hillock where he could see them all clearly and they could all see him. Joseph had brought torches, and, in their flickering light together with the glow of the dying embers of the fire, Nicholas studied each face in turn, not saying a word, noting the incomprehension and the fear. He knew all of them. Most of them had lived in the village all their lives and had worked for his father, as their fathers had worked for his ancestors. They were part of his household. They were Peverells. And yet one of them was Judas.

'You can see what has happened here,' he said. 'This,' he went on, stooping to pick up the remains of the wig and holding it up for all to see, like the executioner at a beheading, 'represents my wife. We have not been married long, but you all know her and her father, Guy Warrener, even though none of you came to his funeral. He was one of you. His daughter, my wife, has done nothing but good. She looked after you when you were ill, taught your children and looked after you at the end. You know her for what she is, beautiful, compassionate, and with no vestige of evil in her. And yet you have done this to her. Now you have me

95

to reckon with. Unless the culprit comes forward and confesses, I shall have you all turned out of my houses. Yes, all of you, even Giles who has farmed my family's fields for as long as I can remember. No one will be exempt. If you know who is responsible for doing this foul thing you must denounce him now, or face the consequences. Come now, don't try my patience. I shall give you but a few moments for the wretch to confess or for someone to tell me who he is.'

They stood there waiting in silent misery. Most of them were in their nightshirts; some in the rough, leather trousers they wore in the fields; all were barefoot, not having had time to put on boots or shoes. But Nicholas felt no compassion for them. One of them was guilty.

Suddenly, Robert Freeman pushed his way to the front of the crowd. Nicholas knew Robert very well. He was a man of some substance, being a freeholder: independent, utterly reliable, the churchwarden. Nicholas looked at him in surprise. He was the last man he expected to come forward.

'You, Robert? Surely this has nothing to do with you?'

'No, my lord. And this,' he said, pointing to the smouldering remains of the fire, 'has nothing to do with anyone here. My lord, you do your tenants a disservice. It is not worthy of you. None of these people would contemplate harming a hair on your head. As for your wife, they would give their lives for her if necessary.'

'Yet someone did this, Robert. How can you be so certain it was not someone from the village? Did you see anyone come up here? Did you see who lit the fire?'

'I didn't see who was responsible, my lord. Like everyone else, I was asleep in my bed. But all I can say is that I can swear on the Holy Bible that none of these good people would even contemplate doing this terrible deed. None of us saw who built this fire because we weren't here; but there is someone who might have done. Master Hoggety, step forward and tell his lordship what you saw.'

Walter Hoggety owned the alehouse. Nicholas had only

96

recently renewed his licence at the last Sessions. Surely, he thought, Walter would not risk his livelihood for the sake of a prank which he must know would cause great offence.

The crowd had now recovered from its fright and was only too willing to push Walter forward. 'Aye, that's right, you tell him,' they shouted, glad that Nicholas's attention was diverted away from them.

'Come, speak up, man, don't be afraid,' said Nicholas, relieved that he seemed to be getting somewhere. 'What did you see from that house of yours?'

'It was after dark, my lord,' said the innkeeper looking fearfully up at Nicholas. He was appalled at suddenly being the centre of attention. 'Not long after dark, mind, but my wife and I go to bed as soon as there are no more customers and people retire early at this time of the year because there's the harvest still to be got in. As I closed the upstairs shutters, I looked down into the field and saw men carrying bundles which they heaped up into a pile.'

'How many men?' said Nicholas.

'Two at that point. There could have been more later but I didn't stop to look. It looked innocent enough to me, especially at harvest time. I thought maybe Joseph had given instructions to use the field for some purpose. I didn't recognise the men but then we do take on strangers at this season to give us a hand to get the harvest in quickly before the weather changes. As I closed the shutters, a man came into the field and spoke to the two men piling up the sticks. Now I recognised this man – not that I knew who he was, mind, but it's the same man who's been riding round hereabouts during the last few days.'

'That's right,' put in Robert Oakes, 'it was the same man who spoke to me up in the churchyard. Vicar saw him too, isn't that right, sir?' he said to Alfred Hobbes, who was standing a little way apart from the rest of the crowd and whose small figure had disappeared into the shadow of some trees.

'Yes, I spoke to him. But he spoke of things I dare not

97

mention, my lord; evil things, and I reckoned he must be an emissary of the Devil and I sent him packing.'

'What bad things?' said Nicholas, his heart beating violently.

'Oh, my lord, terrible things about wanting to find witches and didn't I realise that our own Lady Jane was one of them. My lord, I would have none of it. Don't be angry with me. I sent him on his way, but the damage was done. He'd been spreading rumours all round the countryside and now this has happened. It's the way the Devil works, my lord.'

'You don't have to tell me about the Devil,' said Nicholas, 'I see his work all around me. Did this man give his name? Would you recognise his again?'

'No, my lord. He was not from these parts. He didn't look like a farmer, more a soldier. The upper part of his face was partly concealed by a leather cap which he'd pulled down over his forehead, and the lower part was hidden by his beard. But I would recognise his horse anywhere. His horse was black, well fed and strong; like yours, my lord, but more of the heavy weight about him, like the horses they used in times past when they had to carry a man and his armour. Your lordship's horse is built for speed, as we all know.'

'Why wasn't I told about this man?' said Nicholas, turning to look at Joseph.

'Because, my lord, you have been away and I, for one, have never heard of him before this moment.'

'As my bailiff your job is to know everything that goes on in my manor.'

'Yes, my lord, when it comes to corn and oats and rents and services. It is not my job to watch the roads for strangers.'

He was right, of course, and Nicholas knew he should not speak to the old man like this, but anger was clouding his judgement.

'Who else saw this man?' said Nicholas, addressing the

crowd. No one, except the vicar, Robert Freeman and Walter Haggety admitted to seeing him.

'Did you see him light the fire?' Nicholas asked Walter.

'No, my lord. I was that worn out with running the place – and I must say that I had had one too many tankards of ale to get me a good night's sleep – that as soon as I had closed the shutters I went to my bed. I woke up with the flames, my lord, and by then the men had gone.'

All of a sudden, Nicholas's anger evaporated. He realised that he had made a grave mistake in summoning all these people from their beds. He should have started by talking to those people whose houses were nearest the field, like Walter Hoggety's, for instance. He turned to Joseph, who stood beside him stiff with resentment over Nicholas's recent criticism.

'Joseph, it appears that you were right, after all. These people are not the guilty ones. I am sorry to have caused such an upheaval. See to it that they all return to their beds.'

'I think, my lord, that something more is expected of you. They are waiting to hear you apologise.'

There was nothing for it but to eat humble pie. Nicholas looked at the sea of resentful faces and took a deep breath.

'People, my people,' he began, 'I am indeed sorry to have roused you out of your beds, especially when you must be up early to bring in the harvest. This matter is none of your doing, I can see that now, but I could not ignore such a serious attack on my family. I am indeed sorry for mistrusting you. Now return home, and I beg of you that if any of you catch sight of this horseman and his two accomplices, then come at once to my house and tell us. Now, I shall see to it that you will all be suitably compensated for the inconvenience I have caused you and I trust that you will all accept my apologies. As for you, Joseph,' he said, 'I was indeed too hasty in not listening to you in the first place. I hope that the trust we have for one another will not be affected by this incident.'

99

'That, my lord,' said Joseph stiffly, 'will very much depend on you. I, for one, will always have your interests at heart. Now men,' he said to the crowd, 'away to your beds. We must make an early start tomorrow.'

Leaving Joseph to see to it that the fire was stamped out and the tenants returned to their homes, Nicholas, suddenly overcome with weariness, returned to his house where Jane was waiting for him. Without a word, she led him up to their room where she pulled off his boots and brought water for him to wash off the dust from the journey. Then, clasping her in his arms, he covered her face with kisses.

'Never again do I leave you here alone, my darling one. Tomorrow I shall take you to the bishop's palace where you will be safe. Jane, we are in great danger. Someone is out to destroy us. Why, I do not yet know. But I shall not rest until . . .'

Then, still dressed in his riding clothes, he fell asleep in Jane's arms.

Chapter Nine

'Nicholas, what are you saying? You tell me that the king is coming to stay on the twenty-third of this month and I am to be hidden away in Marchester until you have solved this case single-handed; well, I won't go, and that's the end of the matter. It's the fourth of September today and you know how much there is to do before these visits of the king: the provisioning, the cleaning, the taking on of extra servants – especially the cooks. You know how much the king enjoys what he calls fresh country fare. Think of the last time he came; we took weeks to recover from the upheaval, let alone the expense of it all. No, I must stay here. There will not be any more trouble from the tenants after last night, and with any luck, the troublemaker on the black horse will have moved on.'

Nicholas stared at his wife's stubborn face across the breakfast table. The cold meats and the bread had been cleared away, the servants dismissed and over the ale and the milk which Jane drank, Nicholas had told her about his visit to the king and Cromwell.

'It is not over, Jane. It is only just the beginning and the king wants reassurance that it is safe to visit Sussex. He suspects something is amiss; so does Cromwell, and the king is uneasy. I think Baron Cromwell is the key figure in this case. He is plotting something. He warned me off the investigation and offered, as an inducement, a post on the embassy to the Duke of Cleves should the king decide to marry the duke's daughter. Now why should Cromwell be at all interested in the death of a young girl in rural Sussex? She was not from a noble family. There is nothing about her that would interest Cromwell. But yet, he wants the case dropped. Why, Jane, why? And what does the king suspect? The usual? His Yorkist cousins up to their old tricks? I don't think so; most of the troublemakers have either fled abroad or are waiting trial in the Tower. No, there is something else going on and the king wants someone to find out what it is. And that someone is me. The king knows me and trusts me; and uses me, and doesn't care what becomes of me and my family whilst I carry out his wishes. Jane, we are pieces in a deadly game of plot and counterplot, and I only know one rule in this game and that is how to survive. You and I together, Jane, because if anything should happen to you, then I would not wish to live any longer. And that's why you must go to Marchester, just for a few days until I think it is safe for you to return. In the meantime I will find out the reason for the recent intimidation and catch the person who murdered Kate Bowman. Probably the same person murdered that unfortunate mole-taker.

'The risk I am taking is very real, Jane. If I am seen to be back on the investigation, then we are all in danger. It is not too fanciful to foresee that if I continue with my enquiries into that girl's death, the rumours will increase. Then not only will you be accused of witchcraft but I could face a treason charge. Yes, don't look so horrified. You know we live in dangerous times. One whisper in the king's ear that Nicholas Peverell has been seen riding round the countryside making enquiries, perhaps talking to the king's Yorkist relations, some of whom live near us, and I am for the Tower and Tower Green. Do you not understand now? I am not exaggerating; I wish to God I were.'

Jane could see that Nicholas was deadly serious. She also knew the king and the ways of the court. She knew about the power struggles, the jostling for the king's favours. She had seen how quickly men who had been favoured and given high positions could fall from grace. She'd seen the vultures gather and pick over the doomed man's property and possessions. Hadn't Nicholas, her own husband, benefited from the fall of Mortimer barely two years ago? Already people at court would be watching Nicholas's every move and counting the moments before he, too, fell out with the king and his estates would be forfeited.

'I don't want to be a burden to you, Nicholas,' she said after a long pause. 'I can understand that you want me in a safe place, and what could be safer than in the bishop's palace in Marchester? But I don't think you should continue to investigate this case, which, if you are right, could have political ramifications, without running the risk of your own downfall. Cromwell wants the investigation dropped. The sheriff has already been frightened off. They have tried to frighten you by attacking me, but so far they have not succeeded. Cromwell has resorted to bribery so it must be serious. You could be in real danger, I can now see that. Oh Nicholas,' she said, staring at him in terror, 'you must be as cunning as a fox if you want to continue with this case. For instance, why don't you tell the sheriff you've better things to do than bother with the death of a girl? Pretend to be overwhelmed by the king's visit. Let everyone relax and Sarah Bowman's death will soon be forgotten. As for the mole-taker, no one will take any notice of his death. He will have been buried by now and everyone will already have forgotten him. Then, if you must, proceed with the utmost stealth.'

Suddenly her face crumpled and she jumped up from the table and came round to where Nicholas was sitting, and flung her arms round him.

'Nicholas, I have seen innocent men go to terrible deaths. Please, my dearest love, take no risks. What does it matter if one girl and one lowly mole-catcher have died? No one is going to miss them. But I could not live if anything happened to you; not now, not at this time. Please God, not you.'

Nicholas gently extricated himself from her embrace and pulled her down onto his lap. Stroking her hair, he looked into her eyes, bright with tears.

'Jane, I didn't mean to frighten you. Of course I shall go carefully. I know the stakes are high. And I know the dangers of being the king's loyal servant. But what do you mean about "now"? What's so special about this moment?'

Jane wiped her eyes on her sleeve of her gown and met Nicholas's eyes. 'I was going to tell you before, but too many things happened and the moment wasn't right. But now, with our lives being turned upside down, I think I ought to tell you. I am carrying our child, Nicholas. He's not very big, yet. I have only missed two months, but he's there and already I love him.'

'Jane, you are with child, and you didn't tell me?'

'He's too small, yet, and I might have been mistaken. But I think it's true. Tell me you are pleased.'

'Pleased? My darling, I am delighted. But now one thing is clear – you must leave for the bishop's palace straight away. No more arguments. You are far too precious to stay here where you might be in danger. I'll take you myself to the bishop, then go and see Richard Landstock and tell him I've dropped the case because of the imminence of the king's visit. Whilst you are living quietly with Humphrey Catchpole and his wife, I shall go and see Fitzherbert and tell him to prepare for the king's visit. Jane, you have such a wise head on those slim shoulders of yours. You have always given me such good advice. And now, let me give you some advice in return. Stay at the palace, and look after that child of ours. Our wonderful child; nothing must happen to either of you. Soon, I shall get to the bottom of this mystery and we shall be together again. But take care, my love, and keep out of harm's way.'

'You, too, Nicholas, must also take care. This baby of ours will want to see his father alive and free, won't he?'

104

'He will, my darling. I shall take every care to ensure that nothing happens to any of us. The Peverells have been here for four hundred years and I shall see to it that we are still around for the next four hundred.'

Having seen Jane safely installed in the bishop's palace, Nicholas rode into Marchester to see the sheriff. At first, Richard Landstock was inclined to be wary, but, hearing Nicholas declare his lack of interest in the Bowman case because he had better things to do, he relaxed and became his old expansive self again, full of news about helping the Earl of Southampton round up a gang of robbers hiding out in Marchester harbour. Relieved to be on good terms with the sheriff again, Nicholas took his leave and rode back along the coastal road, passing the turning off to his own manor and continuing to ride eastwards until the turrets of Lord Gilbert Fitzherbert's castle appeared in the distance.

For a moment he hesitated. The game he was about to play was deadly. It only needed one false move and he and his family were lost. His enemies, he knew, were watching him, waiting for the chance to whisper in the king's ear that Nicholas Peverell was disobeying orders and stirring up a hornet's nest in Sussex. Once the king suspected him of disloyalty, even if the evidence was of the flimsiest kind, he could say goodbye to his estates in Sussex and life itself. And now that Jane was with child life had become even more precious. He ought to turn back, now, whilst there was still time, and resume the life of a country gentleman. But two deaths could not go unavenged, and he resented being dictated to by Cromwell and the Sheriff of Marchester. And he would not be intimidated. He had no idea what would be the outcome of his investigations – he was groping in the dark – but his survival instincts were strong and he was aware that he had a lot to lose. But he would not give up his enquiries. Stubbornness, so Jane had told him, was one of his less endearing qualities.

It had only been a week ago that he had paid a visit to

Lord Gilbert Fitzherbert. Less than a week since Sarah Bowman was buried. Much had happened during that week. He'd spoken to the king and Cromwell. Another summons and it would be the end of him, he knew, and the confiscation of his estates. And Jane would be a widow, doomed to a life of poverty and disgrace, and his heir would be fatherless and penniless. Nevertheless, he didn't hesitate for long. Urging his horse on, he rode up to the open gate and across the drawbridge into the courtyard of Tredgosse Castle. There, a charming sight confronted him. A child, no more than seven or eight, he guessed, was playing at sword-fighting with one of the grooms. The swords were only made of wood, but the boy was playing in deadly earnest. Then Nicholas saw that the boy was fighting with the disadvantage of a severely deformed body and the groom was holding himself in check and allowing the boy to do the attacking. When they realised that Nicholas was watching them, they stopped playing and the boy came over to him, his handsome face set in a disapproving scowl.

'You come at a bad time, sir. I am in the midst of a fight to the death with my deadly enemy, Adam.'

Nicholas dismounted and handed the reins of his horse to the groom who, realising that Nicholas was a person of rank, had thrown down his sword and resumed his duties.

'I am sorry to interrupt your fight, but I have to speak to your father on a matter of some urgency. You are Marcus Fitzherbert, I think?'

'Indeed I am; and you, sir, who are you?'

Nicholas told the boy his name and reluctantly the boy put the sword in the scabbard that hung from the belt round his waist and led the way into the castle. Nicholas pitied the boy. Slim, looking younger than his years, he thought, his back was badly misshapen and his legs so bowed and skinny that he walked in a crab-like gait, lurching from one leg to the other. His face, though, when he glanced back to see if Nicholas was following, was remarkably beautiful: small, well shaped, with delicate, pale skin, huge brown eyes and plentiful dark-brown hair cut square round his face. Nature had indeed delivered a cruel blow when he was born.

Once inside the castle, he was taken into the great hall where another child came running up to greet them, a sturdy, well-built boy of about four years old, with dark hair and eyes which were shining with excitement.

'Did you kill Adam?' he said to Marcus. 'Can I borrow your sword now?'

'I didn't have time to kill him because we have a visitor, but you can take the sword,' said Marcus, drawing the sword out of its scabbard and handing it to the child. 'Now be careful and leave old Rufus alone.' He pointed to the wolfhound lounging in front of the fireplace, head between his paws, his ears twitching as he watched the boys.

The young boy grabbed the sword and with a shriek of delight darted towards the dog who, with surprising agility, rose to his feet and fled from the room, the child in hot pursuit beating the straw on the floor as he went along. Marcus smiled shyly at Nicholas.

'You must forgive Justin, my lord; he is just a child.'

'Your brother, sir?'

'My half-brother. My father has not married the lady who bore Justin. She'd like to,' he added with a knowing expression that made him look older than his slight frame indicated, 'but my father respects my mother's memory. Besides, Adeliza is just a common wench; he could not marry her.'

Nicholas had been so fascinated by the two boys that he had not noticed Lord Gilbert come into the room. He came up to them now and held out his hand to Nicholas.

'So, we meet again, my lord, and I see you have already made the acquaintance of my son, Marcus.'

'Indeed I have,' said Nicholas, shaking the outstretched hand. 'And he will soon be a fine swordsman, I think.'

'A bit more practice and we'll have him jousting with the rest of them. There's a fine brain in that head of his, as you will soon find out. He plays chess like a wizard, the lute like Orpheus himself; and the falcons love him and will do anything he asks. Not like that troublemaker, Justin. They retreat onto their perches and feign sleep when he appears.'

Marcus laughed. 'You must not be too hard on him, Father. He is strong and high-spirited and doesn't stop to think. He's only four, my lord,' he said to Nicholas, 'and doesn't know how to deal with animals.'

'He doesn't stop to consider them,' said Lord Gilbert, putting an arm fondly on his son's shoulders. 'And you are too soft with him. Remember, you are my heir. This castle will be yours one day and Justin will be away fighting in the king's wars. You must keep him in his place.'

'Justin will never hurt us, Father. He loves us both. I wish I had just a bit of his strength,' he said wistfully,

'Strength is nothing, Marcus. Even the common labourers have that. A good brain is worth more than a strong body. Now run along and rescue Rufus from Justin's persecution. And order some refreshment for Lord Nicholas. Come, my lord,' he said to Nicholas as Marcus limped away, 'what brings you here again so soon? No more bad news, I hope? Have you caught the wretch who murdered that poor girl?'

'No, and we're not likely to now. The wretch, as you call him, is probably away out of the county. Sarah Bowman's buried and we don't know why she was murdered or who did it. As it happens, I have been away. The king sent for me, and I also had an interview with Baron Cromwell. I have news for you, Lord Gilbert.'

'Then let us make ourselves more comfortable. The tapestry room is more congenial for conversation.'

He led the way across the great hall and through a door into a small room where the walls were covered with tapestries depicting scenes from the hunt. Two chairs with carved wooden arms and cushions on the seats stood on either side of the smouldering fire. Lord Gilbert seated himself in one and indicated the other to Nicholas.

'And how is his majesty?' said Lord Gilbert when Nicholas had sat down. A servant entered carrying a tray with two tankards of ale on it and a dish of small cakes which he placed on a small table in front of the fire.

'His majesty is in splendid health; likewise Baron Cromwell.'

'And the child, Edward?' said Lord Gilbert indicating to Nicholas that he should help himself to the refreshments.

'He thrives. He shows signs of great promise.'

'I thank God for that. It is good to have a son and heir and know that the country will be in safe hands. But what is your news, Lord Nicholas?'

Nicholas helped himself to the refreshments. 'The king sends his greetings and has expressed a wish to pay us a visit later this month.'

'Us?' repeated Lord Gilbert with a look of consternation on his dark face. 'Later this month, you say? Surely you are jesting, my lord?'

'Indeed I am not. He has expressed a wish to become further acquainted with you and he also enjoys using my house as a hunting lodge. Cromwell told me he wants to come on the twenty-third of this month, which doesn't give us much time.'

'My lord, I am appalled,' said Lord Gilbert, getting to his feet and pacing up and down in a state of agitation. 'It will take us months to get this place ready for a royal visit. The bedrooms have not been used for years. Some parts of the castle have been closed off altogether as I have little use for so much space. What am I to do?'

'The king will come to me first. I don't know how long he will stay. It depends how much he is enjoying himself. Cromwell said he only wanted to pay you a short visit.'

'Will he expect entertainments? Banquets? How many courtiers will he bring with him?'

'I don't know, my lord. We never know the king's wishes until he arrives and then he's quite likely to change his mind depending on the circumstances. He will

expect me to provide hunting, feasting and musical enter-
tainment. Fortunately I have an excellent musician who
is used to courtly ways and my wife has a fine voice.
He wants to see you so you will have to be prepared for
any eventuality. Then he might move on to speak to the
Earl of Southampton and discuss the coastal defences. Do
not agitate yourself, my lord,' Nicholas said as Lord
Gilbert's face was becoming more alarmed by the minute.
'You have a fine establishment here; he will be fascinated by its antiquity. He'll suggest all sorts of
modernisation and will probably send you one of his
architects. He likes comfort.'

'Maybe he will be put off by my old-fashioned ways and
not wish to stay here.'

'That would be a disaster for you, my lord,' said
Nicholas, quietly enjoying Lord Gilbert's discomfiture.
'The king is not an easy man to deal with when he is
displeased. He could confiscate your castle and place it in
the hands of others to see that improvements are made.
Having said that,' he added, relenting at the look of horror
on Lord Gilbert's face, 'he is very happy with a plentiful
feast, a soft bed for himself – his servants can share your
servants' quarters – and the use of your stables. Now, be
of good cheer, my lord, you should be honoured by this
royal visit. It's an opportunity to show one's love and
respect for one's king.'

Lord Gilbert stopped pacing up and down, and made a
supreme effort to pull himself together. 'Of course, of
course, I am indeed honoured. Well, well, we shall have to
see to it, I suppose. Ah, here you are, Adeliza; come here,
will you. I have some good news for you. Lord Nicholas
has just told me that we are to expect a visit from the king
at the end of the month. Now, does that please you?'

The woman whom Nicholas had seen on his last visit had
come into the room whilst they were talking. She was as
beautiful as he remembered her, and today she was dressed
in a simple, wine-coloured robe which set off her dark

110

beauty to perfection. She seemed anxious and hardly took in what Lord Gilbert was saying.

'You must curb your son, my lord,' she said. 'He bullies our child.'

'What are you saying, woman?' shouted Lord Gilbert, whirling round to face her. 'Marcus wouldn't harm a fly. What are you complaining about?'

'He took the sword off Justin, who was very upset.'

'Upset? That child upset? Most likely he was beating Rufus and Marcus stopped him. Now stop your incessant worrying about him and listen to what I am trying to tell you. Lord Nicholas has just come back from court and says that the king is to pay us a visit at the end of this month. Good, now I see you have heard me.'

Adeliza had stopped her flow of complaints about Marcus and was staring at Lord Gilbert in horror.

'The king? But we have nothing to offer him.'

'Then we must see to it that we have something. Lord Nicholas says that the king wants to make my acquaintance and look over this fine castle. Now, we must act quickly. We need to take on more servants, cooks ...'

Nicholas stood up. 'I shall leave you now to make the arrangements. I must go back to my house and do likewise. We must show the king that hospitality is not dead in Sussex. We must meet again soon, my lord. Don't hesitate to ask me for help if you should need it. Don't disturb yourselves,' he added. 'I can see myself out.'

Having said his farewells, Nicholas left the two of them discussing the impending visit. As he walked back through the hall, he dropped his leather riding gauntlets on the table and walked out into the courtyard to summon the groom. After waiting for a few moments, he went back into the hall and picked up his gauntlets. Then he stood there listening. Angry voices were coming from the tapestry room, the door of which still stood open. Adeliza was shouting at Lord Gilbert; not about the preparations for the king's visit but a more personal matter about which she seemed to have strong feelings.

111

'My lord, you must now make me respectable and marry me and recognise our son. How can I face the king without some sort of position? He will never sit down to dinner with your whore.'

'Be quiet, woman, we have been over this many times. The king's visit will make no difference to your position. You are my housekeeper; Justin is my bastard. The king understands such matters. He will understand that marriage to you is out of the question. It would dishonour my wife's name.'

'And yet you take me to your bed. You don't think of dishonouring her name then,' she shouted.

'Silence, woman . . .'

Nicholas heard the sound of a slap and a cry from Adeliza. Then a door slammed. Quickly he left the hall. The groom was waiting in the courtyard with his horse. Deep in thought, he rode off towards the village of Monksmere.

In the still heat of the September afternoon the village appeared to have succumbed to an enchanter's spell. The cottages on either side of the dusty track looked deserted, as if the inhabitants had either fled or fallen asleep under the magic. All doors were shut; unusual in this hot weather, thought Nicholas. When the men were in the fields the women and children wandered freely in and out of one another's houses exchanging news and giving a helping hand where needed. But not today. No dogs barked. No dogs chased him down the road as they usually did. No one called out a greeting as he rode past the cottages. He began to feel oppressed, as if he had wandered into alien territory where supernatural forces threatened him.

To the right of the track the outlines of the priory church loomed ominously over the village seemingly warning the villagers that God was watching them. Already the other buildings of the canons were falling into decay as the locals helped themselves to the stones. Soon, Nicholas thought, there would be nothing left of the religious community that had once occupied the site for four hundred years, except the skeleton outline of the tall arch at the east end of the church. That afternoon, the arch appeared to shimmer in the hazy heat, adding to the feeling of enchantment.

With an effort, Nicholas forced his mind away from such fanciful thoughts and tried to concentrate his mind on the task before him. A long time seemed to have passed since he had last seen Kate Bowman at her granddaughter's funeral and he was not sure how to resume questioning her. He had to gain her trust; otherwise she would just clam up and nothing would make her open up to him.

He reached her house. It too, looked deserted. He tied his horse to the gatepost and walked up to the front door. It was closed and no amount of banging summoned anyone inside to open it. His feeling of unease increased. Perhaps he had come too late. Perhaps Kate Bowman had shared the same fate as her granddaughter. And the child? What had happened to him? He walked round to the back of the house where the pig slept peacefully in the sty. It opened one eye when it saw Nicholas, grunted and snorted as it turned over in the straw. It appeared well cared for; so someone was looking after it.

The house had no back door; short of breaking down the front door and forcing his way in, there was no way he could get in. Feeling increasingly alarmed, he mounted his horse and rode off to the Dog and Bell where, he thought, the landlord might be able to tell him Kate Bowman's whereabouts. Or maybe Peter, the sheriff's man, had ridden over with a message for him as they had arranged.

At least the door of the inn was open. He walked into the dim interior and called for the landlord. No one came. Then he saw Eddy. Eddy, the mole-taker's companion, who jumped up from the bench where he was lying and came over to him, a shy smile lighting up his face. Nicholas hardly recognised him; he seemed to have grown several inches since Nicholas had last seen him. His body had

113

plumped out, his face had become less pinched and was now tanned by the sun.

'Come outside, Eddy. It's best if no one sees us together,' said Nicholas.

'Matt's asleep. I'm in charge. Not that many people come at this time of the day.'

'Then it will not lose the landlord any custom if we go and sit under that tree.'

They walked over to the old yew tree that bordered the field to one side of the inn. Someone had installed a rough wooden bench there for customers to rest on in the shade and Nicholas led the way there and sat down, indicating to Eddy to sit beside him.

'Is Matt treating you well?'

'Oh yes, I keep out of his way when he's in one of his awkward moods. Most times he leaves me alone and I serve the customers and wash up the pots. I get all the food I want and a straw mattress on the barn floor by way of payment.'

Nicholas took a few coins out of his pocket and handed them to the boy. 'Here, take these. They will buy you some boots for the winter. Some new clothes too, if you're lucky,' he added, glancing at the collection of rags that covered the boy's body.

'Thanks,' said Eddy, taking the coins and stuffing them in some secret place in the ragged remains of his jerkin. 'I seem to be in luck lately, since old Moley died. I got given two marks last week by another gentleman, like you, riding the same black horse which you used to ride.'

'And shall ride again soon when the groom brings him back from Merrow. Now tell me, Eddy,' said Nicholas, his heart beginning to beat faster, 'what did this man want?'

'He asked about you, sir.'

'What did he want to know about me?'

'Only if you'd been back here since poor Sarah's funeral. I could tell the truth for once and say, no, you hadn't; least-ways, if you had been back, I hadn't seen you.'

114

'Good lad. And if he comes again, you'll tell him the same thing again, won't you?'

'But that'll not be true, will it sir, because here you are talking to me now.'

'He's not to know that.'

'Then I'll be telling a lie and for me to tell a lie it'll cost you two marks. I can't tell lies for nothing, sir.'

'Before I give you any more money, tell me what this man looked like and what else he said. When did you see him and who else saw him?'

'Lots of questions, sir, and not enough reward.'

'Enough of your cheek, rascal. Remember who you are speaking to. Didn't I rescue you from starving to death when the mole-taker died?'

'So you did, sir. And sorry I was to lose old Moley. They buried him mighty quickly, you know. Priest said a few words over him and they shovelled him into his hole and that was that. But I put some flowers on the grave and I hope he's now with God. Still as you say, you did take me on, so I'll tell you what I know.'

'For two marks?'

'Done. Well, up he comes, this man on the black horse. He's a good size, bearded, not from round here. I served him some ale which he drank whilst still on his horse. He didn't say what he wanted you for – well, he wouldn't, would he? Then he told me to hold my tongue and not to tell anyone that I'd seen him; and then he rode off. It was after the funeral. The next day. Late in the afternoon. He took the Marchester road.'

So the man had been prowling around for several days, Nicholas thought. He was sure that this man was the one who had spoken to the vicar back in Dean Peverell and who had started the fire the night he came back from Hampton Court. In the meantime he had been spreading rumours and turning his tenants against him. Where was he now? As long as he was still at large, he, Nicholas, was not out of danger. Neither was Jane. And neither was Eddy. They

115

must not be seen talking together. How much did the child know? thought Nicholas

'Come Eddy, your two marks. Now tell me, do you know where Kate Bowman is? She wasn't at home when I went to see her just now.'

The boy grabbed the coins and looked slyly up at Nicholas.

'Thank you, sir. Mother Bowman's left her house. I feed the pig for her because she intends to come back. She took the child, Henry, with her.'

Nicholas began to feel the excitement of the hunter whose hounds have scented the prey. 'Why did she leave her house?'

'Because the stranger went to see her and threatened to take the child away from her if she spoke to anyone about poor Sarah. I loved Sarah, sir. We got on. I often went with her up to see the canons when they were here. She did some embroidery for them and I killed the moles which were making their hillocks all over the canons' vegetable garden. Sometimes Moley came with us, but most times he let me go with Sarah. I was only a little fellow then,' he said with a shy smile, 'and Sarah looked after me. I can look after myself now, of course.'

'You're doing very well for yourself, certainly. If you continue at this rate you'll soon be able to buy yourself your own alehouse. But let me get this straight; after the man threatened Kate Bowman, she went away. Where did she go to, Eddy?'

'Now that I can't tell you. I really can't. I promised not to tell anyone – and a promise is a promise, sir. I'm to have a bit of that pig, come Michaelmas, if I keep my mouth shut.'

'Eddy, you can have all the pork you want, and a new pair of boots, if you tell me where Kate Bowman is. You know I am her friend. I would never harm her, but I want to catch the wicked man who killed Sarah and I need to talk to her grandmother, because she might be able to help me.'

'Then you mustn't tell anyone I told you. Especially the

116

man on the black horse, because I am sure he wants to harm her. And if he kills her then I shall have to kill myself because I let her down.'

'Eddy, I know you are in a difficult position, but you must trust me. I am going to catch Sarah's murderer; he may have killed Moley, too, if he knew too much. I shall see that the killer swings on Marchester Heath for his crimes. That is what I do, Eddy. I try to keep the peace and bring criminals to justice. Now, are you going to help me? Tell me where Kate Bowman is and I promise I won't harm her. I want to make sure she's safe.'

Eddy stared at him, making up his mind. Nicholas respected him for his integrity. Finally he spoke:

'I think you are a man who keeps his word, sir. An honourable man. Not like Matt, who would sell his own wife for a hundred marks. Well, Mother Bowman's gone to her brother's house. He's a fisherman down at Littlehaven. His name's Amos Carter. He's looking after her and young Henry. They'll be safe there.'

'As long as no one else knows where they are. And that's up to you, Eddy. It's a big responsibility. Just lie low, keep your mouth shut and if the man on the black horse comes back again, tell him nothing about our conversation. Eddy, I will see you are well rewarded when the case is over. No more for now. Matt must not suspect that you are my spy. He would not hesitate to tell the man on the black horse that you are selling me information; and that would be very dangerous for you. Keep everything to yourself and only report to me.'

At last, thought Nicholas, he was making progress. But he must not see Eddy too often. He could be the next one to disappear. And looking up, he saw Matt the landlord standing in the doorway of the inn and the expression on his face was grim.

'Run off now, Eddy,' he said, standing up and pushing the boy away. 'Get me some ale and tell Matt you were just going to serve me.'

The boy ran off and Nicholas strolled over to talk to Matt who had obviously just woken up after a heavy meal. However, he managed to crease his face into a deferential smile when he saw that Nicholas only wanted some ale.

'You're becoming a regular visitor, my lord. Not still chasing imaginary criminals, I trust?'

'No, I have other things to do with my time. But are there any messages for me, Matt? The sheriff's too busy to come this way just now, but one of his men might have been down here.'

'No one's been here from Marchester, my lord.'

'Thanks, that's all I wanted to know. Thank you, Eddy,' he said, taking a tankard of ale from the boy and giving him a coin. 'I hope Eddy earns his keep?'

'Aye, he's a good lad. Trustworthy, too, I think. Mind you, I might change my mind if he stands gossiping with the customers for too long. Be off, boy, and leave Lord Nicholas in peace.'

Nicholas drank the ale, gave the tankard to the landlord and rode off. The day was well advanced and Littlehaven was on the other side of the river, a good few hours' journey as he would have to cross the river up beyond Tredgosse Castle. He'd make the journey tomorrow. Meanwhile it was back to Marchester and the bishop's palace, where he'd see Jane and share her bed that night.

Chapter Ten

It was all Jane's idea. As she put it in her own inimitable way, 'It's no use riding round the county on Harry hoping no one will notice you. You will have to disguise yourself, Nicholas.'

First she insisted on cutting off his hair, which he wore on the long side, then she rubbed a little charcoal on his face, and sent the bishop's steward to find a leather jerkin and some thick breeches, and a leather hat with a large brim to shield his face. Moreover, she said, he must have a new name. 'Farmer Trayford, I think. Robert, or Bobby for short. And you should ride the bay cob, Jack. He's the right sort of horse for a farmer.'

'He's my bailiff's horse.'

'Then he can ride Harry. He must be back from London by now. '

Nicholas began to protest, but he could see the sense in what Jane had said. Hadn't he resorted to disguise on a previous occasion, and hadn't it proved effective? Without it he would not have been able to expose Neville's treachery.

The cob was heavily built with sturdy legs and hairy fetlocks, bred from a long line of knights' horses, but he was willing and good-natured and had tremendous stamina. He clumped along the coastal road to Monksmere in record time and it was not long before the turrets of Tredgosse Castle loomed ahead of him. The road ran round the base of the castle and then turned north where a stone bridge crossed the river Gosse. Once, the canons of Monksmere had collected tolls from travellers but Lord Gilbert had not yet taken up his responsibility for the upkeep of the bridge. As Nicholas rode across it, he looked down onto the decks of two boats making their way towards the town quay further up the river. The sails had been furled and the boats were being propelled along with poles on this last bit of their journey. The river was tidal in its lower reaches, but boats could still get up to Tredgosse, and sometimes there was quite a bit of river traffic. The two bargemen, shielding their eyes from the sun, looked up at Nicholas and shouted out a greeting, and Nicholas waved back. Once across the bridge, he left the main road and took the track leading south to the coast which followed the course of the river as it wound its sinuous way across the water meadows. Lazy cows, too contented to raise their heads and look at him, munched away at the lush grass. A heron stood motionless in the reed beds waiting for a fish to surface. A family of moorhens made their leisurely way downstream and once he caught sight of the dazzling flash of blue from a kingfisher's wings. Soon the sweat was pouring down his back and the cob's neck was dark with a cloud of flies which settled on him drinking the salty liquid. The cob tossed his head irritably and flicked his long tail to remove the swarm on his flanks. The air on this flat, coastal plain was hot and heavy with the oppressive feel of an imminent thunderstorm. The cob plodded on and Nicholas, regretting the fact that he wasn't riding Harry, who was built for speed, pulled his hat down over his face as a protection against the flies. The track followed every bend in the river and the journey seemed interminable.

The sun was overhead when suddenly he caught a glimpse of the sea ahead. The track ran straight now down to the small harbour, and one or two cottages, mere hovels with mud walls and reed-thatched roofs, came into view. Suddenly he was at the end of the track and the beach, with its harbour inlet was ahead of him.

Littlehaven was a small fishing port; a mere collection of dwellings and sheds around the harbour. The doors of the mud-walled hovels stood open to let in the fresh sea air, and children played in the dirt in front of the doors and silent women with babes in arms watched him ride past. Down on the beach, a group of men were mending their nets in the shade of two boats. Nicholas nodded to them and they glanced at him suspiciously. Then he was glad that he had left Nicholas Peverell behind as he would have got nowhere with these men. As it happened, they studied him for a few seconds before, in answer to his question, pointing to a small wooden house near the harbour. This was the alehouse. He thanked them and rode on. The alehouse door was open and he heard a low murmuring of voices coming from inside. He jumped down from the cob and hitched the reins over a post. Then he went into the dark interior where the voices became silent as soon as the men inside saw him.

There were four of them standing together in front of the counter drinking ale from leather tankards. The alehouse keeper stood behind the ale-splashed counter and reached for a pewter tankard when Nicholas, ignoring the stares of the men, went up to him.

'Ale, master? That's all we have. But it is home brewed,' said the man.

'That'll do. And water for the horse?'

'Daniel will see to that,' he said, nodding towards a young boy dozing in a corner of the settle. The boy jumped up and went to see to the cob. Nicholas took the tankard and gave the man some money.

'No fishing today?' he said, looking at the four men.

'Oh, those days are over for us,' said the oldest of the men. 'The youngsters are all out. Tide'll bring them in later. They'll not stay out long. Storms are on their way, so they say.'

'Is business good?' said Nicholas, giving the alehouse keeper some money for a refill.

121

'Middling, master. Now's the time to make a few pence. When the weather changes the boats will be laid up and there will be no money for ale.'

One of the men, small, wiry, with a creased weather-beaten face in which his sea-blue eyes shone out like lamps, suddenly looked at Nicholas as if he had been summing him up before venturing to speak.

'What brings you here, master? Not looking for a couple of lobsters, I think. Mind you, we've just sold a couple of fine crabs to John,' he said, nodding towards the alehouse keeper. 'I'm sure you could persuade him to serve them up to you with some of his wife's home-made bread.'

'Then I'd be obliged if you could fetch me some,' Nicholas said. The landlord hesitated for a moment, then, deciding that Nicholas's money was as good as anyone else's, went off to see to the order.

Nicholas sat down at one of the wooden tables, removed his hat and rubbed his fingers through his short-cropped hair. The boy, having seen to his horse, brought him a wooden platter of fresh crab and a hunk of rough, rye bread. It tasted good; as he ate, the men stood silently watching him.

Finally, the man who had recommended the crabs left the group and came over to him. Cautiously, as if he expected Nicholas to turn on him, he sat down in the seat opposite.

'Ale to your liking, master?' he said.

'It's good. You'll join me?'

He beckoned the boy over and told him to get his companion some ale. 'I like to drink in company,' Nicholas said.

'Have you got business in these parts?' the man said, after the ale arrived and he had drunk it down with relish.

'I was thinking of finding someone with a boat who could take me over to France when I'm ready. Do you know of anyone?'

'France? That's a long way to go. Dangerous too, at this time of the year. What business is it that takes you over there?'

122

'I buy and sell. Sometimes it's wine; sometimes it's good French cheeses. I sell items of fine clothing – hand-embroidered. The French like that sort of thing.'

'Then you are a merchant, master?'

'A merchant and a farmer. I have lands up near the Downs.'

They gawped at him as if the South Downs were in another country, but his answers seemed to satisfy the man.

'It costs a lot to go to France. There's risks. Better to go to Portsmouth and get yourself onto one of the bigger boats.'

'Everything's a risk. Besides, the sea captains of Portsmouth expect a fortune in payment. It'll be cheaper, I think, to sail in a smaller boat from a smaller port.'

The men were looking at him now in great interest. They could smell money. Nicholas's companion watched him finish the crab and wipe his platter round with the remains of his bread.

'None of us have boats big enough to take you across,' he said.

'No one? There must be someone in these parts who could oblige?'

'You'll need Amos Carter. He's out catching fish at the moment, but he'll be back on the tide. He owns that boat down there in the harbour.'

Nicholas went over to the door and looked down into the harbour where a large, clinker-built boat, its sail furled, was moored against the harbour wall.

'That one?' Nicholas said, turning round.

'Aye, that's his.'

'Where does he live?'

'Way along the shore. Largish house – Amos has got a bit of money.'

'Fishing must be good.'

'Aye, that, and more.'

Suddenly, Nicholas became conscious that the atmosphere in the room had changed; it had become tense. The

123

three men at the counter were glaring at the little man sitting at Nicholas's table. The man, too, became aware of their looks, and hastily stood up.

'Best get back to my nets,' he said, drinking down the dregs of his ale.

'Aye, that's enough of your chattering, Ben,' said one of the men. 'You've had your fill of ale. Be off with you, now.'

The little man scampered off. Nicholas picked up his hat, gave the alehouse keeper some money, enough to pay for drinks for the three men at the counter, and went outside. Then, conscious of many eyes watching him, he mounted the cob and rode off along the sandy track which ran along the shore. To his left were sand dunes, to his right the pebbly beach that went down to the sea. The tide was still out; patches of sand had appeared amongst the stones and tiny waves lapped lazily at the water's edge. Overhead the gulls wheeled and screeched to one another as they circled round on the thermals. A scene of utter peace; yet the men had been wary and they had wanted to get rid of him.

He found Amos Carter's house at the end of the sandy track. It was conspicuous by being bigger and better than the other hovels down by the harbour. Amos Carter must be a person of substance, Nicholas thought. And he wondered how he had made enough money to pay for such a prestigious dwelling.

The house stood at the edge of the path with its back to the dunes. The front door was open and a child was sitting on the sand playing with a pile of shells. Nicholas recognised him. It was Sarah Bowman's son. He was named Henry, he remembered. He was a striking-looking boy with dark, curly hair and huge brown eyes which stared up at him in wonder.

'Horse,' he said, pointing to the cob.

Nicholas reined in his horse and dismounted.

'Is anyone here with you?' he said.

The child did not understand and went on playing with the shells whilst keeping one eye on the horse. Suddenly a woman appeared in the doorway. It was Kate Bowman.

'Who are you, and what do you want, master?' she said.

'My name's Rob Trayford. I would be much obliged if you would let me ask you a few questions.'

'I've never heard of you. Come closer. Take your hat off. '

Nicholas did as he was told and, for a few seconds, Kate Bowman stared at him. She looked older, now, he thought. Maybe it was because her head was uncovered and her hair was quite white and gathered at the back of her head in a tight knot like an old woman's. She looked stouter than he remembered her at Sarah's funeral, and her plain, brown dress with a shawl drawn tightly across her chest was not attractive. Her skin was still unblemished though, and her eyes were bright.

'You can't fool me, master. I know who you are. You're Nicholas Peverell. You came to see me with the sheriff. Who told you I was here?'

'Let's say a friend told me. I am glad to find you and the child looking so well.'

She nodded, picked up the child, who was still clutching some of the shells, and looked at him.

'Can we go inside?'

She paused as if uncertain what to do. Then she turned and went into the house, indicating by a nod of the head that Nicholas should follow her.

The room was dark and smoky and smelt of fish, but there was fresh straw on the floor and the furniture was of good quality. Lines of mackerel hung down from the rafters looking like a choir of mournful ghosts waiting to give a performance. Kate Bowman settled the child with his shells at the table that took up most of the centre of the room. Two wooden armchairs stood on either side of the fire where a black kettle, with steam coming out of its spout, was hanging over the flames on a chain.

A tub of water stood by the fire with a ladle hooked over the rim. Kate picked it up.

125

'Will you drink something, sir? There's a hot blackcurrant drink which Amos likes, or water. We have no ale.'

'Thank you, mistress, I have had my fill up at the alehouse.'

'Then sit you down, sir, and tell me why you have come all this way to see me?'

Nicholas sat down in one of the armchairs. Kate perched nervously on the edge of the seat of the other.

'When I last saw you, Mistress Bowman, you were living very comfortably in Monksmere. What made you move down here?'

'Because I didn't feel safe in my own house, that's why. And I was worried about Henry.'

Hearing his name, the child looked up from his game and smiled at her.

'Who or what were you afraid of?'

She shrugged her shoulders and a stubborn look came over her face.

'There's been two deaths in Monksmere, sir. One of them my granddaughter, and the other Old Moley. And I don't know the reason for them dying the way they did. Now, in my way of thinking, people only get murdered if someone hates them or wants something from them, or they know something that could harm someone and that person has to silence them. My Sarah and Old Moley don't fit into any of these things. Who could possibly hate them? Neither of them owned anything of importance. Old Moley was as poor as a church mouse. All I can think of is that somehow one of them or both of them got in the way of someone else. And the pity of it, sir, is that I don't know who that person could possibly be. Old Moley was a bit outspoken and could cause offence, but he was of no importance. No one would have wanted to murder him because he had a sharp tongue. And Sarah? Poor, innocent girl. She was as quiet and gentle as a dove. She harmed no one. And yet, one day, a man on a black horse comes riding up to my house

126

and stands there looking at it. And other people tell me that he keeps asking questions about Sarah, so I decided to come over here. And now you've found me and I suppose it'll be back to the questioning again, and it will be all over Monksmere that I have moved in with Amos.'

'Mistress Bowman, your secret will be safe with me. I shall tell no one. You must trust me. But I want to find who killed Sarah and Old Moley. You may ask me why I do this and the reason is that it is my job to find and bring evil people to justice. I am a Justice of the Peace and I must not let murderers roam freely round the county. If I do that, then we can say goodbye to our peaceful way of life and we shall return to the dark ages. Do you understand that?'

She nodded and Nicholas breathed a sigh of relief. She wasn't going to dismiss him immediately.

'Now mistress,' he went on, 'I shall tell no one you are here. In return, you must tell no one that Nicholas Peverell came to see you. A Farmer Trayford wanted to speak to your brother about a passage across to France in one of his boats. He waited for a few minutes and then rode off. That's all you need to say. If it gets about that Nicholas Peverell is asking questions and has disguised himself, then I shall be in danger and will have to abandon the investigation.'

'I shall tell no one that you came to see me. But, sir, please tell me who is behind this mystery. Who would want to kill my granddaughter and Old Moley? And why should you be in danger? I don't understand.'

'I, too, Mistress Bowman, am working in the dark. But I have to persevere, and I am certain that we shall find out who killed your granddaughter. Now, please, think hard. Can you think of anyone who would want to silence Sarah? You say she had no suitors, was never married, and yet she had this child. Do you think that his father killed Sarah in case she revealed his identity?'

'I don't think so. She said the father was a traveller. He was good-looking and tempted her with gewgaws and frip-

127

peries so that on one summer night, up in the hayfield, she succumbed to his embraces. There's nothing new in that, is there? After he had his way with her, she never saw him again. She never told me his name. I wonder whether she knew it herself. Maids can be very foolish when young men make much of them.

'Now I do know who the father of Sarah was. That's a different matter altogether. I don't know if it's of interest to you, but I will tell you if you've a mind to listen to me. My daughter, my beautiful, wilful Agnes, died when she gave birth to Sarah some eighteen years ago. There's no doubt who seduced Agnes. It's common knowledge in Monksmere, more's the pity. It was him, that wicked lord of Tredgosse, Lord Gilbert Fitzherbert. I call him the devil. He seduced Agnes whilst his dear wife, the Lady Isabella, was still alive. Agnes worked for them, see; embroidered linen, that sort of thing. She was a beauty. Like Sarah. Young, barely a woman. Bowmans are all beauties. You'd be surprised, I think, to know that I've turned seventy. Agnes was just fifteen when the devil had his way with her. When he heard she was with child, he couldn't get rid of her quick enough. He kicked her out and she came home to us. Sarah was born and Agnes, after terrible labour pains, died. And the devil never came near her and ignored Sarah, even though I asked him for help. Well, he's got his come-uppance, hasn't he? Isabella died giving birth to that poor, twisted Marcus, and then the devil takes up with that woman who calls herself Adeliza, and she'll bring him nothing but grief. Mind you, her child, Justin, is bonny enough.'

Nicholas listened intently to what she was saying; but how could all this past history be connected to Sarah's death? he thought. However, he wanted her to continue talking, even if it only showed that he had gained her trust.

'Does Adeliza know about Lord Gilbert's seduction of your daughter?'

'I'm sure she does. The devil spawned many children in the neighbourhood when he was younger. He's long past it,

128

now, and Adeliza keeps him under control. Adeliza, that whore,' she went on, spitting contemptuously into the fire. 'We knew her as plain Alice Butcher, the Earl of Southampton's doxy. He picked her up in a London tavern and gave her to the devil during one of their drunken orgies. I hear she queens it now, up in that castle. She's got the devil in her clutches right enough. They'll be the death of each other, mark my words.'

She fell silent, lost in bitter thoughts. Nicholas looked searchingly into her face.

'Mistress Bowman, think carefully now, could Lord Gilbert have ordered the death of Sarah who, as you have just told me, was his daughter? Could he have been influenced by Adeliza who might have found out that Lord Gilbert had a daughter living in Monksmere who produced a son, not by him, but still related to him? She might have feared that Lord Gilbert, in his dotage, might send for the boy and prefer him to her own child, Justin.'

'The devil wasn't responsible for Henry. I don't think even he would seduce his own daughter, would he? I don't think he could be bothered with Sarah. She was, after all, only one of his bastards. It all happened a long time ago, and most likely he has forgotten all about her. And even if he did want rid of her, why didn't he kill her long ago at her birth? There was more reason then, wasn't there? His wife was still alive and he loved her and wouldn't want her upset. Also, it's easier to kill a child than a fully grown woman. No, if he wanted to get rid of Sarah, then he would have done it a long time ago.

'As far as Adeliza is concerned, this is all ancient history. She probably turns a blind eye to all the devil's previous seductions. She might have been mad with rage, I grant you, if the devil had seduced Sarah, his own daughter, and Henry was the result. I'd not put it past her then to murder both Sarah and Henry, and the devil himself. But she has shown not the slightest bit of concern over Henry's birth, which happened two years

129

ago, remember. If she wanted Sarah out of the way, then she would have murdered her long before. No, there is something else behind this mystery. Something that Sarah knew about along with Old Moley. For once, the devil, I am sure, had nothing to do with Sarah's death. And yet ...'

Here she paused and ran her hands down the front of her dress, tucking in the ends of her shawl which had come undone. 'I can't get it out of my mind that somehow the devil up there in Tredgosse is involved in Sarah's death. Not because of what he did to her mother, not because Sarah had that child over there, but something else. And now, God help me, for the child's sake and my sake, I don't want to know. Because, once I know why Sarah was murdered, then we, too, shall be in utmost danger. And if you, sir, find out the reason for her death, you will be in danger, and your wife, too I think.

'And now, sir, you must leave. The tide will have turned. Amos will be back soon and it's best he doesn't see you here. The men will tell him you came to find him but couldn't wait long. He'll understand that and he'll not worry. But, sir, I beseech you, for my sake and the sake of that dear child, don't come here again.'

'Mistress, I am grateful to you. Here, you must accept these few coins to go towards your bed and board. Please take them.'

He left the money on the table and went out to find the cob, who had not wandered far. He mounted it and gathered up the reins. So, he thought, Gilbert Fitzherbert had not been a recluse all his life. If Kate Bowman was right, the county was probably littered with his bastards. But the landed gentry didn't usually murder their by-blows. Mostly they were proud of them and supported them. The Earl of Southampton was known to be very generous towards his whores. No, they didn't murder their illegitimate offspring; especially eighteen years after they had seduced their mother.

Nicholas rode back towards the port, then, kicking the cob into a lumbering canter, he cut across the water meadows to join the track leading north. Once back on the main road, he turned west, stopping, on impulse, at the Dog and Bell.

It was afternoon and the place was deserted; all except for Eddy, who was curled up, fast asleep, under a hawthorn bush. Nicholas dismounted and hitched the reins of his horse over a post, and walked across to Eddy, who opened one eye when he got up to him.

'Sir,' said Eddy, sitting up hurriedly and scrubbing his eyes with his clenched hands.

'Hush,' said Nicholas, 'pretend you don't know who I am. Just get me some ale. See if there are any messages for me. Just go,' he said as the boy hesitated.

Eddy ran off, returning with a tankard of ale. Nicholas gave him some money and drank down the ale. Then he told Eddy to go back to his bush and pretend to be asleep.

Once more the boy paused, then rummaging around the tattered garment which served as a shirt, he took out a sealed letter and handed it to Nicholas.

'It's for you, sir. I thought it best that Matt didn't see it, so I hid it on my body. The sheriff's man handed it to me and said I was to hide it and give it only to you.'

'You did well, Eddy. Here, take this,' Nicholas said, handing the boy some money, 'and now return to sleep. On no account must Matt know anything about this. Understand?'

'Oh yes, sir. I wouldn't tell Matt anything.'

The boy returned to his bed under the tree and Nicholas mounted the cob and urged him forward. Only when he was well clear of the alehouse did he open the letter.

'Sir,' Peter the sheriff's man began in his large, neat handwriting. 'You asked me to report on anything I consider important. Well, the stranger on the black horse seems to have left the neighbourhood for the time being.

131

Leastways, none of my informants have reported seeing him. Also, the two men who started that fire seem to have disappeared. They, too, were strangers. No person from your village would have done such a thing. If there had been such a person, then your folk would have dragged him before the sheriff without any hesitation. We shall be on the lookout for strangers now. Watch your back, sir; this case is not straightforward, but you can trust your own people. They have a great respect for you and Lady Jane.'

Then he signed the letter with a capital 'P'.

The letter caused him to feel much more cheerful. Someone was on his side. He was not alone. He folded the letter and stuffed it in the pocket of his jerkin. Then he rode home. This time he didn't go straight to Marchester, but went back to his house, wanting to rid himself of Farmer Trayford's clothes before going to see Jane. He could also retrieve his own horse, Harry, from the clutches of his grooms, and return the cob to his bailiff.

As he rode into the courtyard of his manor house, one of the grooms came out of the stable block to take his horse. He was one of the younger grooms and couldn't conceal his nervousness when he looked up at Nicholas.

'Lady Jane's back home,' he stammered. 'Shall I put the carriage away?'

'Certainly not,' said Nicholas scarcely able to believe his ears. 'She goes straight back to Marchester.'

'She'll not agree to it, my lord,' said the groom ducking away from the expected cuff round his ears.

'She'll do as she's told. Now see to it that Jack here gets a good rub-down and some oats. Is my horse back yet?'

'Oh yes, my lord,' said the groom with a sigh of relief to be back on safer ground. 'He's in good spirits.'

'Then let us thank God for that,' said Nicholas, dismounting and striding into the house.

Chapter Eleven

There was no one in the great hall but he could hear voices and the gentle strumming of the lute coming from the kitchen. My God, he thought angrily, there she is laughing and fooling around with the servants only a few days after we buried her father whilst I am sick with worry about her safety. He strode across the hall and into the kitchen. There, before his eyes, was a scene of such beauty and domestic peace that he felt his rage evaporate as quickly as it had arisen. There was Jane, her hair neatly put up under a fashionable French hood which she had brought with her from court. Her simple linen dress was the same colour as her eyes and her face was flushed with the effort of kneading dough on the kitchen table. Mary, their cook, was stirring a cauldron over the fire, and his steward, Cecil Hunter, was seated at the table, trying to compile a list of items needed for the household. On the other side of the table, Balthazar, one foot resting on a stool, quietly played the lute. For once, Nicholas was lost for words. He only wished that he had employed an artist in residence who could capture the scene on canvas. It would be a painting he would treasure all his life.

Jane saw him first and stopped kneading the dough. Cecil put down his pen. Mary stopped stirring the pot and gazed at him in horror. Balthazar fled. Jane removed the dough from her fingers and ran to him with a smile of welcome and such love on her face that his heart melted. How he loved her! He could deny her nothing. He held her close for what seemed eternity, then released her and gazed into her eyes.

'Jane, why do you always defy me?'

'Because there was no need to imprison me in the bishop's palace, even though everyone was very kind. You really have no need to worry about me. None of the tenants would dream of harming me. Joseph has reassured me on that point. I felt I was being unnecessarily protected and there is so much to do here. I have to see that Aunt Anna is comfortably installed in my father's house – you know she is too old to do everything herself – and the king is coming here in just over two weeks' time. Eighteen days if all goes to plan. Just think what we have to provide for him and his retinue. Cecil is desperate with worry. We need extra help. There are beds to air, the rooms to clean. The king likes everything to smell sweet, especially his own room. There is so much washing and polishing that just to think of it makes me giddy. Then there is the provisioning. How many pigs, deer, bullocks, calves, sheep, rabbits, hares, game of all sorts, lobsters, crabs, eggs, hens, geese do you think we'll need? More than we can provide. Cecil must go into Marchester tomorrow and see what can be ordered there. Nicholas, I could not stay in idleness in Marchester a moment longer. Joseph will see to it that his "spies", as he calls his band of loyal men, will report to him if there is any unrest amongst the villagers.

'Now come, my darling lord,' she went on, smiling up into his face, 'Mary has cooked us a brace of partridges, and there are fresh cheeses from the dairy and an apple pie made with this season's apples from our orchard. Let me prepare a cool bath for you and we shall dine together. My lord, I am sorry to have offended you,' she said, making him a mock curtsy and lowering her eyes. He could not help smiling at her coquettishness.

'Jane, I shall do as I'm told, as always. I can never be

134

master in my own house as long as you are the mistress of my heart.'

Over supper, Jane insisted on being brought up to date with the investigation. Once again he marvelled at the sharpness of her mind. If she had been a man, he thought, she would have been his second-in-command, his constable. She showed particular interest in his conversation with Kate Bowman and agreed with him that Gilbert Fitzherbert would not have murdered his own daughter, especially eighteen years after her birth. For one thing, there was no reason to; everyone in Monksmere, it appeared, knew who had seduced Agnes Bowman, Sarah's mother. But the child Henry, that was a different matter. Who was his father? And, what's more, did it matter? If Henry's father had wanted to protect his name, then he would have disposed of both Sarah and Henry as soon as he heard she was with child, not wait for two years. Had Sarah told her grandmother the truth when she said she had been seduced by a charming traveller? Or was there someone else? Someone too important to mention?

'I've just had another thought, Nicholas. Don't laugh at me because it does sound preposterous, but as Thomas Cromwell ordered you off the investigation, could he have fathered Henry? After all, when I was at court, he had a reputation for liking ladies of the lower class of people. The court ladies frightened him.'

'Thomas Cromwell has not been to Sussex, as far as I can remember. He left the closure of the monasteries to his own commissioners. He prefers to stay near the king, otherwise he might be forgotten.'

'Did he never accompany his commissioners?' said Jane, pouring some of the sweet wine to drink with the apple pie.

'Monksmere was too small a religious house to merit the personal appearance of Cromwell. No, I cannot believe that Cromwell was responsible for Henry. And whilst your mind is running along these fantastical paths, no, I don't

135

think King Henry rode over to Monksmere when he came to stay with us, or the Earl of Southampton, and seduced Sarah Bowman. I know King Henry has sired many bastards, but he's always proud of them and supports their mothers. He doesn't murder them.'

Jane laughed and picked up her spoon. Then she put it down again as a new thought entered her mind.

'And yet, Nicholas,' she said, 'both Cromwell and the king had heard of Sarah Bowman. Cromwell wanted you to drop the case; the king was not so definite. He wanted you to keep a sharp eye on Gilbert Fitzherbert. But why should Cromwell want you off the case if he had nothing to do with it? Why should he find the death of Sarah Bowman of the slightest interest? Woman die every day; some of them are murdered. Does Cromwell intervene then? No. There is something very odd about this case, Nicholas. Too many loose ends; none of them connecting.'

'And that, Jane, is the problem. But let's take another look at all of this. There seem to be two problems here: why should Baron Cromwell care one jot about Sarah Bowman's death? And what does the king suspect?'

'Don't forget the child. Who is Henry's father? And does it matter?'

They sat in silence, Nicholas's mind spinning round in circles. Finally he said,

'Maybe trying to find out who Henry's father was could lead us to finding out the motive for Sarah's murder. Maybe we are barking up the wrong tree, but at least it gives us something to concentrate on.'

'And, on the other hand,' Jane continued with mounting excitement, 'the answer might be more simple. Maybe Sarah knew too much. Something she did not realise the importance of. Something which was serious and involved Thomas Cromwell. Maybe there were other people at court who might have known about it or were involved in it. Maybe the king had his suspicions about them but had no proof. Perhaps he wants you to give him that

136

proof, Nicholas. He knows he can trust you.'

'And Old Moley also saw something which might be incriminating. Kate Bowman threw him out of the house after Sarah's funeral. He made some remark about the people of Monksmere. He said they would never tell what had gone on in their village. I should have gone after him then and not waited until it was too late. Sarah and Old Moley. What in the name of heaven is the link, Jane?'

'Eddy knew both of them, I understand,' said Sarah quietly.

'So he did. Then I must get back to him tomorrow and question him further.'

'Nicholas, be careful. If anyone sees you talking to Eddy, he could be the next victim. I think you are being watched the whole time. Is there anyone else in Monksmere you could talk to who would not arouse suspicions? You need to make people open up to you. Kate Bowman trusts you, by all accounts, but you must stay away from her for the time being.'

Suddenly Nicholas started and looked across at Jane.

'Yes, there is someone else. It's just a case of grasping at straws, but it could be relevant. John Woodcock's wife seemed deeply upset by Sarah's death and wanted to take the child back to their own home. Woodcock was very sharp with her. Now, I could go and see Woodcock and I could go as Nicholas Peverell and leave old Farmer Trayford behind. I was given a mill as part of the Monksmere lands when the priory was sold off after the Dissolution and I could talk to Woodcock about getting it started up again. Joseph can find me a miller and I will arrange a date for him to start. It will give me a legitimate reason for going to see Woodcock and I might be able to have a word with his wife.'

'Could he have fathered Henry?'

'No, I don't think so. The Woodcocks have only lived in the house for a year. Before he bought it, it was occupied by the head steward of the monastery. Henry is two years

137

old. The timing's not right. If Henry had been a year old, then, yes, John Woodcock could have been his father, and that would account for his wife's concern for the child, particularly as she is childless.'

'Then you could visit the Woodcocks tomorrow, but I should stay away from Eddy. It would be a terrible thing if he suffers the same fate as the other two.'

The servants cleared away the plates. Suddenly the idea of bed seemed very attractive. Later that night, as he took Jane into his arms, he thanked God that he had a disobedient wife who had come back to him.

As he rode up to the Woodcocks' manor house, he caught sight of her standing at the corner of the house, a wooden basket on her arm. She was obviously about to gather flowers for the house, or embark on some other peaceful pursuit. However, he was not prepared for her start of surprise when she recognised him, and instead of coming forward to welcome him, she turned and rushed away round to the back of the house. He stopped in amazement. Had she mistaken him for someone else? If not, why had she not wanted to speak to him? Whatever the reason, he was immediately on the alert. Something had upset her and he knew then that she was the one person he ought to talk to, but he would have to speak to her on her own.

Meanwhile he could start with her husband. A servant opened the door and he was ushered into the comfortable sitting room where armchairs and small tables placed strategically around the room indicated that this was a place for relaxation and civilised pursuits such as card games, conversation and enjoying musical entertainments. Once again, he marvelled at Sir John's obvious wealth. He had come a long way, and quickly, from his haberdasher's origins.

He did not have to wait long before the door opened and Sir John came in smiling affably. He shook Nicholas's hand and indicated one of the armchairs. A servant brought in wine and two glasses which he set down on the table next to Sir John's chair. 'You'll take a glass of wine, my lord?'

'Thank you. I will drink it with pleasure.'

Sir John poured the wine and handed it to Nicholas. They sipped it in silence. Was there a hesitation in Sir John's manner, he thought, as if he did not quite know how to begin the conversation? Why was he avoiding looking him in the eye? And why was Sir John sitting so nervously on the edge of his chair? Why, in fact, did he look so frightened?

'I've come about the mill,' said Nicholas, putting his glass down on the table.

The effect of this innocuous statement was instantaneous. Sir John relaxed. He settled back in his chair and beamed across at Nicholas.

'Good, good, Lord Nicholas, we should settle the matter now that autumn is on its way and the river will rise. Tell me what you have in mind.'

It was soon settled. Nicholas would send over a miller. John Woodcock would provide a steward. The profits from the mill would be divided between them, the details to be worked out later.

'The canons made a good income from the mill,' said Sir John, 'judging by their account books. They provided flour for most of the bakers around here. There's no reason why we shouldn't enjoy the same benefits.'

They talked on about fields and grazing rights and footpaths and bridges.

'Lord Gilbert will have to see to the maintenance of the bridge soon,' remarked Sir John. 'The canons were good landowners and kept the bridge in good repair. It's a pity Lord Gilbert is not so conscientious. He will also have to decide soon what to do with the old priory church or else there will not be a stone left. Every day I see the rascals over there helping themselves to the stones. It's been there for four hundred years or more and will be demolished in five if he's not careful.'

139

Nicholas knew only too well what Sir John was complaining about. Already the 'rascals' had demolished the old parish church at Dean Peverell and the parishioners were now using the part of the building which was once the monks' quire. He'd forgotten that Lord Gilbert was now the owner of Monksmere Priory.

They discussed other matters of common interest and soon Nicholas got up to leave. He wanted to talk to Joan Woodcock but he could hardly ask her husband if he could speak to her in private, and she was obviously not going to come and speak to him.

Sir John got up and shook Nicholas's hand. 'I'm glad to see you again, Lord Nicholas. When I heard you were off the investigation into that poor girl's death, I didn't think we would see you again. But now I trust we shall see more of you. Am I correct in thinking that King Henry is coming to visit you soon?'

'Indeed he is and will probably pay a visit to Lord Gilbert as well. I am hoping you and your wife will come and have dinner with us and help entertain his majesty. The King likes good company. But where did you hear about his visit, may I ask?'

Sir John chuckled and rubbed his hands together. 'Oh, it's common knowledge, my lord. Anyone who pays a visit to the Dog and Bell will pick up all the news. The landlord is a source of all information. It was he who told me you had dropped the investigation.'

'Then I shall have to be more careful what I tell him in future. But I will see to it that you get an invitation to dinner. I think he will only bring a small retinue as he likes to pretend he is a country squire and enjoys hunting. I don't think Baron Cromwell will be with him.'

He made the remark on impulse but was gratified to see Sir John give a start of surprise.

'Cromwell here?' he said, his florid face paling visibly. 'I understood he never leaves London.'

'He likes to be where the king is and enjoys country air,

140

but I don't think he enjoys the hunt. Do I gather that you are not an admirer of Baron Cromwell?'

Sir John quickly recovered himself and sighed dramatically. 'My lord, it is not my place to express any feelings about such exalted personages. I have neither seen nor spoken with him.'

'Then you are a lucky man. He is not an easy man to to reckon with. But he is one of the king's most loyal servants and protects the king well.'

'Then we must thank him for that, my lord. The king needs loyal men about him in these troublesome times.'

Promising to call again soon, Nicholas was ushered out of the house by a servant who smartly closed the door as soon as he was outside. As he walked down to where he had left Harry hitched to a gatepost, Nicholas looked back and saw Sir John watching him from the window. A pity, he thought; there was no chance of talking to his wife that day. But something was obvious – the Woodcocks had not been overjoyed to see him. He would not forget the look of terror on Joan Woodcock's face when she'd seen him walking up her drive.

The midday drinkers had all left, the afternoon was hot, the air oppressive. Matt, the landlord of the Dog and Bell, staggered off to bed. Eddy, after clearing away the pots and tankards, retreated to the shade of his tree, curled up and went to sleep. When, through the heavy haze of sleep, he heard a horse ride up, he thought it was Nicholas Peverell come to see him, and he began to scrub the sleep out of his eyes before getting up. But it was not Nicholas Peverell, nor the other man. It was Sir John Woodcock, master of Monksmere Manor.

'Sir,' said Eddy, scrambling to his feet, 'do you want something to drink?'

'No, just answer my questions and then you can go back to sleep. Here, take these. They might help to loosen your tongue. There's more where these came from.'

141

He tossed the coins to Eddy, who caught them deftly and hid them away in his clothes. Eddy began to feel uneasy. He'd rather the gentry stayed away from him. It only made Matt furious and he didn't want any more beatings.

'Did Lord Nicholas Peverell come to see you today, boy?'

'No,' replied Eddy, grateful that, for once, he could tell the truth. 'No one's come here – except you, sir, that is.'

'Good. See to it that should he come again and start asking questions, you just keep your mouth shut. You talk too much for your own good. Learn to know when to keep silent or else you'll find yourself in deep trouble. When, in fact, did you last speak to Lord Nicholas, boy?'

Eddy hesitated, wondering whether he should mention that Lord Nicholas stopped by yesterday, for some reason disguised as an ordinary farmer. It was a stupid thing to do, he thought. He'd recognise Lord Nicholas anywhere. Then he decided not to mention it. That letter had seemed important and had come from the sheriff's man. Best not to tell Sir John. Instead he would tell Sir John about Lord Nicholas's previous visit. That had seemed harmless enough.

'Yes, he stopped by for some ale on Thursday.'

'Did he talk to you?'

'Only a bit – he's not after making conversation with the likes of me.'

'What did he say?'

'Wanted to know where Mother Bowman had gone to.'

'Did you tell him?'

'I don't know where she is so, of course, I couldn't tell him.'

'What else did he want to know?'

'Only if I had known Sarah and I said I didn't know her very well. Just that she was kind to me and Old Moley.'

'Did you tell him about her doing work for the canons?'

'Course not. That wouldn't interest him. They've gone now.'

142

'All right. Go back to sleep and tell no one anything; especially don't answer any questions about Sarah Bowman.'

He turned his horse and rode away, looking back significantly at Eddy. Eddy was puzzled as he watched Sir John ride off. He also felt an uneasy sensation – one he'd felt before when he'd found Old Moley's body. He knew what it was. It was fear.

His fear increased when he saw Matt emerge from the inn and come stamping over to talk to him. His face was still flushed with drink and his breath smelt bad as he grabbed hold of Eddy and lifted him up level with his own face.

'So, you're at it again, are you, you little devil? Tittle-tattling to the gentry. Now, I've told you time and time again to steer clear of anyone asking questions. It's none of your business. If you don't stop holding forth to all and sundry I'll be forced to put an end to your chattering one way or another. Next time someone comes asking questions, call me and I'll speak to him. I don't like my pot boy poking his nose into affairs that don't concern him. Let me speak plain,' he said, shaking Eddy's skinny body like a bull terrier with a rat in his mouth. 'Shut your mouth or else I'll be forced to shut it for you. And I shall make sure it will hurt a lot; a bit more than this.'

Then he dropped Eddy on the ground and kicked him viciously in the side. But Eddy was experienced in the art of self-defence and, as he landed, he curled up in a ball and the blow lost some of its force on impact. Matt grunted, bent down and smashed his fist into Eddy's face. Eddy cried out. It hurt a lot and when he wiped his face with his hand, he saw that his nose was bleeding. Matt hitched up his trousers, spat on the bare earth, and went indoors. Eddy lay there whimpering with pain and fear. Then an idea came to him. He'd had enough of all this, he thought. All this secrecy and asking questions and now blows and yells from Matt and everyone scowling at him. Nicholas Peverell

143

hadn't told him that he'd be beaten for talking to him. Well, he had enough money now, from all of them, and he didn't have to stay here a minute longer. What did it matter to him who killed Sarah! No, he, Eddy, had looked after her when she was alive and no one else had done that. And when that mean-faced bastard got her with child he didn't want to know her, did he? Who helped her then? Why he did, little Eddy. A pity he hadn't persuaded Old Moley to leave then and take Sarah with him. They could all be living in peace now in some snug cottage up in the Downs. Somewhere where no one would come asking questions. Now Sarah was dead, and Moley, and by the way things were going, he'd be joining them soon, kicked to death by that monster Matt and his body dumped into the river where it would drift out to sea on the ebb tide. No, he'd hang around no longer. He'd go to see Jude. Jude would look after him. Especially now he had a bit of money. No one knew Jude.

He struggled to his feet and went over to wash his face in the bucket of water standing by the inn. Then he went round to the outhouse where Matt kept the horse and removed one of the stones from the wall. From the hole he pulled out a purse of money. Finally he replaced the brick, said goodbye to the horse and set off across the fields, turning towards the Downs once he was clear of Monksmere.

When Nicholas rode away from the Woodcocks' house he resisted the urge to go back to Dean Peverell. His interview with Sir John had not been particularly fruitful and he was conscious of a feeling of unfinished business. Wanting to think out his next move, he rode over to the ruins of Monksmere Priory and there he felt, once again, the sadness which these abandoned places aroused in him. A whole way of life had been demolished by the stroke of a pen. A ruthless king and his sycophantic servant had ended four hundred years of history. The treasures had been carted away, the lead from the roof stripped off and the

144

bells had been taken away to be melted down for cannons and cannon balls in the Royal Arsenal at Woolwich. Where had Monksmere's canons gone to? he wondered. He knew what had happened to his own monks in his priory. His friend, the prior, had been made Bishop of Marchester, until tragedy overtook him. The other monks had filled the vacancies for priests in the surrounding parishes.

The canons of Marchester, however, were not the same as his monks. These had been priests used to going around the countryside helping out in parishes when needed. They had not been enclosed like his Benedictines. Where were they now? What had happened to their prior? One day he would start to make enquiries. But now there were matters of greater urgency to see to. He turned Harry towards the road. Then he reined him in. Sir John was riding down his drive. Quickly he urged Harry towards the shade of a large yew tree of great antiquity. From there he watched Sir John ride past towards the main road. That meant that his wife would be there on her own. She would have to talk to him now.

He waited until Sir John disappeared then rode over to the house. He left Harry in the same place as before, close to a patch of lush grass, and walked up to the house, ignoring the front door and making his way to the side of the house where there was a stable block and an outhouse. Walking past these, he went to the back of the house where, already, the Woodcocks had started to plant a beautiful garden. Behind a neatly clipped hedge, there was a rose garden, where the overblown blooms were dropping petals over the hedge and onto the neatly tended gravel path. He saw her there, knife in hand, carefully cutting off the dead heads of the roses and placing them in her basket which she had hooked over one arm. She looked very much at home and Nicholas was reluctant to disturb her; but he needed to talk to her.

She saw him then, and put down her basket. He walked over to her smiling reassuringly, but her face, under the large straw hat she was wearing as protection from the sun, had taken on a worried look and her eyes were wary as if he were some sort of animal of unpredictable temperament.

'Lady Woodcock, forgive my intrusion,' he said. I have remembered something I meant to tell your husband, but I have just seen him leave the house.'

'He has not gone far. He only wants to see someone in the village. Why not wait for him inside the house and I will order you some refreshment,' she said, obviously relieved by his explanation.

'I am afraid I cannot wait. I have tied my horse to your gatepost and he will become restless if I leave him there too long. I would, however, be obliged if you could give Sir John a message.'

'Of course, my lord. What is it?'

'Just that my bailiff will call on Monday morning to arrange about starting up the mill. Sir John and I have agreed on terms, but I forgot to tell him when my bailiff will come.'

'I can certainly tell him as soon as he comes home. Is that all that brings you to Monksmere today?'

'Yes indeed. It has been a pleasant morning's ride and I have had the satisfaction of completing some business with Sir John.'

'Then I assume you have given up investigating that poor girl's death, Lord Nicholas?' she said as she picked up her basket and led the way back to the house.

'I am afraid so. We seem to have run up against a wall of silence. No one appears to know anything; no one has seen anything. Most times, in other cases, we are following a lead by now. But not this time. However, this investigation is really the sheriff's business. I only try the wretches. No doubt he'll find a lead one of these days. Sarah was well liked, and no one relishes an unsolved murder – especially when it concerns one of their own community.'

'Yes, Sarah had no enemies as far as we know. But I am

disturbed to hear that the great-grandmother of the child, Henry, has disappeared with him. Sir, do you know where they are?' she said, looking at him beseechingly.

He stopped and looked at her. Yes, there was something between her and the child. Could it be that her husband had seduced Sarah? It was not uncommon for the lord of the manor to take advantage of his position when a pretty girl came to work at his house. Yet, he thought, it simply wasn't possible. The Woodcocks had not lived in Monksmere manor long enough. Unless he had known her before he bought the place. Highly unlikely. The canons would still have been in residence when he came down to inspect the propery with a view to buying it when the canons left.

'Your concern for the child is very commendable, madam, but I am sure Kate Bowman is looking after him properly. I didn't know she had left Monksmere. Probably a change of residence will do her good.'

'As long as no one has forced her to leave or harmed her and the child in any way.'

'But who would want to harm an old lady and her great-grandson?'

'Nobody, I'm sure. No one would want to harm Kate Bowman. We all feel sorry for her. But I loved that little boy and I had hoped that Kate would let us bring him up here as we have not been blessed with any children and we could give him every advantage. She would not let us lay a finger on him, more's the pity. But I pray that he is safe. He is a dear, dear child.'

She began to cry quietly, wiping her nose on the sleeve of her morning gown like a peasant woman. Nicholas felt sorry for her but was very puzzled by the intensity of her feelings. Surely there were other children she could adopt. Many a poor family would be overjoyed to allow someone as wealthy as Lady Woodcock to assist in bringing up one of their children.

'Madam – forgive me if I sound presumptious – Henry

147

indeed is a beautiful child, but there are others who would be readily available for your attentions. The bishop has a home in Marchester for orphaned children. He would value your help in looking after them.'

She dried her tears again and looked up at him angrily.

'My lord, you don't know how much Henry means to me. It is almost as if he is of my own flesh and blood.'

'Then you must surely know who his father is. Could you not approach him?' said Nicholas, risking a rebuff.

His question certainly had an effect on her. He watched as her face dissolved into panic. Her body tensed and she turned, dropping the basket, and ran off to the house, gathering up her skirts in her hands.

'Goodbye, sir,' she shouted back to him. 'I'll tell my husband you called.'

And she ran up the steps of the terrace and into the house before Nicholas could stop her.

He walked back down the drive deep in thought. There certainly was a mystery surrounding the birth of that child and Lady Woodcock knew the answer and was not going to reveal it. But still the question remained. Why should the father of Sarah's child wait two years before deciding to do away with her? Maybe, he thought, whoever the father was, had only just discovered that Sarah had had a child and wanted to dispose of him because he could be an embarrassment but had found the Bowman household too difficult to penetrate and had decided to kill the mother instead. No wonder Kate had decided to leave Monksmere and had told no one, except the boy Eddy, where she was going. She had been right to do so, he thought as he mounted Harry and rode back to Dean Peverell. He resisted the urge to stop and speak to Eddy at the Dog and Bell. It was best if he was not seen talking to the boy too often. Instead he turned north and rode home across the Downland tracks avoiding the main coastal road.

*

It took Eddy three hours to reach Wood Dean, a tiny hamlet tucked away on the lower slopes of the Downs. The sun was setting and he was hot, tired and dusty having crept along ditches and hedgerows, avoiding the main tracks and terrified that Matt had noticed his absence and was coming to get him. He was nearly there now. Skirting the village, he plunged into the woodlands which covered that part of the Downs. Some of the trees were very ancient, he knew. He'd been told by Moley that many of them had been there when Henry V set off for Agincourt and other kings had hunted wild boar under these spreading branches. The great oaks made a canopy over his head and he began to feel safe, knowing that he could come out from hiding now. He could always disappear if he had to into the dappled shade of the trees.

He could smell them long before he could see them. Good, he thought, they hadn't moved on. They'd been here for centuries, they'd told him, and would stay here until all the wood was used up. He climbed over the trunk of a fallen beech tree, skirted a pile of hazelwood branches and walked into the clearing. There he saw the familiar tent-shaped hut with its turf roof and open door. Alison was cooking supper over an open fire. His nose began to twitch like a dog's; his mouth filled with saliva. He could smell rabbit and onions and fresh bread. Beside the hut were heaps of logs and, on the other side of the glade, Jude and Luke were piling turf on the beehive structure of the kiln. As fast as they stopped up one hole in the side of the kiln another one opened and Eddy stood still in the shade of an oak tree knowing he would not be welcome at this moment.

Finally the vents were all blocked and the two men gave a sigh of relief and wiped their faces on the tattered sleeves of their shirts. Jude Burrows had been a charcoal burner all his life, as had his father and generations of Burrowses before them. Luke, his son, would follow the tradition. One day he'd make himself a new hut out of hazel branches covered with turf and would bring home his wife to raise the next generation of charcoal burners.

Eddy stepped out of the shade of the tree and into the clearing. Through clouds of smoke, Jude and Luke walked towards him. With their blackened faces and filthy clothes they looked like two demons out of hell, but when they saw him their faces broke into smiles of welcome revealing dazzling white teeth.

'Eddy, old fellow, it's good to see you again,' said Jude. 'Have you got that devil of a mole-catcher with you?'

Eddy stepped forward and accepted the rough embrace. Then he shook his head.

'Moley's dead. I came by myself.'

'That's bad news. Come over to Alison and sit yourself down. It won't be long before the stew's ready. Luke, watch the kiln. Damp it down a bit more, otherwise all the wood will burn away and there'll be nothing left to sell.'

Eddy followed Jude over to the hut. Alison exclaimed when she saw him and fetched him a bowl of milk.

'Look at the lad,' she said, 'all scratched and torn by the brambles. Come, let me see to those legs of yours. Now drink your milk and we'll hear what you've got to say when you've got your breath back.'

With a sigh of relief Eddy sat down down on a stool and let Alison clean his scratched legs. How fortunate he'd been to come here with Moley, who sold some of his moleskins to Jude for a bit of extra money. Alison turned them into hats and jerkins and coverings for the beds when winter came on.

'Now tell us what happened to Moley,' said Jude when Eddy had finished the milk. Then he told them how he'd found Moley at the edge of the wood. 'Dumped there like a dog,' he concluded.

'Who'd want to do that to Moley?' said Alison, her face creased with concern. 'He'd not harm a fly.'

'Someone must have thought he knew something which could be a bit inconvenient-like. Or he might have seen something which he shouldn't have.'

'Aye, it doesn't pay to know too much,' said Jude,

150

signalling to Luke to leave the kiln and come over and join them.

'Trouble is one can't help seeing and one can't help hearing, but one doesn't know what's good and what's bad. I don't always know the importance of what I've seen but I do know that too many people are asking me questions – wealthy types like Lord Nicholas and Sir John. They give me money too, to keep quiet. Look, I've got a bagful of coins here; all with the king's head on them.'

He took out the bag of coins and handed them to Jude who shook his head and refused to take them.

'Keep hold of them, lad. You'll have need of them one of these days. But gentlemen don't give money away for nothing so you did right to come here. What Moley saw, you might have seen and what he heard, you might have heard and if anyone gets to know this you'll end up dead in a ditch like Moley. Where have you been working since he died?'

'Dog and Bell. The landlord's that bastard, Matt. He hates me. Nearly beat me to death today just because Sir John talked to me. So I didn't hang around any more but bolted off.'

'You did well to come here,' said Jude, glancing across at the kiln where wisps of smoke were again curling out of gaps in its sides.

'What did you and Moley see, I wonder, to bring about all this aggravation?' said Alison as she gathered up four wooden bowls for the stew.

'I don't know, mistress. I went up to the priory with Moley and Sarah to give them both a hand, mainly fetching and carrying. I was always outside in the gardens helping Moley get rid of the moles, and didn't see much of the priests. When I did, they were always kind to me and Moley and Sarah liked them. That's all. That's been my life as long as I can remember. I lived with Moley who told me he found me abandoned on a dung heap and we always minded our own business.'

151

'Then something must have disturbed those priests, as you call them,' said Alison quietly. 'Maybe they were up to something.'

'What, those fat old pussy cats? They spent their time praying and eating and not too much of the praying. It was very peaceful up there, and I'm sorry that they've gone.'

Jude got up to help Luke stuff up the vents in the kiln. Now darkness was falling and the fire under the pot of stew burned brightly, lighting up the glade. From a tree nearby, an owl called to its mate. Bats swooped low overhead, attracted by the firelight. Alison handed him a bowl of stew.

'Eat up Eddy. You'll be safe with us.'

'We'll be starting up the next kiln tomorrow,' said Luke, coming back from the kiln and sitting down on a stool next to Eddy. 'We could do with an extra pair of hands. You'll be able to relieve one of us so that we can take turns to have a rest. It will be good to get away from the smoke for a bit.'

Chapter Twelve

Nicholas walked into the kitchen and saw a stranger sitting at the kitchen table wolfing down a plateful of rabbit pie and hot coleworts. A tankard of ale stood beside his plate. He looked dirty and dishevelled and smelled strongly of horse. As Nicholas entered he looked up and wiped his mouth hurriedly with his napkin.

'My lord,' he said, scrambling to his feet, 'your good wife insisted that I should be fed straight away and she has offered me a night's lodging as I have to be on my way tomorrow to see the Admiral of the Fleet.'

'Tell me your name, sir.'

'Ralph Tomkins. I am one of Baron Cromwell's messengers. I bring you a letter, my lord. He tells me it is highly confidential and I am to give it to no one but yourself.'

Nicholas nodded. 'Give me the letter, Master Tomkins and finish your supper. The ride from London is long and tedious in this sultry weather. My steward will find you a bed later when you've finished eating.'

Ralph Tomkins opened a leather pouch which he wore round his waist and took out a letter sealed with Cromwell's seal. He handed it to Nicholas who left the man to his supper and went into the small room which he used for conducting the business affairs of the estate. He shut the door and opened the letter. It was longer than the usual abrupt message he was accustomed to receive from

153

Cromwell and seemed hesitant, as if the writer was uncertain how to begin.

'Lord Nicholas,' he read, 'I trust you are in good health and likewise your wife, the beautiful and talented Lady Jane. I have been assured by Richard Landstock, Sheriff of Marchester, that you have dropped the investigation into the death of Sarah Bowman. I am pleased to hear it. It does no good to prolong an enquiry into the death of a maid with a bastard child when there are other, more pressing, matters to see to. Suicide amongst such unfortunates as the Bowman girl is, alas, all too common. It is a lesson to us all. We should think carefully about the consequences of our immoral actions before we indulge our passions.'

God damn it, thought Nicholas, what a sanctimonious fellow he is! I wonder if he lectures his royal master in a like manner. What the devil is he getting at?

'You should now, my lord,' the letter went on, 'give your full attention to the king's visit. He is looking forward to sharing the joys of country life with you at your pleasant rural retreat. I trust you will provide him with every comfort and will see to it that nothing untoward disturbs his peace.'

Who does he think he is? thought Nicholas, now thoroughly irritated. Does he suppose I harbour assassins in every corner of my house? I have never met such an arrogant wretch.

'He also wants to meet his Admiral of the Fleet, Lord Southampton, and will attend Divine Service in Marchester cathedral. I have already informed the bishop and hope that he will organise things to the highest standard. His majesty is particularly fond of music and will be highly critical of the choir if it perfoms indifferently. You must speak to the bishop about this.

'His majesty also wants to visit your neighbour, Lord Gilbert Fitzherbert, of Tredgosse Castle. I must admit that the man is a bit of a mystery to me and I want you to see him and make certain that everything is in order when the king goes there. I shall, of course, hold you personally responsible for the king's safety. Having said that, I think you should ask Southampton to send soldiers over to Tredgosse to guard the king when he stays there. You know his majesty likes to hunt and I've heard that the woodlands around the castle abound in wild boar. You must tell Lord Gilbert to see to it that there is a plentiful supply of these animals available for the king's sport. He will, of course, need to be especially well guarded when he is out hunting. You will have to be at his side all the time.

'The king has expressed an uncertainty about Lord Gilbert's loyalty. This makes things very difficult for us, but I know you will do everything possible to ensure the king's safety. I rely on you implicitly.

'Meanwhile, his majesty has expressed pleasure at the prospect of your future involvement in the Cleves marriage. I am sure this will lead to your greater advancement at court, Lord Nicholas, and the increase of your lands in Sussex.'

The letter was signed with Cromwell's signature.

Nicholas flung the letter down on the table. He felt so angry that he could scarcely restrain himself from tearing it up and throwing it on the fire. A knock on the door only made him more irritable.

'Come in, damn you,' he shouted. The door opened and there was Jane dressed for dinner. She stood quite calmly in the doorway taking in the scene.

'What is it, Nicholas?' she said. 'What does Cromwell want?'

'That arrogant scoundrel – read it yourself.'

He pushed the letter across to her. She read it quickly and folded it up neatly when she had finished.

'Yes, he's arrogant; he treats you like one of his servants. But control your rage, my lord. Don't waste your strength. He is anxious about the king's safety and he has reason to be. He does not trust Lord Gilbert, it appears. However, Lord Southampton will be alerted and he will send over some soldiers. We, of course, will guard the king when he is here. But something still puzzles me, Nicholas.

Cromwell is still concerned about Sarah Bowman's death. Once again he warns you off the investigation. What is it about that girl? '

As usual, Nicholas felt his anger evaporate at the sound of Jane's calm voice. Yes, Cromwell was insufferable; but he was powerful. One day, though, thought Nicholas, Cromwell would lose the king's favour, and then ...

'I wish I knew the answer, Jane. But I do know that Cromwell has informers all over the country. We are all being watched. I expect Ralph Tomkins is another one of his spies. Cromwell has a finger in every pie – even in matters relating to the criminal law which is none of his business.'

'I think that he knows more about Sarah Bowman than any of us.'

'What is there to know? She was a young woman. She had the misfortune to have a child out of wedlock, but that is no business of Cromwell's.'

'We don't know, Nicholas.'

'Jane, what do you suspect?'

'I think she might have witnessed something that alarmed Cromwell. What, I cannot imagine. However, Bishop Humphrey has invited us to dinner tomorrow. His servant came just as Tomkins arrived. I accepted, of course. The bishop has many things on his mind.'

'So have we all, Jane. The king's visit has thrown us all into a turmoil. I must see Fitzherbert first thing on Monday morning. Time is passing and I must make sure that he gets on with the preparations for the king's visit. God damn it all, I will also have to try and see Southampton and ask him to arrange for troops to be at hand if we need them. But I can't understand what the king fears now. Most of his Yorkist relations are either in the Tower awaiting execution or have fled the country. There is absolutely no evidence that Fitzherbert is plotting anything against the king. Just a whisper of that would be enough to send him to the Tower. Why, in God's name, am I plagued with all these matters?'

156

'Because the king trusts you, Nicholas. Cromwell thinks he's got you in his pocket because he has bribed you with the promise of future honours if the negotiations concerning the Cleves marriage prove to be successful. And that must be Cromwell's idea, surely. I doubt the king will take to a lady who, by all accounts, has been strictly brought up in a small court, speaks only German, and is reported to be no great beauty.'

'No doubt Master Holbein will do his best to reassure the king on that point.'

'Remember, Nicholas, the proof of the pudding ... Which reminds me, we have pigeon pie for dinner cooked in red wine and our own mushrooms.'

'Give me a few moments to remove these boots and I will be ready to join you at the table. Then let us forget these matters of high policy for the rest of the day.'

It was good to see the church packed out with his tenants on Sunday morning, and good to be conducted by a beaming vicar to their seats in front of the chancel steps. As Nicholas sat down he marvelled how quickly people could change. Only last week nobody had come to the funeral of Jane's father. She had been treated to insults and shunned as a witch. Today, the same people had smiled at them and bowed their heads as they made their way to the front of the church. It was a lesson, he thought, about the fickleness of the mob – for kings too, and their ministers. The same people who cheered at a wedding could also cheer at an execution.

However, those times were past, he thought, as they walked out into the sunshine after the service was over. It was a fine September day. A fresh breeze had blown away the sultry air of the previous weeks and he felt his spirits lift. They stayed talking to the congregation for a long time, wanting to reassure everyone that all was well on the estate and they were all secure in their cottages. It did seem that no one had any previous knowlege of the fire and the burning of Jane's effigy. The perpetrators had not been seen again, nor had the man on the black horse, and everyone was vociferous in affirming their loyalty and affection for the Peverell family. As for Jane, news had gone round about the forthcoming event, as the vicar put it, and they seemed overjoyed at the prospect of the baptism of the heir to the Peverell estates and the feast afterwards up at the big house. They walked back to the house hand in hand pleased that life had reverted to normal, for the time being at least.

'Remember this has only happened because you appeared to have dropped the Bowman case,' said Jane, ever realistic. 'If you hadn't done that, who knows what other methods of persuasion Cromwell might have resorted to.'

'So you have reached the conclusion that Cromwell was responsible for spreading these rumours about us, Jane?' Said Nicholas as they went into the courtyard of the house.

'I think it probable, yes. Who else could have worked so quickly and effectively? His agents are everywhere, as you said. It needs just a whisper in an alehouse to start a rumour.'

'Then I hope he has finished with us now.'

'We're safe for the time being. Remember the king is coming and Cromwell won't want to rock the boat until he's gone.'

'You know, Jane,' said Nicholas leading the way into the great hall, 'if I were king I would appoint you as my chief minister. How did you acquire such knowledge about the workings of the minds of great men?'

'Where else but at court? Remember I was lady-in-waiting to Queen Jane. I watched them all then – the jostling for position, the readiness to believe every slanderous rumour being put around the court. Before Queen Jane died, Cromwell and his ilk were plotting who would take her place. And don't think Cromwell is particularly enamoured of the Duke of Cleves and his daughter. If this marriage takes place, the Howard family will be pushed back onto the sidelines. The Howards hate Cromwell. Also, it happens that the Duke of Cleves is the leading Protestant prince on the Continent and will be a useful ally against the King's Catholic enemies.'

'What a responsibility the man carries,' said Nicholas turning to smile at her serious face. 'If his majesty takes a dislike to the Lady Anne of Cleves what will happen to Baron Cromwell then?'

'Why then the Howards will turn on him and he will have to leave the country; and be quick about it – or face the wrath of his disappointed royal master.'

Dinner that evening at the bishop's palace was a subdued affair. Bishop Humphrey was worried about the king's visit. Over the fine carp his wife had provided, he expressed concern about the service the king was going to attend. The canon precentor, Lancelot Day, shared the bishop's concern.

'What sort of service am I expected to provide?' said the bishop, waving his knife, with which he had carefully dissected his fish, around the company at large. 'Is the traditional Mass still celebrated at the Chapel Royal or will I have to consult some of the reformers' prayer books and concoct an entirely new form of service? At short notice, too. What are your views, Precentor?' he said, looking across the table at the lean figure of Lancelot Day.

'My views, Bishop? I have no views. I only take orders from you. We can't be expected to know what the king likes. We have always been traditionalists at Marchester and I would have thought one of William Cornyshe's liturgical settings would be appropriate.'

'But surely the king will expect something different? After all, he's an expert musician and takes a keen interest in the music for divine service. He will want to hear the latest settings. You'll have to write something, Precentor. Show his majesty that we are the leaders in church music in this country.'

159

The precentor's pallid face suddenly took on a florid hue. He carefully put down his knife by the side of his plate and fixed the bishop with his dark eyes.

'Why should we go to all this trouble to please the king, Bishop? After all, what has he done for us? His commissioners have given us nothing but trouble since they arrived in this county and now, it seems, that our own shrine of the blessed Richard is to be demolished before Christmas. It will cause great grief amongst the common people, Bishop. The precious relics will go to the king and the shrine pulled down and we shall lose most of the income from the pilgrims who come to the cathedral throughout the year to pray before the altar of the saint. Why should I put myself out to entertain the king with new music when we have a perfectly good liturgical setting of the Mass in existence? I'll be damned if I'll do it. My inspiration would desert me and the Devil will prompt me to produce discordant harmonies and rude songs.'

'Good God, be careful what you say, Precentor,' said the bishop angrily. 'If you take this attitude we shall all be dismissed and you will find yourself in the Tower alongside our chancellor. Remember he only once criticised the king, but that was enough.'

'I'm sorry, Bishop, I can't remain silent when the desecration of our cathedral is being contemplated. You can't possibly sit back and watch it happen.'

'What I think, I keep to myself,' the bishop shouted at him. 'I regard it my duty to preserve this cathedral for future generations. The king is coming to worship with us. We must do all we can to give him the best we can offer. Now, will you compose something, Precentor, or will I have to look to Winchester to send me a musician who is able and willing to please his majesty?'

'I find the whole subject deeply distressing, Bishop. I don't think I can eat another mouthful of food at this table. I think I will retire to my house.'

160

'You'll do nothing of the sort. Sit down at once. Remember Lord Nicholas is our guest. He is also a close friend of the king. Do you want to dig your own grave, man?'

The bishop was very angry. He pushed away the remains of his fish and gulped down some wine. Nicholas thought it was time to intervene.

'Let me reassure you, Canon, that the king will expect a traditional Mass setting sung in the usual manner by your excellent choir. Maybe he would appreciate an anthem, if that is appropriate, which you have composed yourself and put aside for such an occasion.'

'Lord Nicholas, I don't write music to order and I don't have any old anthem that I have "put aside" as you say. Writing music takes time and it needs a calm mind – both of which I lack.'

'Maybe we can help you,' said Jane, smiling across at the precentor. 'We have a member of our household who is a very fine musician. I believe you've already met him. His name's Balthazar Zampieri. He came to us from court, having committed an indiscretion with one of the late queen's ladies-in-waiting, and he needs to cool his heels for a while. He came to us for refuge and, as I knew him at court, and appreciate his musical talents, we took him on. Now, he not only plays the lute but composes music of a high quality. He is very knowledgeable about the Italian composers and I'm sure he would help you compose something which will delight the king.'

'Zampieri? Didn't I meet him at that dinner you gave in February?'

'Indeed you did and I seem to remember you got on very well with him. I can send him to you and you could work out something together. You might be able to include one of the king's own compositions. Balthazar knows them all. It would certainly please his majesty. Give him back before the king comes, won't you. The king has forgiven him his indiscretion and will expect to be entertained by him.'

161

'There you are, Canon,' said the bishop, looking more cheerful. 'The Lady Jane has solved your problem for you. Let's have this fellow Zampieri over here straight away and you can pick his brains. Come on, man, relax, and let's enjoy this haunch of venison which the steward's just brought in. Your problems are solved, Canon. Mine are just beginning.'

Later, the bishop and Nicholas sat together in the bishop's private room, the precentor having dashed off to look out some manuscripts. Jane and Katharine, the bishop's wife, went off to talk to the cook about puddings suitable for the royal table. Nicholas felt sorry for the bishop, whom he regarded as a friend. The impending demolition of the shrine of St Richard weighed heavily on his mind and they both knew there was nothing anyone could do to save it. Under the excuse of ridding the cathedral of popish trappings, the real motive for the desecration was the greed of their royal master and his servant Cromwell. Stripped of its crowning glory, the cathedral would never be the same again and thousands of pilgrims would be left desolate. Times were changing, and changing fast, and neither the bishop nor Nicholas were comfortable with the situation.

When the bishop had finally come to a halt in his lamentations concerning the shrine, Nicholas mentioned his own concerns about the case of Sarah Bowman. The bishop seemed pleased to be distracted from his problems and listened intently to Nicholas's account of the two murders at Monksmere and his fears that high officials could be behind them. Both Nicholas and the bishop trusted one another. Nothing said in that little room, Nicholas knew, would ever be reported to the outside world.

'I don't know much about the Monksmere community, Nicholas. As dean I was concerned mainly with the running of the cathedral and the Augustine canons have always been a law unto themselves. Your monks were straightforward. They were proper monks living an enclosed life, and when they were dismissed they retired on pensions. Some of them, I know, found work around here. Your prior of blessed memory was bishop here for a while. But the canons of Monksmere were not enclosed. They were priests living together in a community; neither fish nor fowl, I thought. But they did travel around helping out in parishes where there was a shortage of priests. All of them, and there weren't many, remember, left their priory when ordered to and I don't know where they went. Only one old and infirm canon found refuge in an almshouse at Hardenham which is under my jurisdiction. I don't even know if he is still alive, I'm afraid. When things get back to normal here – if they ever do – I must take more interest in these remoter parishes.

'Now the prior, I do know, went on to great things,' said the bishop, brightening up. 'Somehow or other he had friends at court and became a bishop. He still is, as far as I know.'

'A bishop?' said Nicholas, suddenly alert. 'Of which diocese?'

'One of the big ones, lucky fellow. Lincoln. That was it. He became Bishop of Lincoln.'

'And his name?' said Nicholas thinking back to his previous visit to Cromwell when the Bishop of Lincoln had interrupted their conversation.

'Oh, ordinary name. He'll be Bishop Edward. Edward Woodcock, that's it. I believe his brother bought one of the priory's manors after he left. That was a bit of luck, I'd say, having a brother as prior of a monastery that was about to be closed down, and the same brother going on to be Bishop of Lincoln. Would that we were all so fortunate! Is this any help to you, Nicholas? It's a far cry from a dead girl found on a beach.'

'Not such a far cry, I think,' said Nicholas quietly. 'You've helped me more than you realise. It doesn't solve Sarah Bowman's murder, but it does explain why some one in Monksmere is so concerned about the fate of her child.'

163

Chapter Thirteen

On Monday morning, after a sleepless night, Nicholas rose early. Looking down at Jane, peacefully asleep, he envied her capacity to dismiss all cares before she got into bed and to summon sleep when needed. In his case, the conversation with the bishop after dinner had set loose a host of thoughts which buzzed around in his head like a swarm of angry bees. The knowledge that the former prior of Monksmere had become the Bishop of Lincoln had given him much food for speculation. Now, in the first light of dawn, as he dragged on his breeches, he wondered whether it was really all that significant. After all priors and abbots were coming out of the cloisters all over the country and taking on positions in the government and in the church.

But just suppose, he thought as he splashed water over his face, the prior had seduced Sarah Bowman and had fathered her child. Would the fact that he had gone on to high office and did not want to run the risk of scandal be a sufficient reason for killing her? It seemed highly unlikely, he reasoned as he dried his face and went down to the kitchen to find some breakfast. After all many great men had fathered illegitimate children. Even the Pope and his cardinals were known to have children and had put them forward for advancement. Kings and princes were often proud of their offspring. His own king was said to have been very fond of his bastard son whom he had made Duke of Richmond. No, it was unlikely that the Bishop of Lincoln, whose diocese stretched from the Wash to the Thames, would have gone to such lengths to get rid of Sarah; especially if it should ever come out that he had ordered her murder. That would be a real embarrassment. Not even the king would stand for that. Then Nicholas came back to the same old question which had bothered him since the beginning of the investigation: why wait two years to get rid of Sarah if her murderer considered her an inconvenience to his career? Moreover, what had all this to do with Cromwell? Why should he want to block the investigation into the girl's death? What could possibly be in it for him? No, he decided as he poured himself out a tankard of ale and sat down to eat the hunk of bread he had cut for himself, the bishop's revelation about Edward Woodcock had given him only another piece in the jigsaw, and probably had no connection with the murder investigation.

And yet . . . He could not put out of his mind that in one way or another the solution to the murder of both Old Moley and Sarah was to be found up in Monksmere Priory. Both of them had worked for the canons. They had taken along the boy Eddy to help them. Three people, all had worked for the canons, two of them dead. What had they seen in that place? Sudden death? Immoral acts? Had the prior dabbled in the black arts? Now that would certainly be an embarrassment to his career if that ever got around at court, he thought, as he speared the last piece of bread and drained his tankard. Could it be that Cromwell, one way or another, had got to know about this? If so, why hadn't he confronted the Bishop of Lincoln before? Could it have been possible that Cromwell himself had participated in some satanic ritual in order to placate the forces of darkness? No, that wasn't possible. He could not visualise that ambitious, ruthless servant of an autocratic master putting his own career in jeopardy. Maybe, Nicholas concluded, as he pushed aside his plate and got to his feet, the connection between Thomas Cromwell and Edward

165

Woodcock was no more than a mutual friendship between two ambitious people. And perhaps nothing had gone on at Monksmere Priory. Perhaps it was pure chance that Sarah and Old Moley had both been murdered. But then, maybe not.

It was no use speculating further. Action was needed. He had to find out more about the canons and what had gone on at the priory. The two people who could have helped him in his enquiries had been murdered. But there was still Eddy who had sharp eyes and a willingness to talk when offered money. If he was still alive. The thought struck him as if a stone had hit him. He had to talk to Eddy. Pray God he had managed to stay out of trouble.

He woke up the sleepy groom and ordered him to get his horse ready. He returned to the house to kiss the sleeping Jane and returned to the stables to find Harry in excellent spirits and pleased at the prospect of an early morning ride. He rode down the drive and turned towards Monksmere. Somehow the brightness of the morning and Harry's high spirits did not lift the feeling of dread which weighed him down. What if Eddy was the third victim?

All was quiet at the Dog and Bell. The landlord was just about awake and came stumbling out to greet Nicholas.

'My lord, you are up early this morning. I hope nothing has happened to bring you here. What can I get you? Some ale? It's freshly brewed.'

Nicholas waved the offer away. 'The boy Eddy, is he awake?'

Matt's face darkened. 'That wretch? He's gone, my lord, scarpered. After all I did for him. I took him in when he had nowhere to go and rescued him from a life of misery. All the thanks I get is that, when it suits him, he runs off.'

'Stop whining, man. You made his life a misery and I don't blame him for disappearing. When did you notice he'd gone?'

'Why, on Saturday, my lord. That's when I last saw him. He talked a bit with Sir John and then after I'd told him off for talking to the gentry, he bolted. God knows where he is now.'

'What did Sir John want with him?'

'I'm not the sort of person who creeps around listening to the conversations of my betters. In any case, they didn't stand talking for long. After Sir John rode away I went to my bed. And that's when that young wretch ran away.'

'Did you see him go, landlord?'

'No, I didn't wait. I was too worn out with serving customers.'

'Did anyone send for Eddy? No one came and took him away?'

'I saw no one, my lord. The little wretch must have decided he'd had enough of old Matt and his inn and decided to try his luck elsewhere. No doubt he'll come creeping back to me when he finds the big wide world a bit different from the comforts of a warm bed and a platter of food three times a day.'

'You mean a heap of straw and the scraps from the table. Well, I hope you are right and Eddy has run away. If by any chance I find that he has taken harm I shall hold you responsible. He is just a lad. Too young to work for you and your kind. I shall order a search for him and if we should find his body, God forbid, we shall take you in for questioning.'

Nicholas rode off, his heart heavy. He didn't believe a word the landlord had said and he dreaded finding Eddy's corpse. But one thing was clear. If Eddy had been killed, then the three deaths must be connected. And the link was that all three of them had worked at the priory. If anything had been amiss, they would have known. He had to find Eddy, dead or alive, and there was only one person who could authorise a search. He had to go to Marchester.

Harry took the miles in his stride and it was mid-morning when Nicholas arrived at the sheriff's house. Richard Landstock was in his office. He looked the shadow of his former self and his lugubrious face showed no sign of welcome when Nicholas went in. But, this time, Nicholas was not going to be put off. He sat down at the table and glared fiercely at the sheriff.

'I trust all is well here, Richard. By God, man, you look like a sheep awaiting slaughter. What's wrong with you?'

'Don't press me too hard, Lord Nicholas. I am not myself and things here are not to my liking. But what brings you here?'

'I need your help.'

'I doubt if I can be of much use to you these days. It seems that the office of sheriff no longer commands the respect it once had.'

'What makes you say that?'

'Because my hands are tied. I am being given orders and it goes against the grain.'

'Who gives you orders?'

'I am unable to tell you. Let's just say that certain high-up officials expect me to dance to their tune. I know the king is coming and there are security problems to consider, but we are quite capable of looking after his majesty. I cannot tolerate this interference in my duties. I hope you haven't come to see me about a certain murder investigation. If you have, I can't help you.'

'Richard, you have always been my friend, and we have worked together for a long time, now. Forgive me for saying this, but are you a man or a mouse? Please let us talk in private for a short while. I beg this of you because you are the only one who can help me.'

The sheriff looked at the two men sitting by the empty fire. Nicholas knew them both: Peter, the dark bearded one, was the sheriff's chief constable. Dickon, the younger man, was his assistant. Peter's face had remained inscrutable whilst Nicholas was talking to the sheriff as if he had never had any recent communication with Nicholas.

'You can trust those two. Peter and Dickon are known to you, I think?' said the sheriff.

168

'Yes, we have met before. But now I'd rather they took a short walk down the street. What I have to say must be in confidence. Also, I would be grateful if someone could look after my horse. He's come a fair distance already today and there's more work for him to do before the day's over.'

The sheriff glanced at the two men, who got to their feet and left the room. Nicholas avoided looking at Peter. If the sheriff suspected that one of his men had written to Nicholas, even if it had simply been a note reassuring him about the loyalty of his tenants, then Peter would be in deep trouble.

'Eddy has disappeared,' said Nicholas when they were alone. The sheriff looked up enquiringly.

'Eddy, who worked for Morriss the mole-taker, whose body was found up in Willet's wood. I don't know whether Eddy is alive or dead. If he's dead, then that makes three murders, and the significance of this is, that all three worked for the canons of Monksmere before they were turned out. Now, what went on up there, Richard? What could these three people possibly know that has, so far, cost two of them their lives?'

'Lord Nicholas, I've told you before, I cannot help you with this investigation. I've been warned off it in no uncertain terms. Not only is my job threatened, but even my life, if I disobey orders.'

'In God's name, Richard, who dares to tell the Sheriff of Marchester what to do? No one can order you to drop a criminal investigation. If we do find the body of Eddy, are you going to turn a blind eye to three murders, the worst crime in the criminal law? To countenance murder is a flagrant breach of your duty as a law enforcement officer. Now what are you frightened of, Richard? Who dares to scare you out of your wits?'

'I'll tell you, my lord, as I know I can trust you. I can trust no one else and God help me if you let me down. When the body of the Bowman girl was found and we

169

started to ask questions down at Monksmere, I had a visit from a stranger – the same man who was seen riding around the county spreading rumours about you and your wife. It seems he is a powerful man and commands other men to do his work for him. He's not from these parts, and when I dropped the investigation, and I believe you did likewise, or at least you let it be known that you had come off the case, he disappeared and we have had no more visits. But he said he would come back if he heard that I had disobeyed him and I would lose my job. He even threatened my life. So, here I am, sitting in my room, frightened to death that he'll return. Now you see why I dare not help you.'

'On whose instructions did this man issue his orders?'

'My lord, he said it was on the orders of Thomas Cromwell. I cannot disobey Cromwell, my lord. To do so would be signing my own death warrant.'

Nicholas stared at the sheriff in horror. So, it was Cromwell who had terrorised Richard Landstock out of his wits; Cromwell who was responsible for spreading those lies which had caused himself and Jane so much pain. And was it Cromwell who had had ordered the death of Sarah Bowman and Morriss the mole-taker, incredible as it seemed? And now, had he ordered the death of Eddy? What, in God's name, he thought, was in it for Cromwell?

'Richard, this is monstrous. To think we are being intimidated by this upstart! How can you stand for it?'

'That upstart, as you call him, happens to be, next to the king, the most powerful man in the land.'

'He cannot threaten his majesty's subjects without just cause. Remember Magna Carta; did those barons force King John's hand in vain? We have our rights, Richard; we are not serfs to be ordered around by a royal servant, however powerful he might think he is.'

'But why, in God's name,' Nicholas went on, 'should Cromwell take the slightest interest in this case? Why is he so interested in the death of a country girl that he threatens one of his sheriffs and orders one of the king's justices to drop the case? What is Cromwell frightened of?'

'I wish I could answer that. I, too, cannot understand why Cromwell should bother himself to interfere in what is, after all, a routine murder investigation. It's not as if my lord of Tredgosse has been murdered, or yourself, my lord. Now that would be a cause for concern. But I do know that I don't want to lose my job, so I don't ask questions. And, yes, I am sorry to let you down in this way but I have too much at stake.'

Nicholas looked sadly at his friend and thought – yes, I understand; he can't do any more. But there were others who could.

'There is something you can do, something that would not involve you in person.'

'What's that?

'As the boy Eddy is missing, we have a duty to attempt to try and find him. Should we discover his body, then we have to conduct a murder enquiry. We don't know if there could be any connection between his death, if that turns out to be the case, and Sarah Bowman's. Therefore you can, with good reason, say to whoever asks that you are just doing your job. But first, we have to find the boy. Now, those two men of yours, Peter and Dickon, can I borrow them? I want every hedgerow and ditch in the vicinity of Monksmere searched. I want them to go to the river estuary at Littlehaven and the seashore at Atherington to check whether a body has recently been retrieved. I cannot do it myself and your men have the good excuse that they are merely trying to find a missing person. They can report to me at Dean Peverell, and if I am not there, my wife can be trusted to take any messages. Will you do this for me? Can you spare me two men? If I am questioned, I promise I will keep your name out of it.'

For a moment, the sheriff hesitated. Then he came to a decision.

'I have known you a long time, my lord, and I know you

171

are a man of honour. I would trust no one else. Yes, I will see to it that Peter and Dickon will conduct the search for the boy. But look to yourself. You, too, have much to lose. Think of your wife and your family name. If Cromwell thinks that you are getting too involved, you know what would be in store for you. The *via dolorosa*; otherwise known as the road to Tyburn.'

'I have seen many others travel that road, Richard, and I don't intend to follow in their footsteps. But I cannot ignore an injustice and I have a curiosity to find out what our Lord Privy Seal, otherwise know as Baron Cromwell of Oakham, is up to. Meanwhile, I will speak to the men on my way out, and, if my horse is still willing, ride back to Monksmere.'

'What will you do there? It is a dangerous place for you to be seen prowling around.'

'Have no fear, Richard. I am only going to see Sir John Woodcock about my mill. He's expecting my bailiff today; a fact that has completely gone out of my mind. So, of course, I must apologise for the oversight. Then I must see the lord of Tredgosse about his wild boars.'

'You play a dangerous game, my lord, but I wish you God speed and trust you find the boy alive and well.'

Chapter Fourteen

When Nicholas arrived at Monksmere manor, Sir John
Woodcock and his wife were eating their midday meal.
They asked Nicholas to join them and sent a servant to lay
him a place at the table. Joan Woodcock served him a slice
of game pie and urged him to help himself to cheese. They
appeared relaxed and happy to see him and asked him about
the preparations for the king's visit. Nicholas reassured
them that he would be sending them an invitation to dinner
in due course.

They went on to talk about the mill and Nicholas said he
would send over Joseph, his bailiff, as soon as possible so
that the mill could be in operation when the autumn rains
fell. He apologised for not sending Joseph that day but
pleaded the imminence of the royal visit as an excuse. All
was agreeable; all was as it should be between two
members of the landed gentry who lived near one another.

However, when the meal was over, the conversation
suddenly took a different turn. Nicholas asked whether
either of them had seen Eddy lately. Immediately, the
atmosphere changed. Sir John began to look worried;
Nicholas also thought he saw the hint of fear in his eyes.
His wife looked puzzled.

'Eddy?' she said, looking enquiringly at her husband.
'The boy Eddy who works up at the inn?'

'I think Lord Nicholas means that person. Don't bother

your head about him, wife. He's just a pot boy. No, my lord, I have not seen him lately.'

'Well, it seems he's disappeared. I liked the boy. He was bright and willing and I don't want to think he's come to any harm. The landlord says he has no idea where he is. I don't suppose you have any knowledge of his whereabouts, sir?' said Nicholas.

'Me? What makes you think I know anything about a common pot boy whom I don't even remember seeing lately?'

'Yet the landlord says you were talking to him shortly before he disappeared last Saturday. It was not long after my visit here. He said you rode up to the inn and talked to Eddy. After you left, the landlord went to sleep and during that time Eddy disappeared.'

'Why husband, you didn't tell me that,' said Joan Woodcock, looking flustered.

'There was no need to tell you. I can't even remember the incident it was so unimportant.'

'But now I come to think of it, you did go out just before Lord Nicholas came back to see you about the bailiff. He spoke to me in the garden. You said you had to go out to see someone.'

'Woman, hold your tongue,' said Sir John roughly. 'Lord Nicholas doesn't want to hear about the details of our domestic arrangements. Maybe I did stop to have a chat with the boy. I have a charitable concern for all needy people – widows, orphans, the poor in general. I am think-ing of becoming a patron of the bishop's orphanage in Marchester. Charity comes naturally to me.'

'You are indeed a very kind man, husband. I didn't know, though, that you were considering taking on the Marchester orphanage.'

'I was going to tell you after I've seen the bishop. I would not have mentioned it now had not Lord Nicholas asked about the boy.'

'So, you heard nothing more about him after your

174

conversation with him on Saturday? Your charitable conversation, I should say?'

'No, of course not. I don't own the boy. I know nothing about his whereabouts and, in fact, have not visited the inn since that day. Yesterday was Sunday and we were in church, as I am sure you were. Afterwards we spent a quiet day in our garden making the most of this late sunshine. This is why we came to live here, Lord Nicholas – for peace and quiet. Not to get involved with the goings-on of the local low life.'

'I am glad you find country life to your taste,' said Nicholas, getting up from the table and walking across to the window. 'It must have helped enormously to have the prior of that priory over there as one's brother-in-law. Especially someone who went on to great things. I met him recently, you know, when I went to see Thomas Cromwell. I was introduced to the Bishop of Lincoln, a very powerful man in court circles, I understand. You must be proud of your brother-in-law, madam,' he said, turning to look at Joan Woodcock.

Nicholas noted with some satisfaction that his speech had set the alarm bells ringing in the Woodcock household. Joan Woodcock's face paled and Sir John had to put a restraining arm around her shoulders to stop her from collapsing.

'We see nothing of my brother Edward now that he has moved on to high office. And I can assure you that my purchase of this manor had nothing to do with his influence. It was a straightforward business transaction. The money was handed over to Cromwell's commissioners. No doubt when you next visit London, you will find the transaction recorded in the Court of Augmentations' archives.'

'I was not suggesting anything untoward went on between you and your brother. I merely said it was fortunate to have a relative in such an eminent position. Now, of course, he's even more important as a friend of Thomas Cromwell.'

175

'My brother is an ambitious man. A person of many talents. He will make a fine bishop. The workings of his mind far outshine mine. I am content with the simple life in the country living at peace with my neighbours.'

'And that is to be commended, Sir John. Did any of the canons move on to places of importance?'

'Not as far as I know. The canons were a community of elderly men. There was only a dozen of them, if I remember rightly. Many of them were approaching their end. When they accepted the pensions and left the priory they no doubt found work in the parishes around here and are leading quiet and uneventful lives, like me. They were not all as clever as my brother.'

'Obviously not. And none of them, I should think, attracted the attention of Thomas Cromwell. Unlike your brother. Had he met Cromwell before he became prior here, do you know?'

'I am afraid I can't answer that. As far as I know the two never met until Edward was made bishop. But I do know that Cromwell is always on the lookout for talented men to serve him; and you are one of the most talented, my lord.'

'Thank you, Sir John. I serve my master, the king, rather than his servant. However, Cromwell seems to have chosen well in your brother's case. Edward Woodcock can be reckoned as one of the most powerful men in the land. Another Wolsey, perhaps? Not bad coming from a small religious community in the heart of rural Sussex. I am surprised that Cromwell even heard of him.'

'As I said, my lord, Edward was by far the cleverest member of the family. Everyone knew him.'

'Then I am amazed that he chose to live here. Why did he not seek high office in London? Perhaps as a chaplain to Cromwell, or some aristocratic family. That is the usual route to advancement in the church.'

'My lord, my brother was a humble man. He wanted to serve God in a small community of saintly men. When that community was dissolved by Act of Parliament, he was given his true reward.'

'Hm! Truly amazing! However, thank you for sparing me your time, Sir John. Madam ...' he said, bowing in Joan Woodcock's direction. She was still in a state of agitation and was hanging onto her husband as if her life depended on it.

'Send me a message if you hear of Eddy's whereabouts,' Nicholas continued, 'I am concerned about him. Thank you for your hospitality which I hope to return when the king comes.'

A servant showed him to the door. Harry had been fed and watered and looked hopefully at Nicholas as if expecting to go home. Nicholas mounted him and rode off. As he passed the ruins of the priory church he stopped to look at it once again. How peaceful it now looked with the jackdaws circling round the gaunt outline of the east end. But something had gone on there, he thought, something which had terrified the inhabitants of Monksmere, and, he now believed, caused the death of two people. Three, if Eddy was not found alive.

The Woodcocks knew more than they were prepared to tell him. He felt sure of that. Something had put the fear of God into them. Something involving Edward Woodcock and Thomas Cromwell. They would never tell him, he thought, as he rode back to the main road. He could not bring them in for questioning because he had not the slightest bit of evidence that anything untoward had gone on in the priory. However, Lord Gilbert might be more forthcoming. After all, there were no family connections with the priory, as far as he knew. Surely he would have noticed if anything suspicious had gone on in a priory not a mile away from his castle.

After Nicholas had left, John Woodcock looked furiously at his wife.

'Woman, how many times have I told you to hold your

177

tongue in front of strangers? You are a blabbermouth, an Ipswich fishwife. Don't ever question my actions again.'

'Why husband, what did I say?'

'You contradicted me, woman; that's what you did. You told Lord Nicholas that I went out after he left here last Saturday. You told him I had to meet someone. Don't you see it puts me in an embarrassing position?'

'But I was only telling the truth. You went off to see Eddy.'

'But there was a reason for my reluctance to tell Lord Nicholas every detail of my actions. Can't you see that we owe our good fortune in living here to the kindness of my brother?'

'But what has that to do with Eddy?' said Joan Woodcock bursting in to tears. 'I know I am not clever but I don't understand you, husband. You must give me a proper explanation.'

'Oh hush your weeping and wailing, woman. Are you so stupid that you understand nothing? I told you about the little trouble my brother had when the canons were here, didn't I? Well, Eddy probably knew about it and so did Sarah, I suspect, and that mole-catcher fellow. After all, they all worked up here in the priory and they are not blind or deaf. My brother Edward was anxious that no one outside the priory knew about that "little trouble". When everyone left, he wanted the whole incident buried. Now Sarah and the mole-catcher were always a risk. The time would come, sooner or later, that they would spill the beans. Eddy was a risk, too. All I wanted to do last Saturday was to warn Eddy to keep his mouth shut. And I am now telling you to do the same.'

She gazed at her husband in horror as the implications of what he had just told her sank in.

'Are you telling me that it was you who murdered Sarah and the mole-catcher? And Eddy? Have you now got rid of him, too? Husband, we can't go on like this. It won't be long before Lord Nicholas guesses something was amiss here.'

178

'Not if you don't tell him. No, you fool, of course I
didn't murder Sarah and the mole-catcher. It was up to the
others to do that. And no, I haven't murdered Eddy. He's
solved the problem by disappearing. The brute of a landlord was responsible for that. If Eddy comes back here,
then I don't hold out much hope for his safety. And if you
continue to act the fishwife and blabber our business to all
and sundry, I shall have to send you back to Ipswich. It was
my fault for bringing you here in the first place.'

Joan, her face streaming with tears, stared at her
husband.

'Is it always to be like this? Is the path to bettering
ourselves always to be at the expense of innocent people?
If Edward has done anything he is ashamed of, then he
will spend the rest of his life trying to escape from it.
Is it not better that he should admit his guilt and hope
for forgiveness rather than live in fear that others will
denounce him?'

'Are you mad, woman? Have you no idea of the ways of
the world? Nothing terrible happened up there in the
priory. However, in these times any action can be misin-
terpreted. Do you want Edward to end up in the hands of
the Tyburn butchers?'

'May God help us,' she exclaimed, her face now a
picture of stark terror. 'What did go on in that place?
Please, in the name of our Blessed Saviour, tell me?'

'Tell you, woman? Then you are mad and I must put you
away with other lunatics. Don't you realise the king is
coming and we shall be eating at his table? Keep silent,
woman, and we can continue to enjoy our life here.
Question me in public, or worse, contradict me, then we
are finished. And try to look cheerful. One look at that
stupid sheep's face of yours and the king will suspect we
are guilty as hell. Yes, if you don't guard that tongue of
yours, you and I and my brother will lose everything. And
you will fall with us; remember that. You are a Woodcock,
for better or worse.'

179

'To my everlasting shame,' she said, as, shaking in terror, she stumbled out of the room.

In the courtyard of Tredgosse Castle, Nicholas saw the boy, Marcus, grooming a small, sturdy pony. With its stout legs, long black mane and tail it looked like one of the forest ponies that roamed wild in the forests of Hampshire. Nicholas could see that boy and pony were very close. As the boy bent over to brush the pony's legs, the pony turned its head and nuzzled the boy's twisted back as if he knew it was hurting.

Once again, Nicholas was struck by the delicate beauty of the boy's face, almost like a girl's, with its pale skin and dark brown hair. When he looked up at Nicholas there was a sadness in his eyes as if he had experienced sorrow and pain and knew there was nothing he could do about it. When he recognised Nicholas, he lowered his gaze and resumed grooming the pony as if ashamed of being noticed.

Nicholas dismounted and led Harry over to him.

'Good day, sir,' Nicholas said. 'That's a fine beast you have there. What do you call him?'

'Robin, sir. Because he lived in a forest,' he added, smiling shyly at Nicholas.

'Not from the forests around here, I think?'

'No, my father bought him for me from someone in Hampshire. Robin is a forest pony. He's at home in our woods.'

'Is your father at home?'

'No, he's out hunting, sir.'

'And your mother?'

'I have no mother.'

Nicholas cursed himself for his clumsiness. Of course the boy's mother had died when he was born.

'If you'd like to speak to my father's whore, she's at home. Ring the bell over there and a servant will take you to her.'

180

He then turned back to his grooming as if dismissing Nicholas.

'Will you summon a groom to take my horse, sir?'

The boy straightened his back, wincing slightly as if the action hurt him.

'I am afraid they are all out hunting with my father. If you leave your horse over there, I will see to him when I have finished with Robin. He is indeed a fine steed, sir,' said the boy, looking admiringly at Harry, who, sensing the boy's interest, stretched out his head and nuzzled his arm.

'Thank you. He appears to have taken to you already.'

'I love horses, sir. They are loyal and uncritical. Leave him with me and I will see he comes to no harm.'

Slipping the reins over the post which the boy indicated, Nicholas walked across the courtyard and tugged on the bell rope which hung beside the main door. An elderly man appeared, who conducted Nicholas through the bleak main hall and, after knocking on the door, ushered him into a small room where Adeliza sat doing some embroidery.

She raised her head when Nicholas was announced, and he was struck by her dark beauty. Her morning robe, a rich purple colour, would not have been out of place in the court of the sultan. The collar and the cuffs of the long, loose sleeves were trimmed with panels of rich embroidery encrusted with jewels. Thinking of Jane, with her simple linen dress, up to her elbows in floury dough, he marvelled at the extravagant luxury of Adeliza's attire. Tiny, jewelled slippers protruded from under the hem of her robe, each one costing a fortune. Her unbound dark hair gleamed in the light of many candles as the room had only one small window, high up and admitting very little daylight. The room smelled of some exotic perfume, not at all like the perfumes Jane used which she made herself out of garden herbs and thousands of rose petals.

'Please sit down,' Adeliza said, indicating a chair. 'I am afraid Lord Gilbert is not at home, but perhaps I can help you.'

181

'Madam, I fear I am not in a fit state to sully one of your beautiful chairs. I have been riding hard all day and am unpleasantly hot and dusty.'

'You will, at least, accept some refreshment?'

'Thank you, but I have dined with Sir John and Lady Woodcock and it is my horse who needs refreshment rather than me. However, Marcus is looking after him.'

'He would make a good groom, I think. A more suitable occupation for him than the one his destiny has arranged for him.'

'And that is, madam?'

'One day he will be lord of this castle. He is Lord Gilbert's son and heir.'

She picked up the piece of embroidery which she had laid aside when Nicholas entered the room and began to stab vigorously at a central rose with a sharp needle threaded with scarlet silk. He could not see her face but he guessed at the tension in her neck and shoulders.

'He seems a bright, intelligent boy, madam. No doubt he will be a fitting heir to Lord Gilbert's estates.'

'A fitting heir, my lord? You don't know what you say. He's a miserable crippled creature. He can only ride a small horse and that is with difficulty. Now our son, who is not yet five years old, is out with his father watching the hunt. The grooms will see to it that he is up in the front when the boar is killed. He has no fear and already can use a knife with a dexterity way beyond that of most boys of his age. Yet, the pity of it is that Lord Gilbert refuses to make him his heir. It troubles me greatly, especially as the king is coming soon, I have heard, and Marcus will be the one who sits next to his father at table, whilst Justin has to sit with the servants.'

'His Majesty is well known to love children, madam, and I am sure your son will get all the attention he deserves. But concerning the king's visit, the reason for my coming to see you is because I had a letter from the lord privy seal asking me to make sure that the woods around Tredgosse

Castle are well stocked with animals. The king, it appears, cannot spend all day on his horse looking for the prey as he used to. His leg is troubling him sorely and he wishes to take up a position and shoot arrows at the prey at his leisure. If Lord Gilbert needs more men to round up the boars then I can help him. I shall have to take on extra men as it is – my steward is out today finding more servants and huntsmen – and no doubt Lord Gilbert and I could come to some arrangement to share them between us. Perhaps you could give him that message and also say that Cromwell urges me to warn Lord Gilbert that the king will expect the highest standards of comfort when he comes here. Again, if you are willing, I can send over my steward to instruct you in what are the king's requirements. He is known to leave a house immediately if the arrangements are not to his liking. But, I am sure, in your capable hands everything will be up to the highest standards.'

Adeliza put down her embroidery on the little table beside her and rose to her feet. Her dark eyes looked at him resentfully. Gone was the gracious mistress of the house. Now she had become the angry vixen at bay, facing the oncoming hounds.

'My lord, the arrangements for the king's visit are nothing to do with me. I am not Lord Gilbert's wife. He will never countenance the idea. I am no more than a concubine. He tolerates me because I know how to satisfy his lust. He lavishes jewels and clothes upon me because my beauty arouses him and it pleases him to know that everything I wear, or sit on, or sleep in, he owns. He has bought me, my lord, for one purpose only. The rest, the domestic arrangements, such as they are, are not my concern. If the king is displeased then that is Lord Gilbert's worry, not mine.'

'Madam, take care, I beg of you,' said Nicholas, appalled at her outburst. 'You don't know what you are saying. A visit from the king requires days of preparation. My own house has been turned upside down at the

183

moment and my wife spends all her time giving orders to our cooks and servants. She spends all day in the kitchen and supervises everything from the meat larder and the fishponds to the making of sweetmeats and puddings and cakes. You cannot think of entertaining his majesty and his courtiers in the same way as you would arrange a dinner for a neighbouring landowner. Every meal must be a feast. His majesty likes masques and theatrical performances. You must hire musicians, jesters, and some novelty entertainers. The whole county is at the king's disposal. If you fail to do this, then you are courting disaster. If the king is displeased with the arrangements, then Lord Gilbert will not be lord of Tredgosse Castle for long. And if he falls from the king's favour, then you fall too.'

'I don't care one jot about the king's favour. The jewels I am wearing will keep me and Justin in comfort for the rest of our lives.'

'The king can strip you of everything.'

'Too late. I have already placed many of my possessions in a safe place.'

'And Lord Gilbert . . . Does it not trouble you that everything could be taken away from him – his estates, his titles? The king can make a man the greatest in the realm and can reduce the greatest to a pauper. No one in his right mind would underestimate the importance of a royal visit. If the king is displeased he will take it as an insult. To insult the king is to say goodbye to the world. If Lord Gilbert does not feel up to entertaining the king in an appropriate manner, then my advice to him is that he should leave the country immediately.'

'Lord Gilbert will do what he can, I am sure, but I will not help him. If I am not to be his wife then I cannot be introduced to his majesty in a manner befitting my position and I will not be relegated to the servants' quarters. Do you think I shall enjoy watching that ugly little dwarf taking my son's place at the king's table? No,

184

my lord, if Lord Gilbert wants me by his side in the arrangements he must first make me his wife.'

'Then I suggest you sort out your domestic arrangements as quickly as you can, madam. As things are at the moment you are on the road to disaster, and, what's more, I shall be blamed. I have been informed that the king's well-being is to be my responsibility whilst he is in Sussex.'

'Then you, too, will accompany us on the road to disaster. I am sorry, my lord, but I cannot alter my resolution in order to make your life more comfortable. I must look after myself.'

'Then I must leave you to come to your senses. When Lord Gilbert returns, tell him to be sure to round up all the beasts in his forest for the king's pleasure. I'll come back later to check on the arrangements. Good day, madam.'

Leaving her standing by her embroidery table glaring at him, Nicholas left her and went back to the courtyard where Harry, well fed and watered, was waiting for him. Feeling angry and dispirited, he turned towards home. Disaster was looming ahead for the master of Tredgosse Castle. Unfortunately, he would be the one who would incur the royal wrath if the king was displeased with Lord Gilbert's hospitality.

As daylight faded, Lord Gilbert returned from the hunt. He had ridden long and hard and they had despatched three fine boars. He had worn out two horses and was beginning to think he would have to restock his stables if the king and his courtiers wanted to spend much time hunting. Covered in dust and smelling strongly of horse sweat, he roared at the servants to bring him ale and food. Dinner, he said, had to be soon. His head steward approached and whispered in his ear.

'God damn you, are you telling me that Lord Peverell has been here,' Lord Gilbert shouted, 'and Adeliza has given you no instructions for dinner? What the devil's going on here? Have you gone mad, man? Get on with

185

dinner yourself and make haste. I am famished.'

Angrily he took a swipe at the steward who, used to his master's moods, expertly ducked and scuttled away.

'Adeliza,' he roared. 'Where the devil are you?'

'She's taken to her bed, my lord,' said another servant who was waiting for instructions. 'She says she is not well.'

'In bed? God's blood, I'll make her get on her feet. Who does she think she is? I'll see she comes down to the kitchen immediately. Tell the cook I shall want to eat in one hour.'

'Yes, my lord. But her ladyship said expressly that she was not to be disturbed.'

'Her ladyship? That's a laugh; and you know it's a lie. It's time Adeliza learned her place.'

He picked up the long leather whip which he had used to control the mastiffs and strode off to Adeliza's room where she was lying on her bed calmly eating sugared plums from a china dish.

'Get up, woman,' he roared, his irritation increasing at the sight of her aloofness.

'I am not feeling well, my lord.'

'You were in good health this morning when you serviced me right royally.'

'Maybe I have fatigued myself.'

'Fatigued yourself? Whores don't complain of fatigue. What have you been doing all day? Servicing Lord Nicholas, no doubt. I always thought that pale bitch of a wife of his is too holy to be much comfort in bed. Now, get up.'

He cracked the whip expertly in the air, letting its end flicker across the draperies on the bed.

'Lord Nicholas has a wife who runs his establishment expertly, I hear, whilst I am nothing.'

'Yes, and you came from nothing, remember? And I can send you back to the London brothel where you learned the tricks of your trade. But now I need food and the servants await your orders.'

'Then the servants must do what they please. Whores don't give orders to servants.'

'They do, when I say so,' he shouted, cracking the long whip again. 'Now get down to the kitchen and get me my dinner.'

Adeliza did not move. She glared at him, her dark eyes smouldering with loathing.

'It seems you didn't hear me, my lord. Whores don't order servants around. You will have to order your own dinner, and the king's. It appears his majesty doesn't trust you to look after him properly and sends Lord Nicholas to check on our arrangements. The king doesn't take kindly to indifferent service, Lord Nicholas told me.'

'The king, madam? Who dares to say that he shall not have everything he wishes? You are in charge of my domestic arrangements, remember. It is your job to see that the king is well satisfied.'

'Concubines know their place, my lord. Remember, I am not your wife.'

'Do you threaten me? How many times do I have to tell you that you will never be my wife, and that child of yours will never be lord of Tredgosse.'

'Then you and the king will have to sing for your supper,' she said, turning to select another plum from the dish.

Her insolence aroused Lord Gilbert to fury. He advanced towards her and cracked his whip, this time letting it fall across the lower part of her body which was protected by the thick cloth of her dress. She winced, but she didn't move.

'Will you get up, you bitch?'

'What for, my lord? Concubines start their work when everyone else goes to bed.'

With a yell of rage, Lord Gilbert raised his whip again, this time bringing it down across her shoulders and the open neck of her dress. With a cry of pain she sat up and put her hands across her face.

187

'Please, Gilbert, spare my face. You once said it was as beautiful as a painting of the virgin you had seen in the king's royal chapel.'

'That was a long time ago. Your virginity, madam, was something I never encountered. You were highly skilled in your trade when Southampton gave you to me. Now, get up, I say, before I damage that face of yours. I whip my dogs when they disobey me so why should I not whip whores?'

This time the end of the whip lashed across her face, cutting a deep wound in her cheek, making the blood spurt down the front of her dress. She glared at him in hatred and clutched the wound with her fingers. Slowly she got off the bed.

'I am not one of your dogs. Once you loved me. You could not stop looking at me. Now you are going to kill me.'

As she came towards him spitting out her hatred, he laughed and raised the whip.

'I never loved you, whore. You served me as once you served Southampton and countless others before him.'

'Father, stop,' said a quiet voice from the doorway. 'Think what you are doing.'

Lord Gilbert whirled round and saw Marcus standing by the door, his angelic face looking at him sadly.

'She is very beautiful,' the boy said, 'and don't forget she knows everything. She saw the boat with her own eyes. One word to the king and it will be the end of us all.'

Chapter Fifteen

There it was again. Louder this time. The unmistakable howl of the wolfhounds. They were after the boars, Eddy thought, as he stuffed a lump of turf into one of the vents of the kiln. He had lived with Jude and his family for two days now, and already he felt one of the family. It was unremitting work looking after the kilns and not much time for sleep, but the food was good and plentiful and Alison was like a mother to him.

The howling of the dogs unsettled him. It made him think of the stories Old Moley used to tell him about the great forests up in the north where wolves hunted in packs and lay in wait for unwary travellers. Jude was also worried by the sound.

'Best get out of here, lad, if they come any nearer,' he said. 'The likes of Lord Gilbert don't care what they trample on when they are out for the kill. Kilns'll have to look after themselves. They'll be all right. The smoke puts the horses off but we can say goodbye to the house if they come into this glade. God's curse on them. They've no consideration for poor folk. Stoke up that kiln, lad, block up the vents and the wood will come to no harm, with any luck. Wait till they get a bit nearer, then off to one of the thickets and lie low until the coast is clear.'

Suddenly, the peace of the glade was shattered by the arrival of a large boar, desperate to get away from the

189

hunting dogs. He was a huge beast with a fine pair of tusks, sharp as swords. He stood there, panting, glowering belligerently at Eddy and Jude, ready to take on all comers. The coarse brown bristles stood up along his back like a coat of armour and his small, piggy eyes shot barbs of hatred at them like arrows from a bow.

For a second he stood there, poised for an attack, then, suddenly, he changed his mind. Perhaps it was the smell of the woodsmoke or the sight of Jude with his shovel which frightened him, but whatever it was, he gave a great snort, wheeled round and made to dash back the way he had come. But he had stopped too near a thicket of brambles, and one of the trailing branches had caught hold of his thick coat and held him fast. With more snorts of rage, the beast struggled frantically only to get more and more tangled up in the brambles which wound round his legs like ropes.

'Poor beast,' said Luke, who had come out of the house to see what was going on. 'He'll be an easy target if he stays there. He doesn't deserve a bloody death. I'm going to try to free him and at least give him a sporting chance to escape the dogs. Come on boy,' he said to Eddy, 'give me a hand and watch out for those tusks of his – he'll not be too particular who he sticks them into.'

Eddy and Luke advanced on the boar, who began to lunge around in a frenzy, but he could not free his legs. He could, however, snort and pant and toss his head around with the lethal tusks threatening them with disembowelling if they came any nearer.

Luke advanced slowly, talking softly to the animal, who suddenly stopped snorting and looked suspiciously at him. Carefully Luke advanced further. Then he gave the knife he had brought with him to Eddy and, not taking his eyes off the boar's face, said that when he gave the signal, Eddy was to duck down and cut the briars which held the boar fast. Luke stretched out his hands towards the animal's face as if to stroke it. The boar snorted and glared at him but did not move.

'Now', said Luke quietly, and seized hold of the tusks. The boar squealed with rage and tried to toss him away, but Luke was young and strong and used to carrying huge tree trunks. He held on and Eddy ducked down and hacked at the briars which encircled the boar's legs. The stems parted and the boar was clear.

'Now, get back, Eddy,' said Luke, still holding onto the boar's tusks. 'Let's hope he charges off in the right direction.'

Eddy dashed back to the camp and watched as Luke talked soothingly to the beast before letting go of him. With a snort of indignation, the boar tossed his head, stamped his feet and, much to their relief, wheeled round and charged off the way he had come.

'Well, we've done our best,' said Luke. 'Let's hope he keeps the dogs at bay, or, at least, dispatches some of them before they pull him down.'

Alison had joined them now and she and Jude were both looking worried.

'Best get out of here,' Jude said, 'and make our way up to higher ground. They'll be onto that boar now and will soon be here. We don't want to get in the way of the hunters or their dogs, God damn them!'

Alison picked up the cauldron which hung over the fire and put in it all the pots and pans she could. Together they cleared the hut of the bits and pieces of furniture which made up all their worldly goods, then left the glade and made for the heathland higher up, where, if they were lucky, they would escape the huntsmen as boars preferred the cover of the thick woodlands.

There they hid in a hazel copse and listened to the sounds of the hunt below them. First, the shrill note of the horn to let the hunters know the dogs had picked up a scent, then the crashing of men and horses through the woods, the baying of the wolfhounds and the terrified screams of the animal forced to face his persecutors. Then the laughter and cheers of the huntsmen and the frenzied barking of the dogs. Jude shuddered.

191

'Thank God it's not us they're after,' he muttered.

At last silence, and the woods were filled again with the sound of birdsong. They came out of their thicket and went back to their glade where a scene of utter desolation confronted them. The hut had been kicked to pieces, the piles of wood tossed in all directions as the hounds sought their quarry in all the most unlikely places. One of the dormant kilns had been kicked over and the charred wood ash scattered over the ground. All that remained was the one active kiln which was sending out clouds of smoke as the wood inside was burning fiercely.

'Don't fret, wife,' said Jude, dropping the pile of household goods he was carrying and putting an arm round her. 'We'll survive. It's happened before and, no doubt, it will happen again. Charcoal burners don't exist as far as the lords of Tredgosse are concerned.'

'It's not right,' said Eddy, horrified at the sight of his friends' house tossed aside so contemptuously. 'He's no right to do this. He's just an evil monster. He's got to be stopped and I know how I can do it. I'll go to Lord Nicholas and tell him all I know about that brute. He'll not be so high-handed when he faces the executioner at Tyburn.'

Jude released Alison who dried her eyes and began to reassemble the fire.

'Hold on, lad,' he said to Eddy. 'If it's true what you told us last night about Lord Gilbert and the goings-on at the priory, then you are in great danger. Not only Lord Gilbert's head will roll when it all comes out about what you saw with Old Moley and Sarah, but others, mightier than him, will also have to pay homage to the executioner's block. No, lad, don't you leave here. Let Lord Nicholas work it all out for himself. Save your own skin and let others do the dirty work. Meanwhile, that kiln needs a lot of attention. Most likely all the charcoal's already burned away and we'll have nothing to sell. One good thing about being poor is that it don't take long to rebuild our house.

The bits and pieces are still here and there's no shortage of wood around.'

'But first,' said Alison, straightening up, 'would you go and see if old Eva's all right, Eddy? She lives up that track over there,' she added, pointing to where a track led off from the far side of their glade. 'Most likely the dogs missed her, but I would not like to think of her homeless and night coming on.'

'You don't mean the old witch?' said Eddy, looking at her aghast.

'Well, she might be a witch, I'll give you that, but she's a human being and knows a lot. She knows how to cure the bellyache and once she came here to see Jude when his lungs packed up one winter and I thought he would die of coughing. She even had a visit from Jane Warrener, as she was then, before she married Lord Nicholas. She wanted something to help her father's aches and pains.'

'Go on, Eddy,' said Luke, grinning at him. 'She'll not hurt you. She might give you one of her cordials. I don't expect she's come to any harm. One whiff of her potions and the huntsmen would avoid her like the pestilence.'

Reluctantly, Eddy left the safety of the charcoal burners' glade and went up the track which Alison had pointed out. He could smell Eva's house long before he saw it – a curious aroma of woodsmoke mixed with something that reminded him of the incense he had once sniffed in Marchester cathedral when Old Moley had taken him there to see the tomb of St Richard. Then the track turned a corner and there before him was the hut, crouching by the side of a massive oak tree. The hut actually leaned against the trunk of the tree, he noticed, which provided a solid wall on one side of the house. Smoke was coming from the centre of the turf roof and the front door was open. Much relieved to see the house standing and the fire burning, he turned to go back and report to Alison that all was well with her neighbour. Then he saw an old woman appear in the

193

doorway. She stood there looking at him and curiosity caused him to stay. He had never seen a witch before and Eva was well known in the area. Old Moley had said she was a wise woman who knew how to cure people's ailments. He also said that it wasn't a good idea to get on the wrong side of her because she had been known to cause the death of those who tormented her. She also knew how to cause the death of those people others wanted rid of, provided the right price was paid. She could put a curse on people, too, Moley had said. She just had to think about the person, put the curse on him, and he would die. Her powers were said to be very great and people came from far away to consult her. He wondered what to do next. If he went back to the camp now, without any explanation, she might take offence; so he stood still and waited for the old lady to make the next move.

Suddenly she beckoned to him and then disappeared into the house. Reluctantly, Eddy walked up to the house and stood indecisively in the doorway.

'Come in, boy,' a voice said from inside the house. 'Alison sent you, I suppose. That was kind of her.'

'She was worried about you,' said Eddy. 'You see, the hunt came straight through our glade and our house was kicked to bits.'

'That sounds like the lord of Tredgosse. An evil man if ever there was one. But he keeps away from me. I'm too useful to him. Come inside, boy and let me take a look at you.'

Eddy stepped over the threshold and went into the dim interior of the witch's house. He didn't know what to expect – witches were reputed to be ugly and their houses filthy – but he was surprised by the neatness of the room, the clean floor, the brightness of the fire which provided some light, and the strong smell of fresh herbs hanging in bunches from the rafters. As for the witch, she, too, was not what he expected. She was just an old woman with straggly grey locks of hair and a wizened face under her

194

spotless white cap. The bright blue eyes were looking at him kindly and he felt his fear evaporate. Her only disfigurements were a large protuberance by the side of her nose, and a thicket of tough grey hairs sprouting on her chin. But there was nothing extraordinary about these things, thought Eddy. He'd seen lots of old people with the same blemishes on their faces. Her grey dress was clean and smelled of lavender, and there was only one broomstick propped against the wall. Admittedly there was a cat asleep in front of the fire, but he looked as old as his owner and could barely twitch an ear in his direction when he saw Eddy.

'What's your name, boy?' Eva said.

'Eddy.'

'You once worked for Morriss the mole-taker, I think?'

'That's right. When he died I came here and Jude took me in.'

'You did the right thing, Eddy. Whoever killed Morriss would be after you next. What happened up at Monksmere Priory last year will be coming home to roost now. Great men in high places will fall, mark my words, and you would be an important witness. But you'll be safe with Jude and Alison, and Luke's a good son. Come now, drink some of Mag's milk. It's laced with honey and will do you good.'

With some trepidation, Eddy took the wooden beaker from Eva and cautiously sniffed the contents. He could smell the honey, made from the nectar of wild thyme, and the milk looked fresh and creamy. He drank it down with relish watched by Eva who was looking at him quizzically.

'Don't be afraid, Eddy. I don't only make poisons, you know. I have to eat, too, and my goats make some of the best milk and cheese in the district. Here, let me give you some more. Mag is the queen of the goats. Her milk is famous. Even the lord of Tredgosse's whore orders it for her complexion.'

As he finished the drink, he watched Eva go over to a corner of the room and pick up a wooden basket full of what appeared to be toadstools.

195

'Here, give these to Alison. She can give me the basket back later. You'll do all right for supper tonight, Eddy. Some of these are in excellent condition. Don't stand there staring at them as if they are a gift from Satan. Don't you know what mushrooms look like? Look at this one,' she said, picking up a trumpet-shaped specimen, dark in colour on top, but a pale grey underneath the fleshy leaves.

'These are a delicacy, Eddy. We call them the poor man's meat. All these are perfectly safe to eat. But not all my mushrooms taste as good as these. Would you like to see some of my other specimens?'

'You mean you grow poisonous ones?' said Eddy, very curious.

'I don't grow them. God grows them, but I pick them sometimes when I have to. Come and see.'

She picked up the basket and Eddy followed her out of the house and into the daylight. She walked round to the other side of the oak tree and there he saw a patch of fantastic toadstools. Many of them were bright red, some with white spots. Moley had called them the fairies' playthings.

'Aren't they beautiful?' she said, stopping to look at them in admiration. 'These red ones are not really poisonous; only if you eat them in large quantities. I pick them to make a potion which can cure melancholy. One sip of my potion and a person thinks not of death and despair but of warm beds and fine food and beautiful things. Lord Gilbert is one of my best customers. He calls it the happiness drink. Too much is harmful and can drive a person mad, but taken in small quantities it can improve a person's life considerably. I have known people contemplating the mortal sin of suicide change their minds after just one sip. It is one of God's blessings. Look around you, Eddy, have you ever seen such a wonderful sight?'

As he glanced round the glade, Eddy could only marvel at the fantastic display of colours and shapes. All sorts and sizes of mushrooms and toadstools covered the ground, from the huge red-capped ones to tiny caps perched on

196

thread-like stems. Some grew in clusters clinging to the bark of the oak tree, some were as big as plates, and some as small as thimbles.

'Come over here, Eddy, I have the deadliest of them all. Don't touch them because they are very poisonous. I don't know what was in God's mind when he created them, but maybe he wanted to warn us to be careful. One piece of this one and you will suffer a terrible death – three long days of agony before you die – and not even I have the antidote. They destroy your body inside, and I can't replace that.'

Eddy went over to where she pointed. There he looked down at a strange white toadstool with a pale, thick stem encircled with a collar as fine and fragile as if it had been made of delicate lace.

'It looks beautiful,' he said, 'like an angel.'

'Indeed it is an angel, Eddy. A destroying angel. Admire it, because it is a thing of beauty, but leave well alone.'

'Do you ever pick them?' said Eddy, turning to look at her.

'Only when someone wants a poison, the deadliest there is.'

'Who would want such a thing?'

'Oh, someone wanting to be rid of a sick dog or a cat too old to catch mice. Given in the right quantities it will bring a quick death to an old dog. Animals can tolerate it in small quantities. But not humans. In us it ensures a lingering and painful death.'

'Is it not strange how something so beautiful as these can be so deadly?'

'Yes Eddy. It is often so. Never trust beauty in nature. It can be very seductive, like the song of the sirens.'

Eddy had never heard of the sirens so he went off to admire the other mushrooms. After a while she called him back and handed him the basket for Alison.

'Now you must go back to Alison, and tell her I am fine. Lord Gilbert would never upset me. All these are good to eat, Eddy, although some of them look a bit strange with

197

their shaggy leaves and fat-bottomed stalks. You'll sleep well tonight.'

At the cottage door he took the path back to the camp. Witches weren't all that bad, he thought, as he looked down at the mushrooms in the basket. They just knew more than most people.

Chapter Sixteen

'Eddy might have gone to live with Kate Bowman,' said Nicholas, pushing back his plate and getting to his feet. 'After all, he knows where she's living and he would trust her not to tell anyone.'

It was Tuesday morning and breakfast had been eaten quickly. He had discussed everything with Jane long into the previous night and now it was time for action.

'I'll get over to Littlehaven and take the cob as before. I didn't deceive Mistress Bowman when I last saw her, but there's no point in drawing attention to myself. Harry is too well known in the district.'

'Nicholas, be careful. We still do not know what we're up against, but we do know that Cromwell's spies are everywhere and you have been ordered to keep away from this investigation. We don't want anything to go wrong now – not with the king coming soon.'

'Don't worry, I shall take care to let it be known that I am only trying to find a missing person. Until Peter and Dickon report that they have found Eddy's body, we don't know whether he's alive or dead. I also have a good excuse now to visit Lord Gilbert. I have to see that everything is in order for the king's visit.'

'Why not wait until Peter and Dickon have made their report before you return to Littlehaven?' said Jane also standing up. 'We'll probably hear from them today.'

199

'Because I can, with any luck, kill two birds with one stone. I can see if Eddy has taken refuge with Mistress Bowman and the visit will give me another opportunity to find out what she knows about Monksmere Priory before the canons left.'

'This worries you, doesn't it, Nicholas? You still think there's a connection between what might have happened at the priory and the deaths of Sarah and the mole-catcher?'

'Yes, I'm almost certain. All that speculation about who seduced Sarah and who was the father of her child probably had nothing to do with the reason why she was murdered. What I do know is that what went on at the priory was so serious that everyone living in that neighbourhood has been intimidated into silence. Nothing will induce these people to tell me what they saw, heard or guessed what was going on there. The two eyewitnesses who knew have been silenced. The third will share the same fate if he's found. Already, I might be too late.'

'Then go carefully. A horse and rider are an easy target.'

'Don't worry, my love,' said Nicholas, gathering up his riding gauntlets. 'I have eyes in the back of my head if needs must, and the cob is very particular where he puts his feet and doesn't swerve when frightened. But you, Jane,' he said, looking her up and down, 'why are you dressed for riding?'

He had not observed, until then, that she wore a neat-fitting riding habit, her hair coiled round her head ready to tuck under her hat.

'At last you've noticed,' said Jane, laughing. 'Sometimes I think you are so preoccupied with this investigation that you don't even know I am here.'

'Jane, forgive me,' he said, going to her and taking her in his arms. 'Yes, I am worried about the case and the prospect of the king's visit. But you should not contemplate riding out in your condition. You must not risk yourself and our child.'

'The child is perfectly safe inside here,' said Jane,

patting her stomach. 'He has everything he needs in there. As for myself, all I have to do is to see that Abigail doesn't lace me up too tightly. In any case, he'll have to get used to being carried around on Melissa's broad back. She's as gentle as an old nurse; far too fat and needs exercise. I think she knows I am carrying a child and is extra careful with me these days. I am not going far; only to Marchester to get Balthazar reacquainted with the cathedral precentor. They are going to concoct something special for the king's visit, remember?'

'Remember? Yes I do although it seems ages ago that we dined with Bishop Humphrey; yet it was only two days since. Balthazar rides with you, I assume? I cannot have you riding alone.'

'Yes indeed. Don't worry about us. We are taking along Adam as well because Balthazar might be an expert musician but he is most unsafe on the back of a horse. It would be a disaster if he had to share his horse with a basketful of manuscripts.'

Relieved that Jane would be in safe hands, Nicholas left the house and went round to the stables where he gave orders for the cob to be saddled up. As he swung himself into the saddle he prayed that today he would achieve a breakthrough in the case. So far he seemed to have gone round in circles trying to unravel too many uncertainties. What in God's name, he thought as he kicked the cob into action, had gone on in Monksmere Priory? And who was going to be brave enough to tell him?

He decided to go straight over to Amos Carter's house, avoiding the harbour of Littlehaven where too many people would remember his last visit. He crossed the bridge at Tredgosse and cut across the water meadows which had almost dried out after the long spell of dry weather, arriving at the house shortly before noon. He dismounted, tethered the cob to a tree and walked up to the front door which was closed. There was no child playing in the sand that day and no sign of Kate Bowman. He hammered on the

201

door with his fist and after a long wait she eventually opened it and gave a start of surprise when she saw him.

'Lord Nicholas, why have you come here again? I asked you to leave us alone. All we want is to be left in peace.'

'I hope I won't disturb your peace for long, mistress, but Eddy has disappeared and I wondered whether you've seen anything of him?'

'Eddy?' she said, looking more and more fearful. 'No, I haven't seen him. Why should I? He is nothing to me.'

'Yet he was a friend of Sarah's.'

'Hardly a friend. Sarah spoke to him once or twice when she saw him up in the priory gardens helping the mole-catcher get rid of the molehills. Her work was inside, mending the altar frontals.'

'Mistress Bowman, I must ask you something which is very important. Did Sarah ever mention anything to you about what might have taken place at the priory; something different, something that was out of the ordinary? You see she could have noticed some change in the routine, for instance, and discussed it with Eddy and the mole-taker – an argument, perhaps, a threat, another person injured in anger; that sort of thing. Maybe someone died unexpectedly, or disappeared. Did she mention anything like that?'

Now Kate Bowman looked terrified and became very agitated.

'No, no, nothing happened in the priory that I know about. Nothing. Please go away and leave us to grieve in peace, I beg of you. It's not fair that you come here asking these questions.'

With that, she slammed the door in his face. Reluctantly, Nicholas turned to leave, cursing himself for the inept way he had handled the interview. Of course she was terrified. Someone was going round intimidating the inhabitants of Monksmere and the surrounding villages, and no one was prepared to give him the information he needed. Why should she be any different from the others?

As he prepared to mount the cob he saw someone

walking along the sandy track that led from the harbour. It was an elderly man, thick-set and bearded, and he was carrying a basket. Nicholas waited for him to draw nearer.

'Good day, master,' Nicholas said. The man came up to where he was standing, his basket full of fish, and walked past him neither looking at him nor speaking.

'Is there no welcome for strangers in these parts?' said Nicholas. The man halted.

'We don't like strangers, sir, especially not your sort. I know who you are even though you ride a different horse and you are dressed like the common people. But you are still Lord Nicholas and it bodes ill for the likes of us when you come to see us and ask questions.'

'May I at least ask who I am talking to?'

'No harm in that, I suppose. Amos is my name. Amos Carter.'

'Kate Bowman's brother?'

'Aye, that's so. Is that all you want to know?'

'I am looking for the boy, Eddy, who once helped the mole-catcher. He's disappeared and, as he knew Mistress Bowman, I wondered if he'd come here.'

'We've not seen him. I hope he's not in any trouble. He's a good lad. Uses his brains, too. Most likely he's left the district.'

'Any idea why he'd want to do that?'

'I don't know what goes on in a person's head. He's probably got into a spot of trouble now that Moley's not there to keep him in order. Now, good day to you, sir.'

'Just one more thing and then I'll not trouble you further. You own that boat down in the harbour, don't you? The biggest one there. I noticed it the last time I came here.'

'That's my boat. *Cormorant*'s her name. I go deep–water fishing in it when the weather's right.'

'Do you use it for trading?'

Amos looked at him suspiciously. 'I'll take goods along the coast if I'm asked and if I'm offered enough money.'

'Could you take some bales of woollen cloth over to France for me?'

'It's certainly possible, but could be dangerous. Cost you a lot, though.'

'Then I shall have to think about it. Have you got many customers around here? Lord Gilbert, for instance? Has he ever hired you?'

Nicholas knew he was groping in the dark but he had to keep Amos talking. He wasn't disappointed. At the mention of Lord Gilbert's name, Amos's face became sullen and he spat contemptuously on the sand.

'That devil? I'd not work for him again; not if you paid me a king's ransom.'

'Why, what has he done?'

'Done? Don't ask me, my lord. What has he not done? It's more than my life's worth, though, to tell you about what goes on up in Tredgosse Castle. My lips are sealed. And no one, not even you, Lord Nicholas – and I have nothing against you; they say you are a good man – will ever get me to tell you what I know. If I did, I should be a dead man before night falls. And, what's more, so would Kate and the boy. And you, also, Lord Nicholas.'

'Would the offer of gold persuade you to talk? I could pay you a lot. You would never have to go out fishing again.'

'No, my lord. Once I was promised a fortune and when the time came for payment I was cheated. I received but a quarter of what was agreed. That's why I don't like the gentry and that's why you'll never tempt me with a promise of riches. Good day to you, my lord.'

He pushed his way past Nicholas, who tried to stop him and went up to the door which he kicked open.

'Tell me one thing, Amos,' said Nicholas. 'Who cheated you?'

Amos stopped and turned to glare at Nicholas. 'Who? Why him, the owner of Tredgosse Castle. That's the bastard who cheated me. I risked my life for him. One of

204

these days I'll see him disgraced, and when he falls we'll all be onto him like a pack of hounds tearing apart one of his boars. You'll see.'

'What did he ask you to do?' said Nicholas, his heart beating rapidly.

'That remains my secret. You can do with me what you like but you'll learn nothing from me. You can't touch me because you know nothing. Leave it like that; but get Tredgosse. He's slippery, mind, but we'll all cheer when he's put in chains.'

Then he disappeared into the house and the door slammed shut. Nicholas heard the sound of a bolt slot into place.

Nicholas mounted the cob and rode away. The visit had not been a waste of time after all. Lord Gilbert had done something. Something serious. But he could not arrest a man for committing an unknown offence. Who else would know about Lord Gilbert's activities, he wondered as he rode back to the main coastal road. Cromwell? The king? Did they suspect that Lord Gilbert was guilty of some crime which they couldn't prove? And was that the reason why they had asked him to supervise the royal visit?

He knew that Cromwell and his royal master worked in a devious way. They had used him before and they would use him again. But this time he was working in the dark. No one had accused Lord Gilbert of any particular crime. And, as he rode back across the water meadows, he cursed his luck that once more the king regarded him as a friend and his personal spy. He also cursed Cromwell who had put him into an intolerable position of being responsible for the success of the royal visit when they both knew that one of the king's hosts was unreliable. Nicholas's instinct was to write immediately to Cromwell and advise him to put off the king's visit. But he knew that would be to no avail. Once the king was set on a course, nothing could dissuade him from it. No, Cromwell was relying on him to make Tredgosse Castle safe for the visit, and that meant either

205

proving that Lord Gilbert had not involved himself in any dubious activities, or, if he had, denouncing him and arresting him before the king came to Sussex. And there was so little time left to do anything. Yes, he thought angrily, as he kicked the cob into a reluctant gallop, once again he was to do Cromwell's dirty work for him. And no one at court would feel sorry for him if he failed. But what in God's name was he supposed to do next?

Then he had an idea.

It was Jane's reference to the bishop's dinner that jogged his memory. It was when he and Bishop Humphrey had retired to the bishop's private room after the meal was over and they had talked about Monksmere Priory. The bishop had mentioned that one of the former canons was now a resident in an almshouse in Hardenham. The village was not far from Tredgosse; only a short detour from the coastal road.

He looked up at the sun. There were several hours of daylight left and the cob was showing no signs of weariness. It probably would be a wasted journey, Nicholas thought. The canon would no doubt be old and infirm and his memory unreliable. However it could just be possible that he might remember something about the last days of the priory.

Once over the bridge, he rode past the castle walls and, ignoring the Dog and Bell, took the road which branched off the coastal road about a mile further on. At first he passed through dense woods, then it became a chalk track, firm under foot, which took him up onto the high Downs, where sheep grazed on the short grass and larks twittered overhead. He reached the small village of Hardenham in the middle of the afternoon.

The church was a small, squat building with a square stumpy tower. Attached to it was a long building made of the local flint stone with a tiled roof. Sitting in the sun on a bench by the side of the open door which was at the end

206

nearest the church sat two old men, dressed in the same long black garment which resembled a priest's cassock. They watched him as he rode up, dismounted and hitched the horse's reins over the gatepost.

'Good day to you, masters,' called out Nicholas.

'Good day to you, sir,' said one of the old men. 'Are you looking for something or someone?'

'I am looking for one of your company; a canon of the priory of Monksmere which was closed down recently. Do you know of such a person?'

'Yes, sir. However, if you want to see him then you'd best make haste. He's on his way to meet his Maker and he's almost got to the end of his journey. The warden's inside and he'll show you where he is.'

Thanking the men, Nicholas went into the almshouse, bending his head to clear the low lintel. Inside, the building resembled a large barn which had been divided into several small rooms separated from each other by wooden partitions. He could hear the subdued murmur of voices which sounded like the soughing of the wind through reed beds. To his right there was a small room with a door which stood open. As he stood there hesitating, a man came out of the room. He was younger than the two outside but was dressed in the same black robe which they wore and, in addition, he sported a black, square cap on his head. He was of medium height and strongly built and his manner was brisk.

'Can I help you, sir?' he said, looking Nicholas up and down.

'Are you the warden, sir?' asked Nicholas. The man nodded. 'The Bishop of Marchester told me you have one of the canons from Monksmore Priory here. I would be much obliged if you would let me speak to him.'

'May I know your name, sir?'

'Nicholas Peverell. From Dean Peverell.'

'I am honoured to speak to such an illustrious person. As to the canon, you must mean Brother Gregory. Yes he's here, but only just, if you get my meaning. My wife is with him now. He's received the sacrament and has made his peace with God. Follow me. The others are keeping watch with him in their rooms. They're a bit unsettled but they'll revive when Gregory passes away.'

'How many residents are here?' asked Nicholas as he followed the warden down the room.

'We're ten at the moment; nine when Gregory leaves us,' his guide said.

'Are they all clerics?'

'Not all. They come here at the bishop's recommendation. Mostly they worked in Marchester cathedral in one way or another – workmen, vergers, gardeners, even, who have nowhere to go when they are too old to work. It's a good refuge for them in their old age.'

They had reached the end of the long room and the warden stopped in front of a door.

'This is the infirmary, sir. We have only two persons here at the moment, both on their way out of this world. It's good to die in company,' he added.

He opened the door and they went into a room where neatly made-up beds lined the sides. At the far end two beds were occupied by diminutive figures.

A woman sat by one of these beds and she looked up when they approached.

'Don't disturb yourself, wife,' said the warden. 'The bishop's sent Lord Nicholas Peverell to see Gregory. How is he?'

The woman peered down into the wizened face on the pillow.

'He's holding on. I think he can hear us.'

Nicholas approached the bed. Gregory lay very still, his body looking immensely frail under the blanket which covered him, his breathing as shallow as a ripple of air on a summer's day. Hanging above the bed from a nail attached to the wall was a black cloak together with a flat, black cap. The woman noticed his glance.

208

'That's his cap and cloak, sir. All the canons wore them. That's why they were called the black canons.'

Nicholas nodded. The Augustinian canons had once been a familiar sight in Sussex. The woman picked up the old man's hand which lay on the blanket. She stroked the claw-like fingers, as dry as sticks. The man opened his eyes and looked at her.

'Someone to speak to you, Gregory,' she said. 'Someone from the bishop.'

Gregory's eyes were clear and bright blue and he turned his head to look at Nicholas without any fear. The old man was approaching his Maker in confident certainty.

'Why have you come?' he whispered.

'The priory of Monksmere,' said Nicholas, bending down to bring his face closer to the old man's. 'Can you remember those last days? Cromwell's men came ...'

'God's curse on them,' said Gregory, a ripple of anger disturbing the serenity of his face. 'They took what they wanted but they'll not get away with it. God will punish them. You'll see.'

'What did they take?' said Nicholas, increasingly anxious that the effort of speaking would hasten the canon's death.

'Everything went – the bells, our precious chalice, the lead from the roof. They broke the statue of our lady when they ripped her off her plinth. They were the servants of Satan. He was there, all right, urging them on.'

He was getting more and more agitated, one of his claw-like hands fingering the crucifix round his neck. The woman looked anxiously at Nicholas.

'Best go now, sir. Gregory deserves a peaceful death. Don't excite him. No need to go back to the past. Those days are over now.'

But the old man was unstoppable. 'They took everything, even the blessed Templars' gift to us. Our crowning joy. Pilgrims once came to see it, sir, to kiss the feet of our blessed Lord.'

'He means the gold crucifix, sir,' said the warden. 'He's

209

always telling us about it. One of the local Templars, a crusader, who lived long ago, gave the crucifix, along with a solid gold salver, to the canons of Monksmere in return for their prayers for his soul and the souls of his family. The treasure was beyond price – solid gold it was, although I never saw it. Hush now, Gregory,' said the warden, looking down at the old man whose breathing was becoming very fast and shallow with the effort of talking.

'It's all over now. God will punish the bad men who took your priory's treasure. Leave it to Him. They will not be so peaceful as you when their time comes. You've got nothing on your conscience. Sleep now. God be with you. Come now, sir,' he said to Nicholas. 'Let him go in peace. It won't be long.'

Together, they walked back to the front door. 'I hope you are satisfied with your visit, sir. Please convey our best wishes to Bishop Humphrey and tell him that Canon Gregory has been given every comfort which money can provide. Tell him also that he is always welcome to visit us when he passes this way. It was good of him to think of us.'

Thanking the warden for his help and watched by the two old men who had not left their bench, Nicholas mounted his horse and rode back to Dean Peverell, using the northern road across the Downs.

The old man's revelation about the Templars' gold had surprised him but he could not see that it had any bearing on the case. He knew only too well that Cromwell's men had been ordered to seize all the valuable possessions of the monasteries and nunneries. No doubt the Templars' gold would have been melted down by now to furnish ships for Henry's wars. It would be interesting to find out how much the treasure was worth. He knew that the king had ordered Cromwell to see to it that his clerks meticulously recorded everything that had been taken from the religious houses. It would all be there in the records of the Court of Augmentations. He'd heard that the court's rooms were piled high with the loot. Something as valuable as a solid gold crucifix and salver would most certainly not have been overlooked. It would be easy enough to check when he next went to London. It would be an interesting diversion, that was all. It had nothing to do with the death of Sarah Bowman and the mole-catcher.

Back home, he found Peter and Dickon in the kitchen eating platefuls of cold meats. They had nothing to report. They had searched all the fields and ditches around Monksmere, and the beach at Atherington. No one had seen Eddy. No body had been found. They had to go back to Marchester that day but would resume the search the next day along the banks of the river and its estuary at Littlehaven.

There was also a letter from Thomas Cromwell. The messenger had not waited for a reply. That meant it was an order, Nicholas thought, cursing the man's arrogance.

Chapter Seventeen

Cromwell's letter was terse and to the point. He ordered Nicholas to meet him in his rooms in Westminster palace on the following day. Nicholas looked resignedly across at Jane.

'I'll leave tomorrow before dawn. Have some provisions put up for me, please. It will be a long, hard ride.'

Jane, used to these peremptory summons from London, nodded. But when she looked up at him, Nicholas saw fear in her eyes. He went to her and took her in his arms.

'Don't worry, my love. Harry is rested. I have good horses waiting for me at Merrow. With any luck the weather won't break for a few days.'

'I am not bothered about the journey, Nicholas. You are well used to that. But why does Cromwell want to see you so urgently?'

'It's probably about the king's impending visit. Only two weeks now. Cromwell was always a worrier. He can't trust anyone to do things properly.'

'I'm doing everything possible. The larders are stuffed with game, our stock farms are seething with animals waiting to grace the king's table.'

'I am sure he has no fears about us. It's Lord Gilbert he'll be worrying about, and with good reason. Unless Gilbert stirs himself soon, the king is going to be mightily disappointed. And when the king is put out it bodes ill for us.'

*

212

Nicholas left before daylight and arrived at Westminster just before dusk. He knew Cromwell used the old palace for the business of government as the king preferred his newly built palace at Whitehall for his own purposes. Most of the law courts were situated in the old palace including the Court of Augmentations where the business side of the dissolution of the monasteries was conducted. When Nicholas summoned the porter at the gatehouse of the old palace, he was told that a room had been prepared for him that night because Cromwell had left for the Tower. Nicholas was to join him there on the following day and a boat would be at his disposal. He should be prepared for an early start as the boatman would want to take advantage of the ebb tide.

Although it was late in the afternoon, some of the courts were still functioning. The clerks of the Court of Augmentations would still be at work as there was much to do. Nicholas knew the man in charge of the court – Sir Geoffrey Lancaster, one of Cromwell's minions – and, after leaving his horse to be fed and watered, ready for the return journey, he walked through the warren of narrow streets and buildings to where the court operated.

He found there that work was very much in evidence. Wagonloads of furniture were still arriving from the country and several were waiting to be unloaded in the courtyard. It was a sad sight to see the stacks of chairs and benches and forlorn piles of wooden crosses and statues, some already damaged beyond repair. Nicholas had heard that the royal coffers had been replenished many times by the sale of church furnishings and he remembered how the men had come to his priory and stripped the lead from the church roof and taken away three of the bells to be melted down for cannons in the Royal Arsenal at Woolwich. He had managed to save two of the bells and some of the church plate but most of it had been carted away to this place to be counted, recorded and made ready for sale.

He picked his way through the piles of goods and went

213

into the room where Sir Geoffrey was sitting at his desk surrounded by parchment rolls, giving orders to several clerks at once. Although it looked as if everything was in a state of confusion, Nicholas knew that Sir Geoffrey would have it well under control. He was a small, brisk man, bursting with energy which seemed inexhaustible. He jumped up when Nicholas entered.

'Lord Nicholas, it's good to see you. What can I do for you?'

'Do you hold the records of all the religious houses here, Geoffrey?'

'We certainly shall one day, but we are well behind with the work now. Those idle abbots and priors accumulated so much wealth over the years that we shall soon need to take over more storerooms. But which particular religious house are you interested in, my lord?'

'It's a small priory in Sussex – Monksmere. A community of Augustinian canons lived there and I would be grateful to see the records of the house, if they are available.'

'I will do my best to find them. We are in the process of building a library for all the records but, of course, nothing is yet in place. As it happens, Monksmere was one of the first of the religious houses to be closed so it should not be too difficult to find those particular records. The larger and richer houses are taking a lot longer to sort out. Leave it with me and I will get someone to search out the document. When will you be needing it?'

'Today, if possible. I am staying in a room in Lord Cromwell's apartments and if someone could bring it over, I should be grateful. I shall, of course, see that it is returned before I leave tomorrow. I only need to look at it, that's all.'

'I'll get someone to attend to it straight away.'

Thanking Geoffrey, Nicholas returned to the main building. He was taken to his room, water was provided and, later, a meal delivered. Much later, a knock on the door

214

aroused him. He opened it and found a clerk standing there clutching a parchment roll.

'You asked to see this, sir?'

Nicholas thanked him, took the roll over to the table which he had been provided with, and spread it out.

It was all there, lists of the priory's possessions, everything from the bells to the lead from the roof, the altar frontals and 'two embroidered chasubles worn by the priests at the altar'. There was mention of two small chalices, a silver cross, a silver pyx which once held the consecrated wafers, but no record of a gold cross or salver. The most valuable possessions of the priory, the Templars' gold, were not mentioned.

For a long time Nicholas sat there staring down at the list of goods, then he rolled up the document and went back to Geoffrey Lancaster's room where clerks were still busy working by the light of candles. He handed the roll to the chief clerk and asked for a copy to be made of the list of goods and said he would collect it on his way home the next day.

He returned to his room deep in thought. If the Templars' gold had not been recorded, then it would appear that someone had stolen it. If that were the case, he thought, the treasure was too important, too conspicuous for one of the Augmentation clerks to steal. The men who carted the goods away from the priory would never have dared. Only a powerful man, above suspicion, would take that risk. Was it possible . . .? Was this the clue he had been searching for?

Cromwell was sitting at his desk when Nicholas was ushered into his room in the Tower. He was dressed in his usual sober black gown and cap, preferring the garb of the clerk to the fashionable finery of a courtier. He greeted Nicholas with his customary affability.

'Lord Nicholas, I trust you slept well and my servants looked after you properly.'

215

'Thank you, Lord Cromwell, I appreciate your concern for my well-being.'

'Good, good,' he said, getting up and walking over to the window which looked down to Tower Hill and the streets of the city of London. 'Come over here. He looked back at Nicholas. 'I am just about to see the completion of my work here for the time being. The last of the traitors leave the Tower at any moment. We can watch them set out on their final journey, to Tyburn.'

Nicholas joined Cromwell at the window. Looking down, he saw a large crowd had gathered by the postern gate which gave access to the city. The crowd was silent; men in their working clothes, women with babes in arms, all waiting expectantly.

'Who are the unlucky fellows?' said Nicholas, who hated these spectacles.

'Traitors, my lord. The remnants of those ill-advised men who took up arms against his majesty two years ago. They called themselves pilgrims and marched against the king, defying the royal policy of closing down the religious houses. They wanted them to remain as they were, centres of popery and superstition. The lords Suffolk and Norfolk disposed of most of these rebels; their leader, Robert Aske was executed last year. Unfortunately, one of the ringleaders, Sir Ralph Ingleby fled the country along with a handful of miscreants, but a few did not get away and were rounded up. They have been interrogated and now they go to see the executioner at Tyburn. Ah, here they come!'

The crowd had seen the gate open and began to scream obscenities at the pitiful procession which emerged into the street. There were four men, dressed in rags, emaciated by their long confinement in the Tower, their limbs broken on the rack, tied to hurdles drawn by horses. They were accompanied by guards who urged the horses on swiftly in order to escape the attentions of the crowd who were surging forward to throw offal and stones at the unfortunates. Nicholas walked away.

216

'A terrible punishment. No man deserves that. Why not a swift execution here in the Tower if the law requires it?'

'You talk rubbish, my lord. These men took up arms against the king and his government. What more do you want to be convinced of their treason?'

'They fought for what they believed in. Many people were sorry to see the monks go.'

'Yes, but they didn't march on London carrying weapons. You cannot be soft in this business of government. The safety of the king's realm depends on a firm response to armed rebellion. But come, sit down. Help yourself to some refreshment and let me tell you what I require of you.'

Over the ale and cheese Cromwell came straight to the point.

'The lord of Tredgosse, Lord Nicholas. I want him arrested before the king comes to your part of Sussex.'

Nicholas carefully put down his tankard and stared at Cromwell in amazement.

'On what charge, my lord?'

'Whatever charge you like. You see, I have been informed that Lord Gilbert shows a total indifference to the king's visit. He has made no preparations and has talked unwisely about the king having to put up with what is available. The woman who lives with him, I understand, is not prepared to give the necessary orders to ensure that the king and his retinue are comfortable when they stay there.'

'I agree he is a bit tardy with his preparations, but that is hardly a criminal offence, and much can be done in two weeks if he sets his mind to it.'

'We cannot take the risk, as I see it. You know as well as I do that if the king is displeased it will not be just Lord Gilbert who will suffer.'

'We cannot be blamed for the incompetence of others.'

'Oh we can, Lord Nicholas, we can. You, in particular, will be blamed because you have been put in charge of the arrangements. Now, let us see what we have to do to

217

prevent Lord Gilbert upsetting his majesty. If we arrest him and bring him here, then he is out of our way and the king will not be able to stay at his castle.'

'And his castle stands the risk of becoming forfeit.'

'Quite so. You would be given the stewardship, I think.'

'And his son? And the woman he lives with? And her son?'

'The legitimate son would be made a royal ward. The woman and her son would be turned out and she could return to her old haunts here, in London. That's where she came from, I understand, until Southampton made her his whore and sold her to Tredgosse.'

Nicholas was stunned into silence. He was amazed at the extent of Cromwell's knowledge about other people's private lives. He was also horrified by the callousness of Cromwell's methods of finding solutions to inconvenient problems.

'There is one difficulty which you seem to have over-looked, Lord Cromwell,' he said quietly. 'I cannot arrest a man who has done nothing. And the sheriff, I know, would also object.'

'Oh, why must you be so contentious? It is in the king's interest that Tredgosse disappears for the duration of his visit. It is also in your interest to save yourself from the charge of mismanagement of the arrangements.'

'And in your interest, too, I think. You have overall responsibility for the king's well-being. But I cannot invent a charge just to get someone put out of the way because his presence will be an inconvenience to us. Do you want him to share the fate of those unfortunates which we have just seen setting out on their last journey? And is this to be my fate if I displease the king? And yours, if the king tires of you?'

Nicholas saw that his shot had gone home. Cromwell visibly winced and turned away. He knew the consequences if he fell foul of the royal favour, Nicholas thought. How fragile was the bond that tied a servant to his royal master!

'We must take care not to fail his majesty. He cannot tolerate incompetence,' said Cromwell. 'But come now,' he continued, making an effort to recover his composure. 'You must see to it that Lord Gilbert is charged with a serious crime. You can think up something, you and your friend, the Sheriff of Marchester. Look into his affairs, you've got time. Something might emerge from his past. He might have said something unwise and been overheard. Find that person and persuade him to bring evidence against him. Invent that person if you have to. Bribe someone. You know the form, surely, or do I have to teach you your job? I want the lord of Tredgosse brought here before the king sets out for Sussex. Is that not clear? Do not fail me on this matter, my lord.'

The tide had turned. The boatman was waiting. Nicholas's dismissal was as peremptory as his summons. As the boat bore him back to Westminster Nicholas pondered how on earth he was to confront Lord Gilbert with a totally trumped-up charge. He could not do it. Unlawful arrest was against all the principles of justice. Had the barons who had opposed King John in a previous century forced him to sign the Great Charter in vain? This was England, not the land of the Sultan of Constantinople.

But the fact remained. If he did not do what Cromwell had commanded him to do, what would be his fate? He, too, could follow those miserable wretches along the road to Tyburn. And Jane? And their child which she was carrying? The prospect was too dreadful to contemplate and he cursed the day when he had become the servant of such a king and his unscrupulous henchman.

He collected the copy of the Monksmere roll and rode home by the light of a full harvest moon. Harry was waiting for him at Merrow well rested and eager to get home. It was Friday morning when he reached Dean Peverell. Friday, the twelfth of September. Eleven days to go before the king's visit.

Chapter Eighteen

On Monday evening, after Lord Gilbert had left, Adeliza, angry and in pain because the hunting whip had cut deep into her cheek, summoned her maid, Dora, to tend her. Dora was the only person in the world whom Adeliza trusted. She had been her constant companion ever since she had worked in the brothels of Southwark. Dora had comforted her when men abused her, nursed her when she was sick. She had experienced worse things, she thought ruefully, than the lash of a hunting whip across her face. The rewards, however, had been good and Dora had shared them with her.

Dora entered the room and exclaimed in horror at her mistress's appearance. She went over to the bed and stroked the glossy strands of hair back from the bloody wheal across Adeliza's face. She had seen her mistress suffer all the humiliations which men could inflict on her but she had never expected Lord Gilbert to treat her like this. Her plump, craggy face gazed down at Adeliza in pity which gave way to a surge of anger that he could do such a thing.

'What happened?' she asked, still stroking her mistress's face.

'Fetch clean water, Dora,' said Adeliza, 'and some of that ointment we have which heals wounds so quickly. And bring me a phial of the opiate I gave you. It will help to ease the pain. And then, come and stay with me tonight. I do not want Lord Gilbert near me.'

'He shall never harm you again, madam. I shall see to that. He doesn't know that I am expert in wielding a knife. I shall stay here until this dreadful wound heals and you feel strong again.'

That night they slept soundly until, in the early hours of Tuesday morning, Adeliza woke up. The curtains had been left open as usual, because Adeliza was afraid of the dark, and the moonlight was streaming across her bed. The opiate had worn off and she felt refreshed by the deep sleep. She looked affectionately at Dora, lying fully dressed beside her, sleeping soundly, as she always did. She leaned over and stroked Dora's plain, work-worn face, relaxed in sleep. It was the closest she had ever been to another person. Dora had been a mother to her, a friend and protector. At her touch, Dora woke up.

'What is it, Alice?' she said, reverting to Adeliza's former name in the haziness of sleep.

'Time to move on, Dora.'

'Thank God for that. I cannot abide this place. I hate its master and I hate that twisted wreck of a human being he calls his son – twisted in body and twisted in mind – that's my opinion. Shall we be taking Justin with us?'

'Of course. I cannot leave him here, although Gilbert is his father.'

'How are we going to live? Will you look for another protector?'

'Never again,' said Adeliza emphatically. 'We have no more need of protectors. Lord Gilbert and the Earl have paid me well for my services, as they should. They like to see me decked out in the jewels which they have provided. I have enough precious stones to last us for the rest of our lives. We shall go to London and you could make wonderful clothes for rich women and I would see to the buying of the cloth and sending out the accounts. We shall prosper, you'll see.'

221

'And Justin?' said Dora. 'Do you want him to grow up running a clothing business?'

'He will become a rich merchant,' said Adeliza impatiently. 'He will become head of the guild of clothiers and drive in state with the lord mayor, and I shall be by his side. We shall buy a big house in Cheapside and own a carriage and I shall never again submit to a man's embrace.'

'Alice, madam,' said Dora, scarcely able to control her excitement, 'it is possible, isn't it? You own so much jewellery, your clothes alone are worth a fortune.'

'I have kept everything given to me. I have earned it. I shall sell it all without any regret if it will rid me of men and their brutish behaviour. And there is something else, Dora, something I cannot tell you in detail otherwise you will be in danger. It concerns Lord Gilbert and that little incident at Monksmere Priory I mentioned the other day. Gilbert was involved; not as much as the others, but involved more than enough to send him to the gallows. If I offered this information to the Sheriff of Marchester, or Lord Nicholas Peverell, that would be the end of Lord Gilbert. I would be well rewarded. But it carries a risk. Lord Gilbert would want revenge and, even under arrest, he would pay others to seek me out and put paid to us both. But when the time comes and I know we shall be safe, I will denounce him.'

'When do we leave?'

'This moon will light us on our way tomorrow night. But now we must rest. Give me some more of that cordial and take a sip yourself and we shall sleep soundly. Tomorrow, ask Annie to prepare Justin for the journey. Now sleep, dear Dora. Tomorrow we shall set out to conquer the world.'

The opiate did its work and the two women slept soundly until the moon's light gave way to the sun's.

On that Tuesday morning, Lord Gilbert breakfasted with his son, Marcus. Justin always stayed in the nursery with his maid until Lord Gilbert or Adeliza sent for him. Marcus ate his bread and picked the flesh of his chicken wing with fastidious precision as he hated the feel of grease on his fingers. Lord Gilbert looked up from his plateful of cold beef and watched his son.

'What are you thinking about, Marcus?' he said.

'Only about what needs to be done, Father.'

'You mean for the king's visit? Damn and blast him! And now Adeliza is going to play the invalid.'

'Yes, we shall have to turn our minds to planning King Henry's visit, but we can leave that for the time being. First of all we must consider the problem of Adeliza. You know, don't you, that she will have to go. She knows too much, and now that you have insulted her, she will want revenge. You'll see. Woman always do when they are mistreated.'

Gilbert stared at his son in amazement. Who would have thought that the poor, twisted boy could possess such wisdom?

'What do you think she will do?'

'Why, run away, of course, with her brat and that great lump of a servant. She will survive. She has much jewellery.'

'Then we must let her go, eh? You and I will then have this place to ourselves.'

Marcus sighed and put his knife down carefully by the side of his plate. 'Sometimes, Father, I think you don't deserve to be lord of Tredgosse castle. Where do you think Adeliza will go? To London, of course. There she will see Cromwell who will be delighted to receive her. He wants you out of the way because you know too much. Adeliza will betray us all and tell him everything. Lord Nicholas Peverell and the sheriff will come here to arrest you and you will be despatched to the Tower and the executioner's block. And what will happen to me? The son of a traitor? A useless hunchback.'

'She wouldn't dare. No one would believe her. Cromwell would not give her an audience.'

'Oh yes he would, as soon as he knows who she is. A wronged woman makes a good witness. She has everything to gain. Lord Nicholas might want more evidence – he's too scrupulous by far – but not Cromwell. Now, let me tell you what we must do. I shall order the grooms to saddle up Robin and I shall go riding in the woods this morning. The two women are still asleep, I gather. I think you need more of that medicine which eases painful throats and helps to reduce fever, especially as winter is coming and the dampness from the river will increase. Let me go and order you some more from Eva the witch.'

'And whilst you are there?' said Lord Gilbert quietly.

'She has a good crop of mushrooms this year and we are very fond of mushroom soup, aren't we, Father. Also I know she has several toadstools which she calls the destroying angel and I am never allowed to touch them when I visit her. Adeliza will be ready for food today. We can see that she eats well so that she can build up her strength. But you must treat her gently this morning, Father. When she wakes up, go to her and say you are sorry that you lost your temper. Tell her to rest and we will send up some food. With any luck she will not wake up until midday as I know she has taken some of the opiate.'

'Marcus, how do you know such things? You are a worthy son and heir. Your mind is as astute as that of a person twice your age. Where do you get all these ideas? You have no friends. You don't talk to the servants.'

'You are right, Father. I have no friends. No one wants to talk to a boy with a twisted back. I have sometimes seen you, Father – yes, even you – look at me with sorrow in your eyes, and sometimes there is hatred and bitterness as well. But there is nothing wrong with my mind, nor my eyes, nor my ears. So I observe, I listen. I heard you talking to the prior. I saw the boats. I saw you hand over gold.'

'Damn you, Marcus, are you, too, going to sell me to Lord Nicholas?'

'Oh no, Father, I shall never do that. You are the lord of this castle and I am your heir, aren't I?'

'Of course you are. Never doubt it. We are in this together.'

Marcus left his father and went to the stables where his horse, Robin, was waiting for him. As usual he was delighted to see his master. He breathed softly into his hand and nuzzled his face. Marcus loved Robin more than any other living creature. The little horse did not see his deformity. He only saw him, Marcus, his friend and protector.

Marcus rode up to the woods to the north of the castle and he found Eva near her cottage gathering sticks for her fire. She was pleased to see him because a visit from Marcus always meant a commission from his father, who paid her well. He ordered the medicine and said there was no hurry for it. He would return and collect it later before the winter storms set in. This morning, he said, he wanted to ride further afield, making the most of the last of the summer weather. She wished him a good day, and watched him ride off. Then she left her sticks by the front door of her cottage and went back into the woods to gather more and to look out for any plant that might be of use to her.

Marcus rode a short way until the cottage was out of sight. Then he dismounted, tethered Robin to a tree near some fresh grass, and returned the way he'd come. He walked quickly back to Eva's cottage, taking care to keep to the shade of the trees and to avoid treading on any dry twigs that might give him away. When he saw the cottage he made sure that Eva was not around. Then, quickly, he went to the patch of mushrooms and toadstools and saw what he wanted. Making sure his riding gauntlets covered not only his hands, but also his wrists and lower arms, he stooped down and picked a handful of the delicate white toadstools with the lacy collars round their fragile stalks. These he carefully put in a leather bag he wore round his

225

waist and returned to where he had left Robin. Quickly he rode back to the castle.

Adeliza and Dora slept on that morning until the sun was overhead. It was the sound of someone knocking on the door which roused them. Dora slipped off the bed, patted her hair into place, and unlocked the door. A servant stood there with a tray of wine and warm honey cakes.

'Lord Gilbert sent these,' he said, 'and hopes the lady Adeliza is feeling better.'

Dora took the tray and carried it over to the bed where Adeliza was sitting up and yawning.

'What a surprise! Lord Gilbert is being considerate, for once. I wonder what he wants. Lord, I am so hungry, Dora, I could eat every one of these cakes. Leave me to gorge myself and you go to see Annie and tell her to get Justin ready for tonight. Then you eat as big a breakfast as you can. We shall need all our strength for the journey. Make sure the horses will be ready. We shall need two. Justin can ride up with you on your palfrey.'

The cakes were rich and filling, the wine refreshing. Adeliza finished the plateful. Then, feeling strangely heavy, she lay back on her pillows and dozed until Dora returned.

All day Adeliza tried to rest, but her body felt ill-at-ease and her mind confused. Dora came to see her and tried to rouse her. She had packed a basket of provisions for the journey and Annie had assured her that Justin would be ready for the night journey. Adeliza felt too weary to pay much attention to what Dora was saying. It was all she could do to indicate where she kept her box of jewels and told Dora to see to it that it was packed away with her clothes. Dora began to feel uneasy. This was not like the Alice she knew, always planning the next move, always in control. Now she seemed passive and indifferent to the imminence of their departure.

226

As the afternoon wore on Adeliza began to feel very sick. She closed her eyes, willing her body to remain calm, but the pain started around five o'clock, a pain so sharp that she gasped and called out for Dora. But Dora had gone to the stables to check on the horses.

At half past five, Adeliza began to vomit, a vile, evil-smelling substance that almost filled the chamber pot. She called out again for Dora to come and help her because her bowels were churning and she did not think she could get to the commode in time. It was here that Dora found her at last, too weak to get back into bed. Alarmed, Dora almost carried her back to bed, and ran to fetch water to wash her face and towels to mop up the vomit on the bedclothes.

Adeliza lay back, trying to fight the pain which now racked her body. When Dora returned, she vomited again, the sweat pouring down her face with the effort, her legs drawn up in agony.

'Madam, what is it? What has brought this on? What have you been eating this afternoon?'

'I've eaten nothing,' gasped Adeliza, 'nothing since the honey cakes at noon. And water, of course. Just water, not the opiate.'

Soon she became too weak to leave the bed, but the retching went on and the agonising cramps in her bowels made her gasp in agony. Dora knew then that they would not leave the castle that night. Maybe, she thought, they might never leave it at all.

Leaving Adeliza to rest between the cramping pains, Dora went to the stables to cancel the horses and then went to the kitchen where Maud, the cook, was preparing supper for Lord Gilbert and Marcus.

'The cakes,' said Dora urgently. 'The ones you made this morning and sent up to the mistress. Are there any left?'

'Your mistress ate the whole of the first batch,' said Maud, looking up from the pie she was about to put in the oven. 'As she seemed to like them so much, I made another

227

batch. Here they are. Just a few left because Master Justin also likes them. I'll warm the rest of them up for your mistress's breakfast as I hear she's not well.'

'She'll not be eating honey cakes tomorrow. She's that sick that nothing will stay down.'

'Well, it's nothing to do with my cakes,' said Maud indignantly. 'Here, you try one. Master Justin's been eating them all day.'

Dora took one, sniffed it gingerly, and ate it. Nothing happened. It was, indeed, delicious.

'Maud, did anyone come into the kitchen whilst you were making the first batch?' Dora said.

'Only young Marcus popped his head round the door to see what I was cooking. He'd been out riding in the woods and was mighty hungry. He likes my kitchen, does young Marcus. He says it's the best room in the castle.'

'Did he stay long?'

'No, not that I can remember. He took a sniff at my cake mixture and said he'd come back later when they were cooked. Then the soup I was making began to boil over and I had to go and see to it. When I came back to my cake-making, Marcus had gone. I then put the cakes in the oven and, when they were ready, Lord Gilbert told me to send them up to your mistress.'

Deep in thought, Dora went back to Adeliza who had sunk into a torpor from which Dora tried in vain to rouse her.

That night, in between prolonged bouts of retching during which her body tried vainly to expel any vestiges of food, Adeliza's head cleared from its confusion. She turned her head to look at Dora who had curled up on her bed and had fallen asleep.

'Dora,' Adeliza whispered.

Instantly Dora woke up. 'What is it, Alice?' she said.

'If I don't survive this sickness, and I feel I shall not, look after Justin. Take him somewhere safe – to Jane

228

Peverell's house would be best, she'll know what to do. I fear this sickness of mine is Lord Gilbert's doing. When I am out of the way, he and Marcus will want rid of Justin. Marcus is clever, cleverer than his years. And there is a darkness about him. He would stop at nothing to make sure he inherits this place. Justin was always a threat to him because he is strong and healthy and his father might well prefer him over the sickly Marcus.'

'Hush, my dear Alice, don't talk like this. You are not going to die. You have had a bad upset of the stomach, that's all. Sleep will cure you, just you see. Lord Gilbert will be delighted when I bring him the news that you are better. He is most concerned about you.'

'Lord Gilbert will not welcome the news, Dora. He's only been to see me twice since I've been ill and the last time he left in a hurry because he said he can't abide sickrooms.'

'Men!' said Dora. 'They are all like that. Just you wait and see what a fuss he'll make when he gets ill.'

The griping pains began to tear at Adeliza's body again and she could not summon up the energy to speak. This time her bowels moved violently and she could not get to the commode. Sobbing with pain and disgust, she allowed Dora to clean her body and change the bedclothes.

All next day, Adeliza writhed in the grip of the waves of pain that tore at her body. She had no strength now to sit up and she lay curled up on her side, retching into the dish which Dora had placed there. The flesh seemed to be dropping away from her body, and her skin, once the colour and texture of a ripe peach, took on a hideous yellow hue and her breath smelled foul. Still the pain racked her body as she grew weaker and weaker.

As dawn broke, Dora knew she had to get help. There was only one person she knew she could trust, not the witch Eva who never came to a sick bed, but Jane Peverell, who was reputed to have a knowledge of healing and knew which herbs to prescribe.

229

Seeing that Adeliza had sunk once more into a torpor she slipped out of the room, down to the stables where a groom was just rubbing the sleep from his eyes. She asked him to saddle up her comfortable palfrey which had been given to her for her own use when she went to markets. The groom grumbled at the early start but fetched the horse and helped Dora up onto its broad back. As the sky grew brighter, Dora rode off to find Jane Peverell.

Jane was working in the kithen with her cook, Mary. She now had to organise a large number of extra servants they had been forced to hire to help prepare for the king's visit. She was surprised when one of these servants announced the arrival of 'a person called Dora who's ridden all the way from the castle of Tredgosse'. Wondering why she had come and who had sent her, Jane followed the servant into the great hall where Dora was standing uneasily by the fire.

'My lady, forgive me for disturbing you, but my mistress is very sick, sick nigh unto death, I think, and I've heard you can do wonderful things with your potions so I wondered if you could give me something to help her. The pain is so dreadful,' Dora blurted out.

'Where is the pain?' Jane asked.

'All over, my lady, and the sickness is terrible. She can keep nothing down and her strength is going. Please help me.'

Jane thought for a moment. She could help ease the pain but she would have to see the patient before she could prescribe any medicine. She hesitated for only a moment.

'I'll come and see her myself. Wait here whilst I send for my cloak and a phial of opiate. I hope we shall be in time. I shall go and make ready my horse.'

Jane's horse, Melissa, was a thoroughbred Arab mare, strong and sure-footed. Matching her pace to Dora's palfrey, they rode back along the coast road to Tredgosse Castle.

*

When they arrived, Dora took Jane up to Adeliza's room, using a back entrance and staircase, only used by the servants. When Dora opened the door of the sickroom, Adeliza had not moved. Her body looked as small and as fragile as a child's and her skin had turned a dark yellow. Gone was the lovely woman Dora had cherished. All that was left now was this skeleton covered with parchment-like skin. Jane breathed in the stench of the sickroom and went over to the bed. She looked at the yellow vomit in the basin by the sick woman's head and bent low over Adeliza to smell her breath.

'There is something extraordinary here,' said Jane, straightening up. 'The smell is very distinctive. I think she has been poisoned. What has she been eating?'

'Nothing since Tuesday morning,' said Dora, 'and then just some honey cakes. Later, I put a few drops of opiate in some water and she drank that, but soon she couldn't keep that down.'

'Show me the opiate,' said Jane.

Dora produced the phial which contained a few drops of the heavy, brown liquid. Jane took the stopper out and sniffed it.

'That's quite safe unless you gave her too much. Even so, it would not have this effect on her. The poppies make you sleep, that's all. Who gave you this mixture?'

'The master gets it from Eva, the old witch who lives up in the woods. She knows about these things, but I don't trust her. She's just as likely to put a curse on you as cure you and she never comes to sickrooms.'

Jane nodded. 'I know Eva. She is a friend of mine – a very wise woman. Has anyone been to see her lately?'

'Only Marcus, Lord Gilbert's son and heir. He went to order a potion to ease painful throats. That was on Tuesday when he went to see her, though why the master wanted more of that particular potion, I don't know. We've a shelf full of the stuff and no one's complained of a cough.'

'You say your mistress ate some honey cakes on Tuesday. What time was that?'

'It was noon, my lady. We both stayed asleep a long time and when she woke up she ate the honey cakes and drank some of the wine which the master sent up to her.'

'And did you eat any of the cakes?'

'Not from that particular batch. I tried one that the cook made later and I am all right, as you can see.'

'Then I must go and see Eva immediately. Let your mistress have more of the opiate if she can take it. You might have to force some down her throat, but it will ease the pain. I fear she is very sick. The colour of her skin, her weakness, indicate that her liver is affected and when that happens there is nothing I can do. I'll try to be as quick as I can.'

It had been a long time since Jane had visited Eva to consult her about a remedy for her father's illness. She had the greatest repect for the old woman, knowing that her knowledge of herbs and plants far exceeded her own. She didn't believe Eva was a witch. She knew only too well how easily a skill in healing could be interpreted as magic and therefore the work of the Devil.

Eva was preparing her midday meal when Jane arrived. She was offered blackcurrant wine and some goat's cheese and they sat down at the table and ate together in a comfortable silence. Eva, Jane knew, liked to take her time. Finally, Eva asked her what she had come for and Jane told her about Adeliza.

'Is she very weak?' Eva asked.

'I doubt she will see the sun set today.'

'And what do you think ails her?'

'It looks as if something has poisoned her; some deadly poison which is breaking down her body. The smell is extraordinary, pungent, earthy, like nothing I have experienced before. Now I heard that Marcus came here on Tuesday morning to order a syrup to ease the sore throats of winter. Dora, Adeliza's maid told me. What did you give him, Eva?'

'Yes, Marcus did come to see me and I agreed to make up the usual syrup with the addition of a mild sedative. It's the one Lord Gilbert always buys from me in the autumn. It is quite harmless. I have it ready for him when he wants to collect it.'

'Yet Dora tells me that no one in the household is ill at the moment. Did Marcus want anything else?'

'No, only the syrup. Lord Gilbert probably wanted to build up a stock for the winter. It keeps well. Marcus didn't stay long. I went off to collect wood and he rode away.'

'Did you see him leave?'

'Yes. He rode up into the woods on that little horse of his and was soon out of sight.'

'I wonder ...' said Jane thoughtfully. 'Could he have come back after you had gone? Have you anything deadly poisonous here that he could have taken and then slipped it into Adeliza's food?'

'But, my dear, why should he want to kill his step-mother?'

'I don't know. Maybe he was jealous of Adeliza's son, the boy Justin, and feared lest his father should make him his heir. Or he could have been acting under his father's instructions.'

'I thought Lord Gilbert loved his mistress.'

'Maybe he does, or did, but things might have changed. There are so many things we don't know.'

'Yes indeed, and it's best to leave well alone. But I can guarantee that this particular cordial we are drinking is quite safe and will do that child you are carrying a lot of good.'

'So you know I am with child?'

'It doesn't require the wisdom of Solomon to know when a woman is entering motherhood. I am sure you will produce a bonny child and when your time comes I will send something to relieve the pangs of childbirth. Make sure that you don't put yourself into any danger when riding that beautiful horse of yours. Try to keep her from

233

jumping over too many fallen logs!'

'I'll see she behaves like a docile palfrey. But, Eva, what do you know about Marcus? I would value your opinion. You understand people so well even though you live alone in these woods.'

'People come to see me for all manner of reasons. I get a good insight into human nature from what they tell me. But, as to Marcus, he's a strange boy, not happy, of course, though why would he be with that twisted body of his and the other child so straight and handsome. But he's got a good brain, has Marcus, and he's curious. He comes to see me sometimes just to talk about plants. He was fascinated by the crop of mushrooms I've got this year. There are toadstools amongst them so I told him not to touch them.'

Jane felt her heart give a sudden lurch. 'Show me the toadstools, Eva. He could have ridden back for them when you went off into the woods.'

Eva took Jane round to the back of her hut to the spot under the tree where the mushrooms and toadstools were growing in profusion. Suddenly, Eva gave a cry and ran forward.

'They've gone. Look here. Most of them are gone, the rest just pushed around. Someone has stolen my white angels!'

'Do you mean the destroying angels?' said Jane quietly.

'Yes, yes, beautiful but quite deadly. Do you think . . .?'

'It's possible but we have no proof. What is the antidote, Eva?'

Eva stood up and turned and faced Jane. 'There is no antidote, my dear. All you can do is to pray for a speedy death. How long has she been ill?'

'If she was given the destroying angel on Tuesday at midday – her maid says they slept late that morning – then this is the third day.'

'She will, as you said, be dead by sunset. All I can do is to give you something to ease her passing. This is a wicked

234

thing someone has done. However, I cannot say for certain that it was Marcus who stole these angels of mine.'

'But whoever did this must be caught and punished. Adeliza is enduring a prolonged and terrible death. I must get back to her.'

Leaving Eva standing in the midst of her ravaged patch of toadstools, a look of horror still on her face, Jane rode back to the castle where Dora was waiting for her. One look at the maid's face told Jane that she was too late.

'She's gone, madam. My lovely mistress is gone and there's nothing you can do now. At least she's at peace at last. Her death was terrible to watch.'

Jane dismounted and went across to comfort the maid. When she had calmed down a little, Jane looked at her closely.

'And what does Lord Gilbert say about all this?'

'Nothing, madam, nothing at all, except to say that we must bury her quickly because he can't abide the smell. He's a monster that one. I knew no good would come of her coming to live here. Now I must go to my mistress and lay her out properly. It's the least I can do for her.'

'And what will you do, Dora? After the funeral is over?'

'I shall leave this place immediately and take Justin with me. I promised my lady I would do that for her. The poor soul knew that there was no remedy for her sickness.'

'Come to us, if you wish. There would be a place for you at Dean Peverell.'

'Thank you, madam. It would be good to help with a new baby again.'

Jane gave a wry smile. It seemed the whole world knew she was with child.

'Then come as soon as you can get away. This death will not be unavenged, Dora. My husband comes back from London any time now and he will see to it that the culprit is caught. You will next see him with the sheriff, I think.'

'Thank God you came, my lady. This is an accursed place.'

235

Jane rode home wondering where Nicholas had got to. He should be back here where events were moving fast, not cavorting around with the king's courtiers!

Night fell and Marcus sat with Justin in his room trying to soothe the little boy who could not take in the fact that his mother had been taken from him.

'Hush Justin,' said Marcus, 'she's in heaven now, along with the angels. She's safe and at peace and will be looking down on us.'

'I can't see her, though,' sobbed the boy. 'Which star is she sitting on, do you think? Can I see it?'

'Of course you can. Come, let's go to the top of the tower and look up at the sky and I'll show you where she is.'

Justin stopped crying and began to smile. He jumped up excitedly, taking hold of Marcus's hand.

'Can I say goodbye to Mother's body before I see her soul, Marcus? You said my new Mother is up in heaven, but I still love the old one who is asleep in her room.'

'We'll see her later. Dora is with her now making her look beautiful for her funeral. Now come and see where your new mother is.'

Marcus led the way through the great hall where the candlelight threw shadows on the walls. He picked up one of the thick candles and opened the door to the tower.

'Come,' he said, 'follow me. Don't be afraid. I will light the way.'

Obediently, Justin climbed the spiral staircase after his stepbrother. When they reached the top of the stairs, they went out onto the flat roof at the top of the tower and Marcus pointed out the stars and showed him the bright one where his mother was sitting.

'Can you see her?' he whispered. 'Look how the star flickers. She's waving to you and telling you not to be afraid.'

Justin looked and smiled and began to cry quietly. Then

236

he waved to the star and Marcus took hold of his hand and led him back to the staircase.

'There, now you can sleep peacefully. She'll watch over you tonight. You go first and I'll hold the candle up so that you can see where you put your feet.'

The little boy stepped down onto the first step of the stone staircase. Then the second. Marcus came up behind. With one push, Marcus sent Justin tumbling headfirst down the spiral staircase. He stood there listening to the boy's scream, the sound of his body bouncing off the walls of the staircase. Then a thud. At last, silence. Marcus ran down and looked at the body crumpled on the stone floor at the bottom of the stairs. Justin's head was lying at a curious angle, and Marcus checked that he was dead.

He went to his father's room where Lord Gilbert was waiting for him.

'Justin has had an accident,' Marcus said. 'He's fallen down the tower steps. We can bury him with her tomorrow.'

Lord Gilbert looked at his son in admiration. 'Then it will be you and I together from now on; and you will be my most worthy heir.'

Chapter Nineteen

Eddy stared at the smouldering kiln, waiting for the next puff of smoke to appear from a vent in its wall. Luke and Jude were working hard now with winter approaching and the demand for charcoal increasing. It was very quiet, just the faint chatter of the wood pigeons nesting in the oak tree above him. He glanced round. He was on his own; all the others were up in the woods collecting wood to feed the insatiable kiln. He was in charge now and Jude had given him strict instructions what to do. He was to block up all the vents and keep the wood burning at the slow temperature required to turn wood into charcoal. Too much air going into the kiln would burn the wood up too quickly and then he would be in real trouble.

He felt a sudden sympathy with the kiln. He, too, was smouldering with pent-up rage which he could not stamp out however hard he tried. The image of Lord Gilbert's huntsmen contemptuously kicking over the kiln and the piles of wood which he and Jude had so carefully built up still haunted his mind. What right had anyone to destroy someone's livelihood? He remembered vividly how the men had stamped out Alison's fire and overturned her cooking pot which they had tossed about as if it was worthless. What did they care, he thought savagely as he stuffed some grass into the tiny hole which had suddenly appeared in the side of the kiln, that the pot contained a whole day's food for the four of them? And of all people, he thought, Lord Gilbert should be the last one to make enemies. He was soon going to need all the friends he could find. Not that he had any friends. Everyone hated him and his whore and his evil, twisted son, Marcus, who might look innocent enough, but he, Eddy, knew he was capable of every sort of wickedness. He remembered how he had once seen him put a harmless, domestic cat in a sack, hoist him up to hang from a branch of a tree and then poke it with sharp sticks. Eddy had watched him smile as the terrible howls of the animal faded into silence.

It was time, Eddy thought, that Lord Gilbert was denounced, whatever Luke and Jude said. Someone had to bring the devil to justice and Eddy knew he was the one person who could do that without risking his livelihood. All those people down in Littlehaven, Amos Carter and his friends, Kate Bowman, even that cunning old fox John Woodcock who lived in Monksmere, who must have known what had gone on at the priory, had everything to lose. But who should he tell? And who would believe him? And how could he leave his friends in the lurch, as they had trusted him to help care for the kiln and had given him shelter when he had felt like a hunted animal?

He stood at his post all day until the others came home and relieved him. Then the idea came to him. Eva had been kind to him. She might be a witch, but she had never harmed him. She would tell him what to do and where to go.

Now the others were back he was free to do what he liked until Alison called him for supper. Telling them he would not be long, he went up into the woods to Eva's cottage. She was at home, as she always was at this time, making herself a hot cordial out of the blackberries which were growing all around her in lush profusion. She looked up as he approached her, and nodded to him to come and sit by her on an upturned log. Then, as if she had been

239

expecting him, she handed him an earthenware beaker of cordial and waited for him to speak.

'I've been doing a bit of thinking, Eva,' he said as he gave her back the empty beaker.

'Oh, and what have you come up with?'

'That I ought to tell someone what I know about the goings-on back there in the priory, and about that black-hearted lord of Tredgosse Castle.'

'I wondered how much you knew about him. He is indeed a bad man, Eddy, and if he finds you he'll kill you without hesitation. Best to stay with Alison and Jude and shut away in that head of yours whatever it is you know.'

'I can't do that, Eva. These things won't stay shut away. It's not right that he lets his hunters destroy people's property. They should respect people like Luke and Jude. They are good men and provide us with what we need. He deserves to be destroyed, but properly with a trial and all that so that everyone knows he's guilty. Not murdered. That's what he does.'

'I see Old Moley taught you a thing or two. You're right, of course, but you can't go, Eddy. It's too dangerous. If Tredgosse's spies get wind of you they'll hunt you down and kill you, just as they hunt down the wild boars.'

'Will you go, Eva, and tell someone? I'll tell you what I know.'

'Me, boy? Oh no, no one would believe old Eva. And besides, my legs are so stiff that it would take me an age to get where I ought to go.'

'And where would that be?'

'To Jane Warrener, of course; or rather, Lady Jane now that she's married Lord Nicholas. She's good, Eddy, and clever. She'll tell her husband who'll get the sheriff and they'll arrest Lord Gilbert and send him for trial in London.'

'And then what will they do with him?'

'Send him along the road to Tyburn and join the others on the field of execution.'

'That's right. That's what I want. I want everyone to see him suffer like he's made others suffer. I don't want him to die alone and unseen.'

'Well, don't worry about that side of things, Eddy,' said Eva, refilling the beakers. 'Let the law do what it has to do. But you must not go to Lady Jane's house, Eddy. You'll be seen and stopped.'

'But Luke and Jude can't go. They have to look after the kiln and Alison has to look after them. I'm the only one.'

Silence fell. Then Eva looked thoughtfully at Eddy, got up and went into the cottage, reappearing holding a pair of stout boots.

'If you must go, make your way across the Downs and keep away from the coastal road. You will have to leave when the others are asleep. The sky will be clear tonight and there is a full moon to give you light. Here, wear these,' she said. handing him the boots. 'They will protect your feet. Give them back to me one day if you remember. When you get to Lady Jane's house, tell the servants that old Eva sent you and that you have something important to tell their mistress. Don't let them turn you away. Go carefully, now, and take this. It's only a cordial made out of my own honey, but it will give you strength. Be polite but be determined and you will succeed. I shall think of you.'

He took the boots and the small pottery jar of cordial and decided to hide them on his way back to the camp and collect them when he set off later.

'It's a good seven miles to Dean Peverell,' Eva said. 'You'll not miss Lord Peverell's house; it's the biggest in the neighbourhood. Give yourself two to three hours as the going will be rough. Try to get there at sunrise. The further you are away from Tredgosse before daylight the better your chances are of not being discovered.'

Eddy thanked her and ran back to join the others for supper. That night he couldn't sleep but lay there quietly listening to the others snoring. When he judged the time was right, he got up and crept away to where he had hidden

241

the boots and the jar of cordial. Then with his back to where the sun would rise, he crept through the woods, and out onto the Downs towards the village of Dean Peverell.

When Nicholas arrived home on Friday morning, a pale streak in the sky was heralding the coming of dawn. He had made good time on his journey from London and the moon had provided enough light to see by. All was quiet when he led Harry to his stall. The servants were not yet up. He gave Harry some food and water and rubbed the sweat off his glossy coat. Then he left him for the stable boys to give him a thorough grooming when they stumbled down from the hayloft where they slept above the horses.

He went into the house, helped himself to a jug of ale, cut himself off a piece of cold beef and a hunk of bread and went up to the bedroom where Jane was still asleep. He went quietly into the room and looked at her whilst he munched the food. She looked so beautiful with her unbound hair spread over the pillow and her face so calm in its repose that he didn't want to wake her. He wanted the moment to last for ever and her image to be imprinted on his mind.

But the moment did not last long. Scarcely had the sun appeared over the horizon than Jane opened her eyes, saw him and sat up suddenly.

'Nicholas, you're back at last. What have you been doing? And what are you eating? Oh my love, let me get you something more appetising than yesterday's bread and broken meats.'

She swung her legs out of bed but Nicholas put down the plate and tankard on the side table and went over to her. He sat down on the side of the bed and gathered her up in his arms. He buried his head in her hair and held her closer breathing in the fragrance of the fresh herbs which she had strewn on her pillow. She felt so soft, so full of sleep, like a small animal waking up in its lair.

'My love, I have missed you so much, but I couldn't get away. I saw Cromwell and have learned much that I needed to know. And now I have a task to do which is not going to be easy.'

'Can't it wait just a little while?'

'Everything can wait until I have completed the most important task of all, that is to look at you and show you how much I love you.'

Gently he removed her night robe and gazed at her long, slender body which in the pale light of dawn looked white and mysterious, like that of an enchanted princess. He stroked her beautiful hair and kissed her firm breasts, already a little swollen, he noticed, as they prepared to provide sustenance for their baby.

Still half asleep, Jane responded to his ardour, and he, fully dressed in his riding breeches and jerkin, made love to her, rejoicing at her cries of pleasure. When they were both satisfied, she opened her eyes and looked at him in wonder, her face glistening with the sweat of their exertions.

'Nicholas,' she said reproachfully, 'your boots. You've made love to me in your riding boots filthy with the mud of London.'

He laughed. 'My darling wife, I would find a way to make love to you even if I were clad in a suit of armour. Damnation,' he exclaimed as someone was knocking urgently on the bedroom door. 'What is it? Come in, if you must.'

The door opened and the face of the youngest of Jane's maids stared at them. She seemed terrified at the sight of them and scarcely able to deliver her message.

'Madam, my lord, I am so sorry, I didn't know ...' she stammered, anxious not to say too much as she stared at her mistress lying naked on the bed and her master lying beside her with his breeches unfastened.

'What is it, Sophie?' said Jane kindly as she sat up and draped the sheet around her shoulders.

'Cecil told me to tell you that there's a person wants to

see you, madam; a boy,' she said, wrinkling her nose in disgust. 'Says it's urgent. Cecil tried to send him away but he won't go. Says he walked all night and he's exhausted. He says that even if we turn him out he'll simply sit down in the front of the house until you come to see him.'

'Well, don't send him away. Give him something to eat and I'll speak to him when I'm dressed.'

'Did the boy give his name?' said Nicholas, suddenly alert.

'Just said he was called Eddy and someone called Eva told him to come and speak to you,' the girl stammered.

'Then I shall come straight away,' Nicholas said, jumping off the bed and tying up the laces of his breeches. 'You did well to disturb us. Don't be alarmed. Go back to the boy and look after him.'

Eddy jumped up from wolfing down a plateful of bread and cheese when Nicholas came into the kithen, followed by Jane, dressed in a morning robe. Eddy wiped his mouth on his sleeve and looked at them anxiously.

'Sir, I had to come. I hope you're not angry with me but you were kind to me when I worked at the Dog and Bell. I've been thinking about things, you see, and I don't think it's right.'

'What's not right, Eddy?' said Nicholas, sitting down opposite him.

'It's Lord Gilbert, you see. He's a bad, wicked man and gets away with things. He lets his hunters come riding into our glade and they kick over our kiln and destroy all the work we've done. '

'Where have you been hiding?' said Jane, coming to sit next to him at the table.

'Up with the charcoal burners, Luke and Jude, in the woods above Monksmere and Tredgosse Castle. Alison lives with them and looks after us. They were kind to me after Sir John Woodcock threatened me and I had to run away. I wanted to come to you before, but Jude and Luke

244

told me not to because they said it was too dangerous, but old Eva said I should come and see you, Lady Jane, and she gave me these boots to wear, and told me not to let your servants send me away.'

'What do you want to tell us, Eddy?' said Jane, nodding to the servants, who had come crowding into the kitchen, to leave them.

'Why it's about Lord Gilbert. You see he has no right to destroy Luke and Jude's property, not after what he's done. He should've kept very quiet if he wanted to escape justice. But it's too late, now. He's got to be arrested. You see, he knew what was going on up in the priory. He knew, like we all did, that those men which that devil the prior was sheltering, were traitors. And, instead of reporting the prior, he paid Amos Carter to bring his boat up to his own jetty at Tredgosse and take the men away. Now, that's not right, is it? He knew who they were.'

'And who were they, Eddy?' asked Nicholas quietly.

'Well, I didn't know all their names. But Sarah knew because that devil – the prior, I mean – kept on at her until she shared his bed. He forced her, otherwise she would have lost her job and so would Moley and me and Kate would've been turned out of her house. He liked her in his bed, did that randy old goat, and he got her with child – you know the child who's called Henry. Anyway Sarah, used to going in and out of the prior's rooms, could see what was going on and could hear people talking. She said the men were soldiers mostly because they had swords and daggers and armour and frightened the canons out of their wits. Their leader she called Sir Ralph and he wanted to sleep with her too, but the prior wouldn't let him and wanted rid of them all. So he got Tredgosse to pay Amos to take them over to France.'

So that was it, that was what the prior had been up to, harbouring the fugitives from the northern rising which people were now calling the Pilgrimage of Grace. Sir Ralph

245

was almost certainly Sir Ralph Ingleby, their leader after Robert Aske was executed. So the black canons of Monksmere Priory had been harbouring a nest of traitors. Black indeed, he thought, and black their prior who was now his grace the Bishop of Lincoln.

'But why, Nicholas,' said Jane quietly, 'did the prior risk everything to shelter fugitives? Surely any sensible man would have reported them to you or the sheriff.'

'Because, Jane, they wanted to restore the monasteries and the Pope's authority. They were not evil men, but foolhardy. And they are, without doubt, most certainly guilty of treason. Probably the prior hoped to get them out of the country where they could join up with the French king and other exiles who want to overthrow our king. If they succeeded, then the prior would be safe in his priory for life and would be well rewarded by the victors. But it did not work out like that.

'Now, Eddy,' Nicholas went on, turning to look at the boy who was scraping up the last few crumbs of his breakfast as if they were the last he'd get. 'What you have told us is very important. You did right to come here and you must stay here now with Lady Jane. Eat and sleep your fill and we shall look after you. You can help the grooms in my stable.'

'But Luke and Jude – I must go and see them and tell them not to worry about me. They are my friends.'

'I shall see that they are told. You must not leave this place. But now I must away to the sheriff and then I shall arrest Lord Gilbert on a charge of treason. Then it will be safe for you to go out again.'

'But Nicholas, one other thing,' said Jane, looking anxiously across at her husband. 'Why did Cromwell make the prior a bishop after he was turned out of the priory? Given that Cromwell knows most things which go on around here, he must have had some idea that the prior was sheltering armed men in his priory. Why give an arch-traitor an important bishopric?'

246

'That's what I intend to find out,' said Nicholas grimly. 'Now Eddy, I want you to think carefully, have you ever heard of the Templars' gold?'

Eddy looked up. 'Of course, we all knew. People used to come and look at it and say prayers to it.'

'Then what happened to it?'

The boy looked blank. 'I don't know. I expect it was all taken away with all the other stuff.'

'Nicholas, what are you thinking?' said Jane.

'The unthinkable, my love.'

'You mean that Cromwell . . .?'

'Hush, I have no proof.'

'The bishop would know.'

'Indeed he would and I intend to ask him,' said Nicholas, standing up, and calling for the servants to come.

'He would never tell.'

'Oh yes he will, when he stares at the executioner's axe.'

Nicholas found the sheriff in his house in Marchester. This time he was greeted warmly and listened to all that Nicholas told him. Finally Nicholas said, 'I have to arrest Tredgosse.'

'On a charge of treason?'

'Yes.'

'Your only evidence at the moment is what a young boy has told you. He could have made it up.'

'He could, but I am sure he is telling the truth. He worked up at the priory. He saw the rebels. His friend Sarah knew who they were because she lived with the prior and their leader wanted to seduce her. The mole-taker saw everything too. The three of them knew too much.'

'Why wait two years to kill the girl and the mole-taker?'

'Because she was a growing threat to the prior who is now the Bishop of Lincoln, one of Cromwell's henchmen.'

'Still, why wait so long? If I were in the prior's shoes and about to be evicted from my priory and hoping for high office I would have them put out of the way immediately.'

247

'He probably thought they were too insignificant to bother with, and too frightened to tell anyone. Indeed the whole neighbourhood of Monksmere was terrorised into silence, if you remember. Even you and I were intimidated and ordered off the case. There is more to this than meets the eye, Richard, and I think I know who is behind all this. But we are dealing with men in high places, all traitors, and thieves to boot. But we cannot make a mistake. As for Lord Gilbert, rest assured that there are many witnesses to his treacherous activities who will now come forward without hesitation once I have him under lock and key. Now, if I may make a suggestion, would you send Peter and Dickon to Littlehaven. I want them to get Amos Carter and his friends, who took the rebels over to France, and Kate Bowman, who knew what was going on at the priory, and also knew who was the father of Sarah's child, to testify against Tredgosse. When they know he's under arrest, and I am going to do that straight away, they will not hesitate to come forward and denounce him.'

The sheriff agreed to do what Nicholas wanted. With Lord Gilbert under arrest, he could not be blamed if anything went wrong. Lord Nicholas was now in control, he thought, with a sigh of relief. He began to gather his men and gave the necessary orders. Meanwhile, Nicholas mounted his horse, fresh from his stables, and galloped off to confront Lord Gilbert.

No one came out of the stables to take his horse. All the doors were shut and the castle looked deserted, as if the inhabitants had been stricken by a pestilence. Overhead two seagulls floated aimlessly around in the still air. When they saw him they swooped down to take a closer look, then wheeled away, soaring upwards as if he, too, were doomed. For a moment he stood there as if under an enchanter's spell, then, brushing aside these fancies, he tethered his horse to a post in the middle of the courtyard and walked across to the main door. But before he reached

248

it, one of the small side doors opened and a plump, middle-aged woman came running out. She looked terrified and kept looking back nervously over her shoulder.

'I'm glad you've come, Lord Nicholas,' she said. 'There is terrible wickedness in this house. Lord Gilbert has just returned from burying his wife and that dear boy, Justin, who that devil child murdered. He is with his father now, plotting more mischief, I'll be bound. Not only have they murdered my dear mistress and her son but now they'll want rid of me and the other servants. No one dares to go into his room to speak to him. Thank the good God you've come.'

'Is he in his room, now?'

'Yes, he's shut himself away with his devil child.'

'Tell me your name.'

'Dora. I used to look after my lady Adeliza until that monster poisoned her. Your wife was here yesterday and saw her just before she died. Has she not told you?'

Nicholas thought back to his return home that morning. There had been no time to ask Jane what she had been doing whilst he had been away.

'I've only just returned from London and have not had time to speak to Jane. I've come to arrest Lord Gilbert so you will have nothing to fear now. The sheriff is on his way and they will take away your master for trial in London. Now show me where he is.'

She took him into the great hall at the same time as Lord Gilbert appeared from one of the small rooms that opened off from the far end of the hall, next to the door that concealed the staircase leading up to the tower and the castle ramparts. The boy, Marcus, was with him.

'What do you want, Lord Nicholas?' he shouted.

'I've come to arrest you. The sheriff will soon be here so there's no point in trying to escape.'

'What is the charge?'

'High treason. Lord Gilbert Fitzherbert, master of Tredgosse Castle, we have proof that you helped the king's

249

enemies escape from this country where they had been plotting treason against their lawful sovereign. We know you allowed the rebels to embark from your own jetty and that you hired a boatman from Littlehaven to carry them across to France.'

'Who says so?'

'We have many witnesses who are not afraid to testify against you. Now, please come quietly. You would be foolish to resist.'

'I shall never be taken from this place. The lords of Tredgosse have never recognised anyone's authority but their own. I shall not take the coward's way out and be dragged to the execution field at Tyburn. If you want me, you will have to take me by force.'

He ordered Marcus to stand back out of his way. Then he reached up and took down a huge broadsword that hung on the wall next to a suit of heavy armour. Grasping it with both hands, he swung it above his head and, with a shout of rage, hurled himself at Nicholas. Taken by surprise, Nicholas had barely time to draw his own sword, a rapier of fine Toledo steel, light, supple, as deadly as a striking cobra. Stepping aside to avoid Gilbert's charge, he whirled round to face his antagonist. He was conscious that several of the household servants had appeared and were standing round the edge of the hall watching the scene. Not one of them came forward to help their master.

Gilbert's second charge was more controlled and the blade of the broadsword flashed fire as it came towards him. One cut from that weapon, Nicholas knew, could sever his arm. One sweep of that blade could remove a man's head from his body. His rapier felt light and ineffectual in his hand, but he knew it was sharp and could pierce a man's body to the heart, especially when, like Lord Gilbert, he was wearing no armour. So he waited for the attack and parried the great blade, the clash of metal upon metal resounding round the hall. Then, before Gilbert could raise his sword for another chopping blow, Nicholas advanced on him, whirling the rapier to dazzle Gilbert, aiming always at the centre of his body. It was a case of a fencing master against a butcher. Both weapons were equally deadly, but in this case the rapier in the hands of a fit man was the deadliest. Gilbert was old and fat, the result of soft living. Nicholas realised he would tire quickly as long as he himself could keep clear of the heavy blade. All he had to do was wait for his opponent to flag and then seize the opportunity to plunge the steel into his body.

Again he dodged the next slashing blow, then advanced on Gilbert who began to retreat. Nicholas knew he must not be allowed to go back into his little room at the end of the hall. He could slam the door and take his own life, preferring to kill himself than be hauled away ignominiously to face trial and execution. This Nicholas did not want to happen. Traitors like Gilbert had to be taken alive, interrogated to reveal what they knew, and then tried before a lawful court with a jury giving a verdict and a judge passing sentence.

Slowly and inexorably Gilbert was driven back to the far end of the hall. Then Nicholas saw one of the servants dart forward and open the door leading up to the ramparts. That was where Gilbert would be forced to surrender. To climb a spiral staircase backwards trying to wield a broadsword in such a confined space was an impossible feat for an ageing and unfit man.

The next time Gilbert raised his sword, Nicholas lunged forward and ripped the sleeve of his jerkin. The point went in deep and blood began to flow down Gilbert's arm, dropping in crimson spots on the stone floor like petals from the overblown roses of late summer.

Gilbert gave a scream of pain and rushed forward whirling the great sword at Nicholas with renewed vigour. Again Nicholas dodged the blade and pressed forward, driving Gilbert back towards the open door. Unable to retreat further, there was only one place for Gilbert to go. He mounted the bottom stair of the spiral staircase.

251

Now Nicholas had the advantage, but he knew that he must not let Gilbert dash up the stairs and out onto the roof where he could throw himself off the castle ramparts. He had to keep him fighting every step of the staircase. Slowly, Gilbert retreated up the stairs, slashing at Nicholas who remained just out of reach. The great sword was too unwieldy to be much use in the confined space of the staircase and several times the blade crashed against the stone walls, making a deafening noise.

Up and up they climbed, Nicholas pressing the attack and waiting for his chance to cripple his adversary further.

'I have you, my lord,' he shouted. 'Throw down your sword. Can't you see it's no use to you here.'

'I'll never surrender to you, Lord Nicholas.'

'Then you are a fool. Do you want to die like a dog without the chance to make your peace with God? What chance will you have when you face your Maker with the blood of Sarah Bowman on your hands, and that of the Lady Adeliza? You, carrying the stigma of treason? Throw down your sword. Listen, I think I can hear the sheriff arriving.'

'You'll never take me alive. As for making my peace with God, I'll take a chance. He has never done anything for me. He took away my beloved wife, he gave me a deformed son. What do I care about God! I hate him and he can go to hell for all I care. Satan suits me better. He and I understand one another. I'll be content to serve him in the next world.

'As for that wench, Sarah Bowman, for your information as you seem to think I am about to die, I didn't kill her. Yes, I seduced her mother – not that she put up much resistance – but I didn't kill her daughter, mine too if what she said was true. Why should I kill Sarah? No one would believe her if she had informed on me. You'd better speak to that old goat of a prior – I hear he went on to high office. You see, the Devil looks after his own. Now that prior had every reason to kill Sarah Bowman.'

'So now you add blasphemy to your list of crimes,' said Nicholas, lunging at Gilbert, who stood on the stair above him with sword raised. 'What hope is there for you in the next world? I pity you, Lord Gilbert.'

With a shout of rage, Lord Gilbert brought the sword down towards Nicholas's head, but quick as a flash of lightning, Nicholas drove the rapier upwards towards the mighty body poised above him. Now he had no choice; he could not take him alive. The point of the rapier slid into the soft part of Gilbert's body at an angle which took the blade up under the rib cage and into the heart. Gilbert dropped his sword and stood swaying above Nicholas on the stair, blood streaming down his wounded arm and spurting from the wound in his chest. Then he toppled forward onto Nicholas, forcing him down the stairs. They arrived at the bottom in a tangled heap with Gilbert's blood pouring over Nicholas, who looked up and saw the sheriff.

He disentangled himself from Gilbert's body and stood up. He was bruised but no bones were broken. The sheriff looked down at Gilbert's body.

'Pity you had to kill him, my lord.'

'I had no choice. It was him or me.'

'But now he can't confess to killing Sarah Bowman.'

'He didn't kill her, Richard. He told me that just before he died. Apart from anything else, she was his daughter, not that that would have worried him. She was just too unimportant for him to bother about.'

'Then who the devil did kill the girl?'

'I think I know; and I'm going to get him. But I need more evidence. However, Lord Gilbert deserved to die; and he was lucky to die so swiftly. He killed his mistress, or allowed his son to kill her. And he also allowed him to kill his stepbrother. Incidentally, where is Marcus? He's only a child but he's got the mind of Satan and we must not let him get away.'

Marcus stood watching the fight. He saw the servants

253

waiting, doing nothing to help his father. He saw one of the servants open the door to the tower and he knew what was going to happen. Lord Nicholas was younger and fitter than his father; the rapier was far superior to the broadsword in a confined space, and he knew the Sheriff and his men would arrive at any moment as Nicholas Peverell would not have come without support. It was time for him to leave Tredgosse Castle. But first he had to have some means of supporting himself. He knew what he had to do, and he knew where to find it.

Quickly he went up to Adeliza's room and tipped the contents of her jewel box into a leather pouch. Then he went down to the stables and saddled Robin. He could not leave the castle by the main gate as he knew he would ride straight into the arms of the sheriff and his party. But there was a back way out of the castle which led out into the woods and then up to the Downs.

He mounted Robin and left the castle by the back gate. Then, kicking Robin into a gallop, they tore along the wooded track.

'Faster, faster,' he shouted to the little horse, beating it with the whip he had taken from the stables.

The animal whinnied with fright. He was not used to this treatment. Then, when he felt the lash of the whip again, he panicked and bolted off, leaving the track and making for the dense woodland where he would have to slow down. A fallen log blocked the way. Robin, in a state of terror, cleared it with one leap. Marcus hung on.

'Stop this, you stupid beast,' Marcus shouted, trying to force the horse onto the track again. But Robin, ears flattened to the side of his head, dashed on, determined to rid himself of this fiend on his back. Straight ahead was a great oak tree which had been standing there for centuries. One of its vast branches had dipped low with the weight of its years; even so there was just room for Robin to get under and make off into the clearing. But not enough room for his rider. Too late, Marcus tried to jerk the horse to the side

254

of the tree, but it was no use; Robin went straight towards the branch. Marcus took the full force of the branch on his chest. It swept him off his horse and onto the forest floor where he died instantly, his neck broken and his chest shattered. The pouch containing Adeliza's jewels spilled open and the rubies and diamonds lay scattered on the mossy ground.

Chapter Twenty

On Saturday, after a dinner eaten in haste, the sheriff left Nicholas and Jane and returned to Marchester to write his report. There was now no shortage of witnesses eager to testify against Lord Gilbert. It was as if the whole countryside had relaxed and could now talk freely about his wickedness. As for the prior and the canons of Monksmere, no one could say a good word about them. Even Sir John Woodcock denied all knowledge of his brother's activities and said that it all happened before he bought his manor, and, in any case, as he put it, 'I am not my brother's keeper.'

Just before he set off, the sheriff turned to look at Nicholas.

'Well, Lord Nicholas, what now?'

'I shall leave for Hampton Court immediately. I believe the king is staying there at the moment to avoid the stench of London.'

'Then God speed you, and come back safely.'

'We shall meet again soon, I think, Richard, when the King comes here in ten days' time.'

'Then I shall pray that the preparations proceed smoothly, as I am sure they will in Lady Jane's capable hands. And you, boy,' he said, looking down at Eddy who, in his new position as groom, was holding the reins of his horse, 'serve Lord Nicholas well, and he will treat you well. It's not often that a groom gets a chance to look after the king's horses.'

Eddy bowed, and, at a nod from the sheriff, released his horse. 'Thank you, sir. I think I shall prefer looking after Lord Nicholas's horses to watching the kilns of the charcoal burners.'

Nicholas arrived at Hampton Court in the early hours of Sunday morning. He was conducted to his usual room in the gatehouse as he was well known and no questions were asked. The servant said he would inform the king about his arrival as soon as his majesty woke up, which, on a Sunday, was early, as his majesty always took Communion at eight o'clock with his chaplain before attending divine service in the Chapel Royal at half past nine

Nicholas threw himself down on the narrow bed and tried to compose his mind to sleep as he was desperately tired, but his brain would not relax. It was one thing, he thought, to denounce the Bishop of Lincoln – there were plenty of witnesses prepared to testify to the presence of armed men in the priory – but it was quite a different matter to denounce the king's chief minister. The more he thought about it, the more impossible it seemed. He was quite sure that the bishop and Cromwell had made some sort of pact – Cromwell was to be given the Templars' treasure in return for his connivance at the prior's treasonable activites – but he had not a jot of evidence to support this damning accusation. However, first things first, he thought, as sleep came to him just before dawn. Pray God that the Bishop of Lincoln had not flown the nest.

He was summoned to join the king in the ante-room of the Chapel Royal just before the service was to begin.

'Well, Peverell,' said the king, smiling affably at Nicholas, 'you have news for me, I believe?'

'Yes, your majesty. Serious matters ...'

'They always are when you appear. Well, today they

257

must wait until after divine service. We must not keep the good bishop waiting.'

'May I ask which of the bishops is officiating this morning?'

'Why, Edward, my most esteemed Bishop of Lincoln. It is his turn this week to keep me in our good Lord's favour. Why do you look so alarmed, Peverell? It's not like you to look so agitated.'

'Your majesty, I beg you to listen. The bishop who is about to take this service is an arch traitor. He sheltered rebels in his priory at Monksmere after the northern rebellion was suppressed. Sir Ralph Ingleby escaped to France from there. Gilbert Fitzherbert arranged the transport of the rebels over to France. Lord Gilbert is dead, he was killed by me on Friday, resisting arrest, but the bishop lives and enjoys your favour and he is the one who should be brought to justice as he masterminded the rebels' escape.'

The king motioned the ushers away and called for the captain of his guard. He looked at Nicholas keenly.

'Have you witnesses to support this accusation, Lord Nicholas?'

'Most certainly, although the bishop did his best to silence them. The girl, Sarah Bowman, whom I mentioned before to your grace, was one of them. The prior seduced her, she bore him a son and she observed everything that went on in the priory. She cannot testify now, of course, the bishop saw to that, but she told others and many other people have now come forward and said they had also seen armed men in the priory. They are not afraid of making statements now that they know Lord Gilbert is dead and when they know that the bishop is safely locked away in the Tower awaiting trial.'

'The bishop's brother, I think, lives in the manor which he bought when the priory was closed down? Would he not testify?'

'He does indeed own the manor, but he bought the place after his brother left. I think he knew something had been

258

going on at the priory when his brother was prior, but he did not actually see the rebels. Others saw everything, armed men, Sir Ralph Ingleby, terrified canons.'

'My God, Lord Nicholas, I do not doubt that you are right. I always wondered what happened to Ralph Ingleby. So, the bishop harboured a nest of vipers! For the usual reason, I suppose, to safeguard his interests should the rebels get support from the Continent and drive me off my throne. Captain Pickford,' he called to the captain of his personal bodyguard, 'let the bishop conduct divine service. We must not miss the choir's singing. Then, arrest him. No trouble, mind. We must have him alive.'

The captain looked stunned. 'But your majesty ...' he stammered.

'Do you question my orders, Captain? Just do as I say. Now, Lord Nicholas, let us go up into our Royal Pew and enjoy the music. And watch the bishop say his last public prayers.'

From the Royal Pew, Nicholas stared down at the richly ornamented chapel where Prince Edward had been baptised the year before. The candles lit up the heavily decorated interior where the tall figure of Edward Woodcock stood in front of the altar which was covered with a lavishly embroidered cloth. The air was heavy with incense as the king still preferred the traditional rites. The bishop's chasuble, decorated with gold embroidery and encrusted with jewels, glittered in the candlelight which cast flickering shadows up on to the intricate fan-vaulted ceiling.

Nicholas glanced at the king. Nothing seemed to disturb him as he closed his eyes, the better to appreciate the sweetness of the choir's singing. He remained deep in prayer throughout the service as the bishop's voice went on unfaltering. He had a beautiful voice, Nicholas thought, strong and resonant. A pity it would soon be stopped in such a brutal way.

At last the service was over. The king and Nicholas

259

stood for the blessing and then watched, as the guard entered and seized the bishop. The words were said. The bishop was arrested on a charge of high treason. The king nodded to Nicholas and they went down the stairs from the Royal Pew back into the ante-chamber where soldiers were dragging away the terrifed bishop. When he saw Nicholas with the king, he stopped and fought the guards to let him speak.

'I am not the only one,' he shouted. 'Look around you, your majesty. Why should I suffer and not the other one?'

'Who else knew you were sheltering rebels?' said Nicholas as the king looked on impassively.

'Ask your chief minister, Thomas Cromwell. He knew. He wanted the gold, you see. He took it with my agreement. In return he said he would keep silent. His men killed that girl, Lord Nicholas, and the other witnesses. Why don't you arrest him?'

'Take him away,' said the king, turning his back on the scene as the bishop began to scream abuse at Thomas Cromwell.

'Shall we arrest Baron Cromwell, your majesty?' said Nicholas as the bishop was dragged away.

'No, not yet,' said the king after a pause. 'His turn will come, I think.'

'Should you not at least question Cromwell?' said Nicholas, alarmed that Cromwell was going to go free.

'For what purpose? He will certainly deny everything. He will say that the bishop made these accusations to save his own skin. Do we know Cromwell appropriated some of the priory's treasure?'

'I checked with the Court of Augmentation's list of goods taken from Monksmere Priory. The treasure, which they called the Templars' treasure, was not recorded.'

'As were a lot of other things, I suspect. I am surrounded by thieves, Lord Nicholas, and traitors. Much of the monastic treasure has gone into the coffers of my loyal and faithful servants. It is not difficult to melt down the gold

260

objects and hide it away from my inspectors, who, most likely, have not been able to resist a bribe in return for their silence. We live in a wicked world, Lord Nicholas, and I trust no one. Except you, and so far, you have never let me down. No, let Cromwell remain at large for the time being. He is useful to me at the moment as he is in the middle of conducting the negotiations for my marriage to the Lady Anne of Cleves. I cannot let anything upset those arrangements now. Thomas has told me that he has found me a fine, fat, Flemish mare with good child-bearing hips and I look forward to servicing her. And I shall want you to go with him to conduct her to my presence when the formalities are over. No, let Cromwell get on with his work. I feel that one day his ambition will overreach himself and he will follow the bishop to the Tower.'

The king had paused at the entrance to the ante-room. Now he turned and put an arm affectionately round Nicholas's shoulders.

'Oh, how weary I am of all these troublesome matters. How I am looking forward to enjoying your company and that of your beautiful wife in your rural retreat! I knew you would sort out all these disturbances in your county. I never trusted Tredgosse of course. The man was too much of a recluse and such men are dengerous. Now I suppose I shall have to appoint a steward for the castle, until I make up my mind what to do with it. Have a safe journey, my lord, and I look forward to seeing you soon in happier circumstances.'

'Your majesty?'

'Yes, what is it?' the king said, summoning one of his ushers to attend him to his state rooms where he was to receive the ambassador from the court of the sultan in Constantinople.

'Do you think Cromwell ordered the girl to be killed, and the other witness, and arranged for the intimidation of my household and that of the sheriff? '

'I expect so, Lord Nicholas. Probably the orders came

from him but with the agreement of the bishop, I should think. Don't worry about it. All will come out in the interrogation, but then, we can't always believe everything people say under torture, can we?'

'But in this case ...?'

'In this case, I think we shall ignore what the bishop says. Remember my marriage to the fair Lady of Cleves cannot be put in jeopardy. Cromwell has some delicate diplomacy ahead of him as the Duke of Cleves is not yet certain he wants to entrust his daughter to me. But I shall not fret about it. There are plenty of fair ladies at court who would please me well if Cromwell fails to get the Duke's consent. However, I fear the fathers of these fair ladies are not too enamoured of Baron Cromwell and would rejoice if the Lady Anne does not please me and I would have to take his office away from him. Let us leave Baron Cromwell to his own devices – for the time being, that is.'

Epilogue

The king had worn out two horses, he had enjoyed an excellent day's hunting in Nicholas's well-stocked woods, and he was in a good mood. Dinner was in progress and the king had done justice to the haunch of venison and pigeon pie. As Nicholas surveyed the company seated around the table in his great hall, he felt proud of Jane and his servants who had toiled away ceaselessly to make the king comfortable. The Bishop of Marchester and his wife were there and several of the cathedral dignitaries, the sheriff and his wife, and the Earl of Southampton. He also felt a moment's panic when he thought about the cost of it all. Already he had discussed with his bailiff which fields he would be forced to sell to pay for the king's stay.

The meat courses had been cleared away and sweetmeats were being served including a huge model of Hampton Court made with marzipan and decorated with preserved fruits. The king yawned.

'Come, Lord Nicholas,' he said. 'Let us take a stroll around your gardens before darkness falls. I would like to breathe the fresh air of Sussex. Oblige me with your arm as my leg plagues me tonight.'

Picking up one of the flaming torches which the servants were putting in their sconces in preparation for nightfall, Nicholas led the way out of the house and through a wicket gate into the first of his gardens. It was the herb garden and the night air was perfumed with the scent of rosemary and thyme and sweet majoram. The king breathed deeply.

'A beautiful night. One I shall remember, I think. I shall sleep easily in my bed tonight, Lord Nicholas, because I feel safe under your roof.'

Darkness was indeed falling. Above them the waning moon shone brightly and the clear sky was scattered with stars which glittered like diamonds. In the second garden, the orchard, where fruit hung ripe on the trees and grass was damp underfoot with the recent rain, Henry stopped and listened. High on the bough of an apple tree a nightingale broke into rapturous song.

'How clever of you to find me a nightingale, Lord Nicholas. You never cease to amaze me. Now where is the barn owl? I must see a barn owl when I come to the country.'

As if on cue, with a great flapping of wings, a barn owl flew into the garden and perched on a tree near to where they were standing. The owl's flat, white face shone out of the darkness like a benevolent spirit and he surveyed them with his strange, unblinking eyes.

'Maybe it's the spirit of Wolsey, come to haunt us,' the king whispered.

'Maybe. More likely it is an omen that all will be well in your majesty's kingdom from now on.'

The king laughed. 'I doubt it, Lord Nicholas. But at least there will be peace here in Sussex tonight. I look no further ahead than that.'

'Your majesty has been beset with enemies recently. From now on we shall have to maintain constant vigilance throughout your kingdom.'

'Well, you seem to have a nose for traitors, Lord Nicholas, but I know I can leave Sussex in your capable hands. As for Tredgosse castle, I propose to pay it a visit tomorrow and hunt some of the wild boar which frequent the woods in those parts. Then I propose to hand over the castle to you, my lord. I am sure you will look after it well.

264

Make it comfortable for your wife and when your son arrives, he will have a fine castle to look forward to as part of his inheritance.'

'Your majesty,' said Nicholas, taken aback. 'You do me great honour.'

'Nonsense, modesty doesn't suit you. You deserve to have it. The county should be peaceful from now on. I have decided to let the Woodcocks stay in their manor. I hear he's been doing good works in Marchester, founding an almshouse by all accounts, and his wife helps run the foundlings hospital. If he keeps his nose clean I shall have to make him a Justice of the Peace like you and you can both sit together on the bench at Quarter Sessions. I am not a vindictive man, you know. Punish the ring leaders and let them be a warning to others who might think of rebellion.'

'And Baron Cromwell? Was he not a ringleader? Did he not steal the Templars' gold? The bishop insisted that he did when he was being interrogated. Was he not hand in glove with the bishop when he was prior of Monksmere? Did he not send his spies to intimidate my wife and me, and the sheriff? Was he not responsible for the murder of Sarah Bowman and the mole-taker?'

'Why do you keep on about Thomas Cromwell, Lord Nicholas? I see you are not as merciful as I am. Cromwell might be guilty of all those things which you have listed so passionately, but we have no proof. Oh, I know the late Bishop of Lincoln denounced him emphatically, but he was under duress. People in his position are wont to heap the blame on someone else. Usually it's their ruler, but in the bishop's case it was the chief minister.'

'As I said before, Nicholas, because I shall address you as such from now on because I regard you as my beloved friend, Cromwell is useful to me at the moment. You will have to work closely with him over the negotiations with the Duke of Cleves. Rest assured we shall watch him closely. One slip and we won't show him any mercy then. Now, let us follow the example of that beautiful barn owl

265

and fly away from this enchanted garden and go back into the house where I look forward to hearing that other nightingale, your beautiful wife. And afterwards, as I feel so well, I shall ask her to partner me in a sprightly galliard.'